THE LIES
HAVE IT

Praise for *Dead Light District*

"*Blood and Groom* was a delightful discovery, it featured the tough-as-nails, but still self-aware Sasha Jackson as a private investigator uncovering heinous crimes. *Dead Light District* stays true to the character. Edmondson keeps the tone light with occasional jokes and sarcastic wit, and her series character is worth the attention for those who appreciate contemporary P.I. fiction." (*Bookgasm*)

"A missing-person case that goes terribly wrong will have readers chuckling and cringing as they read Jill Edmondson's latest mystery, an intriguing tale. Edmondson develops it in style with unexpected twists and turns. Jill Edmondson is a writer to watch." (*Guelph Mercury*)

"Five Stars out of Five." (*Examiner.com*)

"Jill Edmondson takes the reader on an engaging ride, characters are smart and sassy, dialogue is snappy and situations will make you laugh out loud. PI Sasha Jackson brings a unique blend of Janet Evanovich's Stephanie Plum and Robert Parker's Spenser to the page. Five Stars for humor, action, pace and characters that are sure to delight!" (*Donna Carrick, author of The First Excellence ~ Fa-Ling's Map*)

"Sasha Jackson shows compassion and wits like never before in *Dead Light District*, the gritty yet warm portrayal of Toronto's underworld. I'm excited to see where this series takes us next. Sasha Jackson, you are one sleuth I want to watch." (*Robin Spano, author of the Clare Vengel Undercover series*)

"Sasha Jackson, is once again solving a mystery with a combination of her intelligence, tenacity, and (amusing!) snarkiness. Dead Light District is a lively and exciting read. I recommend it for those who like a fast-paced mystery with an amusing tone. The story is about a serious subject (prostitution) but the author has balanced it with plenty of humour, quirky characters, and a compelling mystery." (*Bookish Magpie*)

Praise for *Blood and Groom*

"A sparkling debut." (Sleuth of Baker Street)

"Toronto's sexiest new detective." (*Paul the Book Guy*)

"*Blood and Groom* is a sprightly read – a promising start to a new series and a fresh writing career." (Joan Barfoot, *London Free Press*)

"Blood and Groom's main character, newly licensed downtown Toronto P.I. Sasha Jackson, has enough sass and quirk to hold a reader's interest." (*Quill & Quire*)

"The style is fresh, well-paced and uses dialogue that feels real… Edmondson shows the storytelling skill to turn this debut into a Toronto-focused series with room to grow." (*Hamilton Spectator*)

"A quick, entertaining read best enjoyed with double vodka tonics and morning-after grilled cheeses." (*She Does the City*)

"Romance and finance combined to deadly effect." (*Dublin Evening Herald*)

"A fast-paced, soft-boiled novel with a strong, distinctive voice and a sassy protagonist." (*Sherbrooke Record*)

"The book is fast-paced… the quick and funny style that appeals to fans of Janet Evanovich. There's a lot of promise here and we'll look forward to Sasha Jackson's next adventure." (Margaret Cannon, *Globe & Mail*)

"Jill Edmondson's *Blood and Groom* is a fast-paced whipcrack of a book – a little self-aware, a little edgy and a lot of fun." (*Bookgasm*)

"It took a surprisingly long time for Toronto to come up with its own street-savvy female gumshoe, but Sasha Jackson is beginning to look like she was worth the wait. Crafty, tough, and tenacious, fledgling private eye Sasha's an interesting update on the Hammett/Chandler model. Sasha's hard-bitten enough to make her forays down those mean streets a worthwhile stroll, offering enough modern touches and originality." (*Thrilling Detective*)

THE LIES HAVE IT

A Sasha Jackson Mystery

Jill Edmondson

IGUANA

Editors: Greg Ioannou, Jade Colbert, Colborne Communications
Front Cover Design and Illustration: Jennifer Stellings
Back Cover and Interior Design: Jack Steiner
Author Photo: Iden Ford
Printer: Webcom

Library and Archives Canada Cataloguing in Publication

Edmondson, Jill
    The Lies Have It / Jill Edmondson.
(A Sasha Jackson mystery)
Issued also in an electronic format. Forthcoming.

ISBN 978-0-9866838-1-7

I. Title. II. Series: Edmondson, Jill. Sasha Jackson mystery.
PS8609.D67D43   2011C813'.6   C2010-902412-5

1 2 3 4 5   15 14 13 12 11

Printed in Canada

To D. with love. You're still here!

Acknowledgements

Hearty thanks to Patricia Côté, Mimi Whalen, and Deirdre Fitzpatrick. I couldn't ask for more amazing friends!

Warm fuzzy appreciation to the folks who made the whole thing happen: Greg Ioannou, Jade Colbert, Jennifer Stellings, and Jack Steiner. I have some terrific people behind me. Thank you!

I'd also like to thank the wonderful team at Iguana Books. Great people with creativity, know-how, and patience in spades!

Finally, I'm really lucky to have Derek on my side. Without him, there wouldn't be a book.

Author's note

This is a work of fiction. I know because I made it up. However, The Pilot Tavern is real, and the second-floor party room called The Stealth Lounge does in fact exist, plus there's an awesome rooftop patio known as The Flight Deck. I'm forever coming across people who tell me they have special memories (albeit occasionally fuzzy ones) of hanging out there over the years. If you've never been to The Pilot, you owe it to yourself to check it out.

Saturday, September 29, 7:00 pm

"See a penny, pick it up, all day long you'll have good luck," my friend Jessica said, as she leaned over to grab the shiny copper coin on the sidewalk. We were heading into The Stealth Lounge, the private party room on the second floor of The Pilot Tavern.

"See a penny, let it lie, then bad luck will pass you by," I replied.

I've never let it cripple me, but I do happen to be a tad superstitious. Penny or not, I didn't have a great feeling about the evening ahead of us.

Bound for Glory, a sado-masochist fetish club, was booked into The Stealth Lounge tonight. The same group had rented the place two weekends ago, and poor Jessica had been the only bartender on duty that night. Dear friend that she is, Jessica had suggested that I pinch-hit at the bar with her this evening. I do have a real job as a private investigator, but all too frequently I find myself needing to supplement my income. Friends take pity on me, and occasionally offer me casual jobs that even welfare recipients would turn down, but I don't have that much pride. Besides, The Pilot's one of my favourite watering holes.

"Hand me the knife, will ya?" Jess asked as she dumped a bunch of citrus fruit on the bar.

She got busy slicing lemon and lime wedges while I stocked the beer fridge. We were in the midst of setting up the bar for the evening when Ian Dooley, the guy who spearheaded this dominance and submission social club, arrived.

"Hey, I'm Ian," he said, leaning against the bar. His voice was a little on the high-pitched nasal side, and had more than a hint of a Maritime accent.

I expected some wimpy little milquetoast with a sign on his forehead saying "beat me." Instead, when I looked up, I saw a hefty guy in his late thirties. He was tall, easily six feet two inches. He was wearing a red plaid shirt and faded jeans, and had thick scruffy, dark hair and a firm jaw. He looked like Paul Bunyan's long-lost cousin.

"Nice to meet you. I'm Sasha and this is Jessica." I wanted to be polite, but I didn't stick my hand out for him to shake. Something about a dude who hosts fetish parties gives me the heebie-jeebies.

"Ian and I met couple of weeks ago," Jess said.

"Oh yeah," I said.

"It should be a pretty good crowd tonight," Ian said. "I've really been putting the word out. A lot more people were invited for tonight than last time."

"Sounds good."

"I'm gonna start bringing stuff up, but can I leave this behind the bar for now?" He handed me his jean jacket and a Nike backpack. I tucked them onto the shelf where Jessica and I had stashed our purses.

"Could one of you unlock the back door for me?" Ian asked.

"I guess so. Jess, do you have the key?" I asked.

"Can you grab it?" she replied. "My hands are sticky. It's under the drawer of the cash register."

"Okay."

"Thanks," Ian said. "It's a lot easier to bring things up the back stairs. I can pull my truck right up to the back door."

Ian headed out to collect the accoutrements for the S&M funfest. Jessica checked to make sure the cash register had enough change for the night, and I stocked up the straws and swizzle sticks.

Once we got everything set up behind the bar area, Jessica and I took a moment to freshen up.

"Do you think this colour is okay on me?" Jess puckered as she applied a shiny coat of Candy Apple lip gloss.

The bright red tone flattered her complexion and suited her chestnut hair, but I'm not one to toss off compliments freely.

"Yes my dear," I mumbled through the bobby pins I was holding between my teeth. "All the bondage boys are going to be begging for you." I was alliterating while trying to get my hair to co-operate, but gave up, and just stuck it into a random pile at the back of my head. My hair's a lost cause these days. A good chunk of it was burned during a fire a few weeks ago, when I wrapped up one of my more unusual cases. The case had started with a missing hooker and had ended with me dousing out flames on my head. All in a day's work. I had some hair extensions put in, but right now they seem like more bother than they're worth.

By nine o'clock, The Stealth Lounge had been transformed into a spank-me paradise. The stocks were in place, a St. Andrew's cross had been set up, and the lights were dimmed. An upside-down hangy thing that Jess had described to me after the previous event was set up. I looked it over, and could not figure out who was supposed to use it or how. Ian reclaimed his knapsack and went into the men's room to change into his party clothes. He came back shirtless, wearing only a black leather "kilt" and black lace-up army boots. I couldn't tell if he was wearing socks.

He passed his knapsack back to me, flexed his muscles and asked, "Whaddaya think?"

I checked him out from head to toe, and really didn't have any opinion, except for flinching when I noticed his pierced nipples. Ouch.

"So, is it true that men don't wear anything under their kilts?"

Shortly after nine o'clock, the first few partygoers began to straggle in.

"Coupla Stolies, neat," commanded a man in a leather hood as he dropped a fifty dollar bill on the bar. He groped and grabbed at his partner while I poured their shots of vodka. The man looked like he wanted to devour the woman for breakfast, and she hung onto his arm like the ditz I'm sure she is. After the guy paid and scooped up all his change, I gave my hands a quick rinse. Everything about this evening felt grimy. It suddenly seemed like my uncareer had been downgraded from unconventional to uninspired. I reminded myself that I had options. I could go back to school and train as a nurse or something.

The next twosome to belly up to the bar were in character, and they dashed the career choice I'd just made. She was Florence Nightingale in a micro-mini and see-through blouse. A cute little nurse's cap with a red cross on it was perched jauntily on her head. Her partner was dressed in green hospital pants and a white lab coat, and looked ready to give her a cervical exam.

The Missing Hooker case I had worked on this past summer had exposed me to the world of commercial sex. I had learned more than I wanted to know about what people do behind closed doors. However, my education in non-traditional sex is mostly anecdotal, and I've never actually *seen* anyone acting out their fantasies like I was seeing here tonight.

In fact, in another former job of mine, I'd talked people through their wet 'n wild fantasies, but that had been on the telephone. I usually played solitaire or surfed the Internet while horndogs got their rocks off, but I digress. Tonight was a real eye-opener.

Ian greeted guests as they arrived, high-fiving some of the guys. He pointed out the coat rack to the left of the entrance where people could dump their jackets and bags, and then he steered people towards the bar to order themselves a glass of liquid courage. Yet another couple walked in, and they too were dressed to role-play. They were in leather from head to toe, though she had on considerably less of it than he did. The red-haired chick had a studded dog collar around her neck, and her partner had a leash attached to it. He didn't pull the leash taut, but the message was clear.

They came straight to the bar and I asked them something along the lines of "what's your poison" although I reworded it – some jackass in this crowd may have taken the cliché literally. Jess threw a smirk my way as she handed a Corona to a wrinkly old man wearing nothing but assless leather chaps and a pair of handcuffs dangling from his left wrist. I didn't watch to see where he kept his wallet. The master and slave duo in front of me looked at the array of bottles behind the bar.

"Johnnie Black and Coke. On the rocks," Master said. I was about to ask his pet what she'd like, when her master continued, "She'll just have water." I didn't ask if I should pour it into a bowl or serve it in a glass. The girl never even made eye contact with me.

I have to admit, the people – at least those who were permitted to speak – were rather nice and generally polite. But with some customers it was hard to hear their orders – the music was blaring, and leather facemasks aren't especially conducive to enunciation.

I flirted with a couple of the wussier-looking guys, correctly guessing they'd respond well to a stern dominatrix, a role I'd learned to vocalize all too well during that period of financial meltdown when I'd briefly worked at an X-rated call centre. There's something to be said for transferable skills. You'd think that someone with my rather sullied curriculum vitae would be blasé about bartending at a fetish party. I wasn't necessarily offended by what was going on, but it was beyond my ken, although sort of interesting and rather surreal. Right now, I kind of wished I were a pothead. A joint might have helped make sense of this night. Alas, I'm not a toker.

I made the next customer beg me for his bottle of micro-brewed light beer.

"Are you sure you want it?" I purred as I uncapped a bottle of organic lager. "How badly do you want it?" I held the bottle just beyond his reach.

"Oh Mistress, you know I want it…bad…Please, please tell me you're going to give it to me," the guy replied.

A couple feet away, Ian, who'd been watching this whole transaction, gave me a thumb's up.

Jess rolled her eyes at me, and poured a Scotch on the rocks for a woman wearing nothing but Saran Wrap.

"Careful not to spill any on your lovely outfit," Jess deadpanned as she handed the Saran Siren her libation.

Although the night had started off rather slowly, by eleven o'clock, the party was in full swing. I suppose, if one were to choose, The Stealth Lounge is the ideal setting for a fetish party. The walls are painted one shade lighter than black. There are several oversized, ornately framed mirrors hung at odd angles behind the bar. I glimpsed at myself in them, and thought for the hundredth time that it would have been funny to replace them with the convex and concave mirrors found at funhouses and carnivals. I checked my reflection and was satisfied with the appearance of the slender, blond girl in a slim-cut, short, black skirt, and a scooped-neck, clingy, white top who smiled back at me.

The furnishings of The Stealth Lounge run to glass and chrome, the upholstery is a velveteen zebra print. Pairs of loveseats at right angles to each other are at the far end of the bar. Exposed ceiling beams, with their guts painted matte silver, give the room an industrial feeling. Blue-tinted lighting completes the mood. The music – all techno heavy instrumental, with throbbing, reverberating bass – comes over an audio system with crystal clear sound. Yeah, I guess if I were to host an S&M party, this would be the place to do it.

Couples and trios had started to pair off, and they were strapping, whipping and spanking each other with reckless abandon. Most of this pheromone themed hand-to-hand combat took place in the loveseats near the back. Those who hadn't yet met the bolt to go with their nut were milling about the bar area like dogs in heat. No doubt some of the sexual tension came from folks who had miscalculated the targets of their pick-up lines. One dominant trying to pick up another dom was just not good for anyone.

"Hey Jess," I said, "maybe next time we should offer sticky name tags and pass them out at the entrance: S for submissive, D for dominant, B for bondage, and Y for why the Hell don't I find another job?" Jess laughed.

Moose, a florist by day and The Stealth Lounge's doorman by night, was busy manning the entrance. I imagine it's rather difficult to be macho and intimidating when you smell like roses, but Moose seemed to be doing okay. A dark-haired Latino behemoth, Moose checked IDs and names on the guest list, plus he had the unenviable task of screening people for dress code infractions.

"Oh c'mon, lemme in! I wanna check it out!" slurred a skanky looking bit of trailer trash who looked like she'd be right at home in a bowling alley.

"Sorry, but your name's not on the list." Moose's face was impassive.

"Wassa matter? I don't look sexy enough? Here, how's this?" she wailed as she unbuttoned her shirt and flashed her saggy boobs at poor Moose and the folks standing near the entrance.

"Lemme in!" She cupped her breasts and continued to demonstrate her lack of both dignity and self-respect.

Her toothless Neanderthal of a date tried to finesse his way in with a bribe. He slipped two dollars into Moose's palm and said, "That oughtta take care of things."

Moose scooped the Neanderthal into a headlock with his right arm, and firmly gripped Skanky's wrist with his left hand, and unceremoniously ushered them downstairs. A twenty might have worked, but not a deuce.

"That woman was unreal, wasn't she?" he asked me when he came back into the bar. I chuckled and slipped him a shot of vodka. He tossed the toonie onto the bar as a tip.

The bar area was quiet for a moment; everyone's drinks had been replenished. Jess and I leaned back against the beer fridge and simultaneously sighed, smirked, and surreptitiously stared at the group before us. A rather pudgy woman was prancing around wearing a nippleless pink teddy on top and nothing, *nothing* on the bottom. She had a fluffy purple feather boa around her neck and was asking guys to slap her cottage cheese butt. Ian, ever the gracious host, happily obliged, while I averted my eyes and tried not to toss my cookies.

Jess had seen most of this crowd at the previous soiree and she filled me in on whatever catty gossip she had about them.

"See that guy?" she asked, indicating a well-preserved senior with giant nipple rings, "he's into golden showers, giving and receiving. I think he left alone last time. Can you imagine being into that?"

I cringed. "Never, no way, not in a million years."

I folded my arms across my chest, and pressed my knees closer together than words in a dictionary. Right now, I kind of wished I were wearing a medieval chastity belt.

Jess continued, "See those two bottle blonds with black roots over there? Wearing fishnets? They're looking for a third chick who likes to talk dirty and wants to be paddled. Do you ever think of switching teams? I could introduce you."

"Ha ha. Piss off, Jess, or I'll give Assless Leather Chaps your cell number. Besides, Derek satisfies me more than anyone in this room ever could."

Derek Armstrong is the new man in my life. Our romance is still in its nascent days, but I swear that since we started seeing each other, the skies are bluer, the sun is brighter, and the birds sing more sweetly. Oh barf. I don't do well with mushy sentiments, but Derek really rocks my world. I couldn't imagine doing any of this kinky stuff with him, although handcuffing him might be fun. And maybe gagging him, but that's only because there are times when I'm not even remotely interested in him for conversation. *Sigh*. Derek had left on Tuesday to work on a trial out of town, and I was really starting to miss him.

Beyond the bar area, in the dimly lit corners of the room, there was a lot of yelping and moaning going on. Ian and several people were clustered around the stocks, and another group was parked near the upside-down hangy thing, so I still couldn't see how it was being used. Perhaps it was best not to know. A moment later an *extremely* sexy man wearing nothing but a skimpy pair of red underwear approached me. He set down his role-playing toys – a gaudy looking crown and sceptre – on the bar.

"How ya doing?" the Regal Romeo asked.

He was so handsome and cocky standing there in his undies without even a hint of self-consciousness. It unnerved me and I got all tongue-tied.

"Great! The fun sure seems party...I mean, it seems like everyone's having a good time."

He winked at me and said, "How about a Bombay martini? Shaken. Really dry, with a twist. By the way, everyone around here calls me King Arthur."

"Good to meet you. I'm Sasha." I tried to look cool, holding the martini shaker in one hand, and shaking it in rhythm with the music. This guy's smile was electric, and he radiated sex appeal. Why do guys like him instantly make me feel self-conscious? I tried to think of Derek, but His Royal Hotness in front of me was just too yummy to ignore. Besides, there's nothing wrong with *looking*. I sucked in my tummy and tried to look cool. The charade came to an abrupt halt as my hand slipped, and the lid from the martini shaker flew off, splashing icy gin all over the front of my top.

"Guess I'm the top contender in the wet T-shirt contest." I discovered the hard way that my clingy little white T-shirt is fairly transparent when it's wet. Oh dear.

I measured out another couple of ounces of gin and started again. "Interesting crowd. I guess you know most of the people here," I asked, holding the shaker a little more tightly this time.

"I've talked to most of them online, but this is only my third or fourth party with this group. I go to whichever parties I can. It's a great community. Everyone's completely at ease."

I tried not to stare, but his undies left *nothing* to the imagination. Some lucky woman was in for a treat later tonight.

"Oh. That's interesting. I never really thought of it as a community," I said, effortlessly demonstrating my stellar conversation skills.

"Yeah, Ian hosts this group –"

"They're called Bound for Glory, right?" It was a safe bet that the fetish group hadn't named themselves after a Woody Guthrie song about a train. Was that a Woody song?

"Yeah. And there're lots of other groups and chat rooms too, you know, like Second Life, FetLife, sites like that. I belong to those as well, but I prefer this group because all their events are downtown."

"How convenient."

I passed the cocktail to King Schlong and was instantly repulsed. He reached into the front of his undies and whipped out a gold Amex to pay. Eeeeeewwwww! The credit card was warm.

"It's on the house, handsome," I forced a smile and nudged his card back to him. I washed my hands again, this time with scalding water.

Around 1:30, the party started winding down. Some people paired off with others to go to hotel rooms, and a few partiers invited their sex slaves home for a night of obedient lovemaking. Only three or four people left alone, including the Golden Shower Guy and King Arthur of the Red Undies. Other than them, the fetish crowd seemed to be batting just under a thousand. Ian was practically chained to Minerva, a raven-haired barracuda with never-ending cleavage who had shown up around eleven o'clock. Minerva looked like she had a long list of commands in store for Ian later tonight.

"I've packed up everything I can for now," Ian said. "I'll come back tomorrow afternoon for the rest of the gear."

"That's cool," Jessica said. "Everything will be locked up when we leave, but I won't be here tomorrow. I'm starting my vacation in about half an hour, as soon as this shift ends."

"Well then, bon voyage. Is there someone else I should speak to tomorrow?"

"Just ask whoever's on duty downstairs to open up the second floor for you."

"Thanks. Can you pass me my jacket and my bag, please?"

I handed Ian his things from behind the bar and bid him adieu.

By 2:30, thanks to some help from Moose, we had cleaned up, cashed out, and were ready to go home.

"Just let me set the alarm, then we're outta here," Jessica said.

"Do either of you want a ride home?" offered Moose.

"Absolutely," we both answered.

"I'll get the lights," I said.

"Here, Sasha, don't forget your phone."

"Duh." I stuck it in my purse as Jess locked the door behind us.

Sunday, September 30, 2:58 am

I was feeling pretty icky after serving a fetish crowd all night. I tiptoed through the house, careful not to wake my dad, who was sound asleep, and marched right down the hall to the bathroom.

I drew a bath so I could mentally and physically cleanse the night from my body and my memory. I'm not exactly a prude, but whips just ain't my thing. It occurred to me that that could be a great country and western song title. I started humming as I filled the tub, and dumped in half a bottle of baby oil and a package of scented foaming bath beads. I stuck a bath pillow behind my neck and flipped through this month's issue of *Billboard*. I had already read it, but I was so tired, all I really did was look at pictures and captions, and get suds all over the pages. I stayed in the water until it turned cool and my skin had become prune-like.

I heard my brother Shane stumble in around half past three, and head straight to his room. He's always exhausted after a Saturday night at his restaurant. I'd have to wait until morning to tell Shane about my *bizarro* bartending experience. Shane has been in the food and beverage industry for years, but I doubt he's ever seen the likes of what I had tonight.

I towelled off and dusted a liberal amount of talcum powder all over my body, and then I spritzed enough Versace on myself to drown out the lingering scent of *eau du trashy*. I left my bedroom window open a crack so I could enjoy the cool breeze coming from the early autumn night. It was almost four in the morning, and I was snoring softly before my head even hit the pillow.

Sunday,
11:15 am

"Can I get a large orange juice, please, and a coffee?" I said to the waiter as I took my seat at a sunny patio table. Toronto was currently experiencing a welcome blast of, ahem, Aboriginal Peoples' summer, and patios all around the 'hood were jammed. Today's brunch was at Kilgour's, near Bloor and Bathurst, one of the Annex's hidden gems, and home of the best eggs Benedict anyone could ever ask for.

Jessica and Lindsey had gotten here before me and were already on their second cups of coffee. No doubt Jessica needed the caffeine as much as I did.

"Sorry I'm late. I slept through the alarm."

"I could hardly drag my ass out of bed this morning. That was quite a night," Jessica stifled a yawn as she spoke. "At least I'll be able to sleep on the plane tonight."

"So, tell me all about the fetish group," Lindsey said.

"I have no idea where to begin," I said.

"I can sort of get my head around the dominant and submissive part of it, but the role-playing stuff I just don't get," Jessica said.

"Like the ancient cowboy?" I said.

"Exactly. This grey-haired old dude, he had to be at least 168, was all tricked out like a wrangler from the Old West," Jessica said. "And this chick – she was probably in her early thirties and pretty good looking – well, she was letting him bronco bust her or something. Giddy-up." We both snickered.

Lindsey gave us a look of utter disbelief.

"You should have seen them, Lindsey," I said. "The girl was down on her hands and knees, and the old guy was whipping her ass like there was no tomorrow."

Our waiter, who happened to be delivering our meals at this exact moment, gave me a quizzical look, then asked if anyone needed ketchup. We all said no, and he walked away, no doubt wondering about the rest of our conversation.

"Wow. I hope you earned good tips. Tell me at least the money made it worth your while."

"Meh. They tipped okay, but they weren't exactly big drinkers. I probably made more money for less hassle back at the slut mines." If nothing else, the phone sex job had paid well, and had given me a unique insight into human nature.

"All this talk about kinky sex makes me want to become a born-again virgin," Lindsey said.

"It was surreal," Jessica said. "But enough about that. What's happening in your world, Lindsey? Any appointments today?" Lindsey, who is a real estate agent, usually has to devote most Saturday and Sunday afternoons to open houses and viewings of resale homes priced well above average prices. Such is the Toronto real estate racket.

My purse started ringing.

"Hello," I said, fumbling to grab the phone before the call went into voicemail.

"Hi, is Ian there?"

"Sorry, wrong number." I clicked off. A moment later, the phone rang again, and the same guy asked again for Ian. "Sorry, it's still the wrong number," I said and hung up. I took a closer look at the BlackBerry and realized *toot sweet* that it wasn't mine.

"Ooops," I said. "I think this is Ian's phone. I must have picked it up last night by mistake."

"Shit happens. I'm sure he'll call the bar looking for it," Jessica said.

"I bet he's got some juicy stuff on it," I said, flipping through the menu. "Maybe some kinky photos…."

"You're not really going to poke your nose in his business, are you?" Lindsey said.

"Of course not. I'm just saying I could, if I wanted to. That's all."

"About the last thing I want to see after last night is pictures of kinky sex," Jessica said. "Anyhow, Lindsey, what have you got on this afternoon? Want to tag along while I do some impulse shopping?"

"My afternoon has unexpectedly opened up," Lindsey said. "I kept today free from clients because I was supposed to go to some rah-rah-rah political group hug at around four, but it's been cancelled."

"You mean the community BBQ or picnic or whatever with Mr. Plastic Fantastic wannabe mayor and his Barbie Doll wife?" I asked.

I was only half listening to Jess and Linds. My thumb was poking through the text messages and callers list on Ian's phone. I wanted to get his BlackBerry back to him as soon as I could. I know how lost I'd be without mine. I scrolled through the directory to see if he had a home number or a work number stored in his contact list.

"I know these political events are pretty lame, but they're good for networking. There's always a chance I'll get a listing out of it," Lindsey said. "Besides, Shane's an ardent supporter of Tim Nealson."

"I know." My brother had never before shown even a slight interest in politics, but that was before he started working for himself. Now, as a small business owner, he was becoming something of an activist, at least at the municipal level.

"Why's it cancelled? The election's only three weeks away. You'd think Nealson and whatsherface would be out there glad-handing everyone and taking pictures with cute little babies," Jessica said.

"Gwendolyn. The missus is Gwendolyn. She was in a car accident this morning," Lindsey said.

"Uh-oh."

"I don't think it was very serious. All I heard on the radio was that she'd been in a fender-bender and was taken to hospital."

"Yikes. Not exactly what the Nealsons need to deal with right now," Jessica said.

"Sometimes I think she campaigns harder than he does. She gets her name into every news release and every sound bite. If Tim Nealson gets elected mayor, I have a feeling his wife will be the one who's really running City Hall," I said.

"It may not be such a slam dunk. Cooperman and the Italian Stallion are gaining in the polls," Lindsey said.

"And the right-wing blowhard has a loyal following."

"Anyhow, I'll have a chance to do my bit to support Nealson later this week," Lindsey said.

"Oh yeah, he's doing that dinner at Shane's place," I said.

Shane's place is a wonderful restaurant called Pastiche. It's a five-star fine dining room with five-star service offering five-star cuisine at five-star prices. Luckily, I usually eat here for free.

"I'm kind of surprised to see this side of Shane. He's normally so passive, but Nealson's positions on small business and taxes have won him over. Shane's really excited about the shindig at Pastiche," Lindsey said, more to Jessica than to me.

"What night is it again?" I asked.

"This Thursday. It's being arranged by some group called the Egg Business Improvement Association," Lindsey said.

"It's not egg, you idiot. It's E.G.G., which stands for Elm, Gould, and Gerrard streets," Jessica said.

"Whatever," Lindsey retorted pithily.

"I totally get why Shane supports Tim Nealson, but honestly, none of the candidates in this campaign really bowls me over. I don't think any one of them is cut out to be mayor," I said.

"I hate to sound like a bimbo, but can we get off this topic?" Jessica said. "It's a bit heavy for me right now. Keep in mind, less than twelve hours ago, I was watching people in leather and Saran Wrap paddle each other. I'm still suffering from the aftershocks."

"I think I'm permanently scarred from last night, too. I can't get rid of the images," I said, flipping again through Ian's phone.

"For crying out loud Sasha, that's not a toy. Why don't you just call back the wrong number? Maybe whoever that was has another number for Mr. Spank Me."

"There are times I don't feel I deserve to call myself a sleuth." I hit recall. The wrong number dude was a guy named Andy.

"There seems to be a mix up, and I somehow ended up with Ian's phone," I said. "You're the last guy who called this number, so I thought maybe you could help me track down Ian."

"He has a land line," Andy said. "Why don't you call him at home? His number is –"

"Just a sec, let me find something to write with." I dug through my purse. Wallet, a hairbrush, some tampons, two tubes of lipstick, a ring of keys – some legal, others not – gum wrappers, my iPod, a broken pencil, a golf ball – not sure from whence that came – a few hair scrunchies, a green marker, and my own cell phone, way down at the bottom of my bag. "Okay. Fire away."

I scribbled the number in Kelly green felt-tip on a paper napkin. When I hung up, I immediately called Ian's home number and left a message for him to call me.

"So are you all packed for your trip, Jessica?" Lindsey asked.

Jessica was booked on an overnight flight to London Heathrow for a family reunion planned around her great grandma's hundredth birthday.

"Pretty much. Just a couple last-minute things. I have to make a pit-stop on my way home, and then I'm all set."

"Since I'm free, I can drive you to the airport, if you like," Lindsey offered.

"Thanks, but no need. I'm carpooling with my cousin Zack and my aunt and uncle."

"What did you decide to get Great Granny for her birthday?" I asked. "It's gotta be pretty hard to shop for someone's hundredth birthday."

"I got her a pair of argyle socks."

"Tell me you didn't…" I said.

Long before Jessica was a twinkle in her daddy's eye, Jessica's great-grandmother had both legs severed just below the knee after an unfortunate incident involving railroad tracks and too many glasses of dry sherry. The old bird never bothered with prosthetics and has spent the last forty-plus years in a wheelchair.

"You're positively deranged. GG's going to write you out of her will."

"The old broad still has an off-the-wall sense of humour. Zack is giving her a pair of tap dancing shoes," Jessica said.

"What in the hell is she going to do with any of it?"

"She'll use the socks as mittens, and the tap shoes will probably become a doorstopper or bookends."

My jaw dropped as the waiter came by to clear our plates, and to offer coffee refills or dessert.

"I'll pass. It would be extravagant to have dessert after eggs Benedict," I said, in a rare instance of self-restraint.

"Before I forget, here's the key to my apartment and the key to my mailbox," Jessica said.

I tucked them into my wallet.

"Thanks again for offering to cat-sit and apartment-sit for me," she said. Jessica's big fat lazy Himalayan cat Bella was like a baby to her. I'm kind of neutral on cats, but this twenty-pound ball of grey and white fur, with a face that looked like a ping pong paddle, was okay. Low maintenance and occasionally affectionate. "And help yourself to whatever you want. *Mi casa su casa.*"

"No sweat. I'll enjoy the peace and quiet," I said.

"Hey, I resent that," Lindsey said.

Lindsey is my brother Shane's girlfriend – actually, they're engaged now. Even though Shane and I are both in our early thirties, we both still live at home with our resignedly indulgent and frequently befuddled dad Jack. Lindsey stays at our place two or three nights a week, so the Jackson abode is often pretty busy. Moments of solitude are cherished for their rarity.

"Well, if you weren't allergic to cats, you could apartment-sit and use the place as a love nest," I replied.

"Bella doesn't eat much. Just measure out a scoop of cat food every day and make sure the water bowl is full."

"I think I can manage."

"And the litter box is in the bathroom."

"I know," I said.

"Yeah, but you've got to change it as often as you can. It starts to stink really quickly. The ventilation in the bathroom is terrible."

"No worries," I said.

"So what time do you have to meet your new client?" Lindsey asked me.

"In about half an hour. We should get the check."

A Mr. and Mrs. Edquist had left me a message on my office number yesterday morning, but I wasn't able to schedule a meeting with them until this afternoon.

"Do you know what kind of a case it is?" Jessica asked.

"Yeah. A teenage girl who ran away from home. It promises to be frustrating. Runaways always are."

Sunday,
2:05 pm

"We've been wandering all over the city looking for her," Mrs. Edquist said.

"And you're certain she's in Toronto?" I asked.

Mrs. Edquist, in a basic pair of navy gabardine slacks and a rather ugly white and blue polka dot blouse with batwing sleeves, was sitting on the edge of a neatly made bed in a standard room at the Best Western Hotel downtown. Her hair was neatly combed and a few grey roots were poking through. Her husband, a seemingly affable, middle aged man with a bit of a paunch, was pacing back and forth in front of the window, and I was in the beige vinyl club chair beside the bolted-down television. Mrs. Edquist was calm and business-like right now, but her red-rimmed eyes told me she'd cried more than a few tears of worry over her daughter this morning.

"Her friends all said she was coming here. Macy always talks about getting out of Peterborough and coming to the big city. She says small towns stifle her."

Macy is the sixteen-year-old angst-ridden, angry Goth offspring of Mr. and Mrs. Small Town Middle Class. Peterborough, about an hour and a half from Toronto, began as a farming town, then became a factory town of sorts, and now was mainly a university town. Mom and Pop both had administration jobs at Trent University, she in the Registrar's Office and he in Alumni Affairs. The daughter in the photo looked like she would prefer hanging out in dodgy back alleys with a bunch of skinheads rather than trying to decide on her eventual major. Her dyed black hair was shaved about an inch above both ears. She had on way too much black eyeliner, and seemed to be sneering at the camera.

"Well, Mrs. Edquist, a lot of runaways end up here. Has Macy taken off from home before?"

"Please, call me Phyllis."

"And call me Harold. Or Harry if you prefer. She's taken off four or five times in as many months," Mr. Edquist said. "But she always comes back in a couple of days. This time it's different. She's been gone almost a month."

"We had to come here to look for her. We couldn't just stay home and wait for the phone to ring." Mom's voice cracked a bit.

"The Toronto cops were no help?" I already knew the answer. There was little the police could do since, at sixteen, Macy was no longer a child.

"No. We tried, and they were sympathetic, but impotent. We've put up posters all over downtown. We've canvassed the streets where we've seen kids hanging out. None of them could help us," said Phyllis.

Pierced and tattooed teens hanging around the usual inner-city haunts wouldn't be inclined to speak to such examples of Suburban White Bread under any circumstances. Rebellious youths would stay mum out of spite just because the Edquists had "Conformist Parental Units" written all over them.

"Where have you been looking?" I asked.

Mr. Edquist rattled off a list of neighbourhoods and intersections. Parkdale, the Eaton Centre, Yorkville, College Street.

"And when have you been doing this?" I asked.

"Since the week after she left."

"No, I mean, what time of day?"

"We hit the streets right after breakfast, and keep going, off and on all day, until suppertime, maybe five thirty or six."

"That's your mistake. The goths and punx and emos and phreaks don't even start to come to life until noon. I'll begin looking in the late afternoon and go until two or three in the morning."

"Thank you so much for helping us. Harold and I can't take any more time off work. We've used up all of our vacation days. We're not exactly poor, but we can't afford to take unpaid time off work. We still have a mortgage."

I was reluctant to bring up the subject of my fees.

"Today's our last day in Toronto, we're going to check out soon, and drive home. We both have to be back at work tomorrow."

"I'll give it a whirl, but only for a couple of days. I don't want to waste my time or your money."

I gave them the contract I had tucked into my purse. The bleeding heart in me wanted to help these folks. Sympathy prompted me to shave about twenty percent from my usual rates. They gave me all the info they could on Macy Edquist, plus a few more photos. We shook hands, and I bid them farewell, already feeling guilty that I would be profiting from their pain and worry.

Such is life. I've got to make a living. I can bartend at fetish parties only so often.

Sunday,
4:29 pm

Back at Dad's house, I started digging through my closet. No one could ever accuse me of looking like a suburban middle class parent, but I didn't exactly blend in with the chip-on-their-shoulder teen set either. I knew no one would talk to me if I looked like a square, so I dug through some of the clothes from my rocker chick band days. A faded and frayed, ratty old pair of black jeans - held together by little more than a hope and a prayer - looked anti-establishment enough for the job. A ragged Ramones T-shirt and no bra seemed to fit the bill, complemented by a battered old pair of Doc Martens boots that were out of style enough to be retro. I swapped my blue leather purse for a tan canvas US Army Surplus bag with a Union Jack patch sewn onto it, and mussed my hair a bit. I washed off my usually subtle make-up and then smudged a lot of black eyeliner around my eyes and headed downtown to pretend to be a cool older chick who belonged on the scene. Sort of.

I got off the 505 streetcar just south of the Toronto Coach Terminal. A handful of ragamuffins in dirty clothes with safety pins poking through every facial orifice were panhandling a block from the bus station. They had a scrawny, mangy husky with them. The dog look marginally cleaner than the five teens, but that's only because he could lick himself. Clearly these losers were too apathetic to shower even once a week.

"It's not much, but I'll give you ten bucks if you answer a couple of questions for me."

A punk dude with dirty blond hair answered, "Ten bucks each?"

"Hell, no. How about twenty for the group? You can get Rover there some dog biscuits. He looks hungry."

"Whadup?"

"Anyone seen this girl? Name's Macy. She's sixteen,

came here about a month ago. From Peterborough."
I passed around the few snapshots Mom and Pop had
given me.

"I seen her around the Eaton Centre coupla times,"
Dirty Blond said.

"Know where I can find her?" I asked.

"Nope."

"Does she have a usual hangout? A usual crowd?"

"Dunno," they mumbled in unison.

"I think I seen her hanging with a bunch of cutters,"
said a girl with torn fishnet stockings and lime green
streaks in her platinum hair. "They usually chill somewhere around Kensington Market."

"Thanks a bunch." I handed the girl two tens and
started walking towards the market.

"Word."

Describing Kensington Market is a pretty tall order.
First of all, it's not a market per se, but a neighbourhood
in downtown Toronto, loosely bordered by Spadina to
the east, Bellevue to the west, College Street to the north
and Dundas to the south. Yeah, the druggies and the
skinheads hang out here, but to leave the description at
that would do the neighbourhood a disservice. It's like
the area has a split personality and alternate versions of
itself appear throughout the day. Buskers, panhandlers
and artists are generally here around the clock. Ditto
a few neighbourhood drunks. However, the area has
some super-cool funky shopping, especially when
it comes to vintage clothing and army surplus. The
presence of these stores is no doubt a response to the
presence of aging hippies and artists.

The street life in Kensington has changed little over the years. The same few buskers are always on the same old corners, strumming acoustic guitars and hoping the open guitar case would fill with people's spare change. As for the disaffected Gen-X layabouts, well, they're interchangeable with new teens from one year to the next. They all have the exact same ways of being non-conformist, anti-establishment rebels.

The first teens I talked to were sitting on the steps of a vacant storefront. A guy and a girl, both about seventeen, each appeared malnourished and dirty. The guy had a newish looking tattoo around his neck. It was supposed to be barbed wire or thorns or something, but the amateur job looked more like a string of the letter " *C*" in *Old English* font. The tattoo itself was puffy and red, and I'd wager that within a day or two, buddy would be in need of penicillin for the pus about to ooze out of his newly inked neck.

"Hey, wassup?" I asked, trying to sound casual.

"Yo," answered Ink.

"Know many of the people who hang here?"

"Why ya asking?" He sort of thrust his chin out when he answered. His twiglike girlfriend stared blankly at me.

"I'm looking for my little sister. Her name's Macy." I passed them the photo. "Seen her around?"

"Maybe," Ink said. The Twig just shook her head. Twiggy had a bunch on short scars on the inside of her forearms. It was plain to see she was into self-mutilation. Each scar was about an inch wide, and they ran perpendicular to her veins, up and down the length of her arms, from wrist to elbow. God, I hoped Macy wasn't into self-inflicted pain, although the kids by the bus station had alluded to Macy hanging out with a bunch of cutters. This didn't bode well.

"You see, our mom was in a car wreck. She might die any day now. Macy's been on a tear for a couple weeks. She doesn't even know about the accident."

"Mighta seen her a while ago, but I dunno. The last few days was a blur." His girlfriend giggled a bit.

"If you see her, gimme a call." I gave them a piece of paper with my cell number on it. I had no illusions they'd see Macy, nor did I think they'd put my number in a safe place where they wouldn't lose it, but this is my job. It just takes one person out of a string of dead-ends to help me crack a case. Maybe Ink and Twiggy would be the ones. And maybe leprechauns are real. After I gave them my cell number, I thought fleetingly about Ian and his BlackBerry. I thought it was odd that he hadn't yet returned my call. I made a mental note to try calling him again later.

One great thing about Kensington is the food. Over the years, Kensington market has been populated by various groups of New Canadians: Eastern Europeans at the turn of the century, Portuguese in the 1950s, Jamaicans in the seventies, and more recently Latinos from Central and South America. You can get wonderful empanadas and gorditas on one block, on another you can stock up on goat roti, around the corner you can find an unending selection of cheeses that'll knock your socks off, and there are a number of Asian grocers with a wide array of unidentifiable legumes, fungi, and dried shellfish. The neighbourhood smells wonderful and repugnant all at once. This is the Kensington

Market suburbanites visit on a casual, lazy Saturday, or where tourists – consulting dog-eared copies of Lonely Planet travel guides – come to take in a heady dose of multiculturalism.

Kensington Market is also an edgy urban enclave, long popular with counterculture groups, from Rastas to punk rockers to artists. I've had my share of hanging in Kensington Market over the years, but it was usually related to something from my band days. Some of my first gigs when I was playing the Toronto music scene were at Graffiti's, a bar that paid so very little that any starving new garage band who wanted to play there could. As I poked in and out of storefronts and taverns, I recognized more than a few nameless faces, pickled barflies who never seem to leave their usual barstools. I recognized a white-haired Irish man who had once been one of the best Flamenco guitar players in Canada. For the last decade or so, ever since he lost his wife to lung cancer, he's been trying to slowly kill himself with copious amounts of whisky and his own three-pack-a-day nicotine habit. The woman a few stools over from him reportedly had once been a wildly popular call girl. She now seemed threadbare all over, from her clothes to her hair to her teeth. But if you checked her out with half-closed eyes, and let your imagination fill in a few blanks, you could see that she had once been very pretty. The word on the street was that she was now on welfare and was HIV positive.

A young girl with black stringy hair was walking just ahead of me. I knew the odds were slim, but I picked up my pace to catch up with her.

"Hey Macy," I said, tapping her on the shoulder.

"Huh?" The girl jumped a bit.

"Sorry, didn't mean to startle you. Thought you were someone else." The girl's face was rather cherubic, despite the blood-red lipstick and slashes of black eyeliner. Anyone with naturally chubby cheeks would never be convincing as a Goth. "From behind, you resembled the person I'm trying to find." I shoved Macy's picture in front o her.

"That doesn't look like me."

"I know, I said from behind. Same height, same hair. Any chance you've seen her?"

"Nope." And with that, Cherub walked away.

As an older, inner-city neighbourhood - established back in the days when Toronto had a population in the low thousands - Kensington Market remains rather small and claustrophobic. I guess, back in those horse-and-buggy days of yesteryear, no one had planned ahead to make Kensington vehicle friendly. Finding a parking spot around here is a bitch, but then, only an idiot would choose to drive here. The narrow, one way streets are hellish for drivers to navigate, but with the crowds and congestion, cars can rarely move at much more than fifteen or twenty kilometres an hour, so pedestrians are fearless about zigzagging across the street mid-block. It could even be argued that cyclists pose a greater danger to walkers than cars do, given that many bikers ignore stop signs, or ride the wrong way on Kensington's one-way streets. I narrowly escaped being plastered to the road by a stoned slacker on a pimped-out BMX.

"Whoaaa, sorry lady," he intoned in a sleepy voice, as I jumped back from the curb.

I walked to the next block and waited for the light to change, but I needn't have bothered. There was absolutely no vehicular traffic in Kensington Market today. One of the cool things about Kensington is that on the last Sunday of every month – in other words, today – the neighboured is a car-free zone. Pedestrian Sundays in the Market are wonderfully busy and laid-back. I traipsed around a while longer, and talked with another dozen teens or so. I got a lot of shrugs, was told to fuck off twice, and one guy asked me if I wanted to do a few hits with him. He failed to specify hits of what, and I was afraid to ask.

All in a day's work. I was tired and hungry, so I decided my brother would love to treat me to dinner.

Sunday,
7:51 pm

"You know we have a dress code, right?" Shane asked when I walked through the back door into the kitchen of Pastiche. He shook his head at my scruffy sartorial choices. Shane was standing over a hot stove stirring a curry coconut broth for the mussel dish featured on tonight's prix fixe menu.

"Yeah, I don't exactly class up the joint, do I? I can eat in the kitchen." I said.

"Pass me a bowl." Shane pulled a tureen out of the

refrigerator, and ladled out a serving of the soup du jour. He had his back to me and busied himself for a moment adding this and that to the dish.

I ate standing up, leaning against one of the prep tables. Not the most elegant way to eat soup, but gift horses and choosy beggars – and I eat at Shane's place for free. A bit of cool soup dribbled onto my shirt. I left it there; I thought the stain might lend me some unkempt credibility with the street kids I was planning to canvass after dinner.

"Damn, this is good. Sweet and spicy? I can taste lemongrass."

"Yeah. Chilled Spicy Thai Watermelon soup with Crabmeat. There's lemongrass, cilantro, Serrano chilli, and ginger. You like it?"

Shane knew he didn't have to ask. The fact that I was practically inhaling the bowl showed how much I liked it, but Shane is a chef and he loves to hear feedback on his latest creations. "A mouthful of heaven," I said.

"This week, except on Thursday when we're having the Nealson party, the restaurant's doing a theme on Asian-inspired dishes. With a twist, of course. You can try some mussels if you want."

"Bring 'em on." We chatted while I ate and Shane cooked and fretted, and occasionally barked at the kitchen staff. Frankie, the line cook, told Shane to take a flying leap, to which Shane said something about hell freezing over. It was all good-natured. A salty, weathered army vet, Frankie – probably more so than anyone else on staff – keeps Shane from completely losing his mind on busy nights.

"You know, Sasha, the Asian menu theme reminds

me of my friend Percy."

"Do I know him?"

"Probably not. A good guy. We worked together years ago at that Italian place in Woodbridge?"

"I remember the place. That's where I got food poisoning."

"How many times do I have to tell you that wasn't my fault?"

"I lost five pounds in less than a week."

"It saved you the trouble of going to the gym, didn't it?"

"Yeah right. Anyhow, what about Percy?"

"He opened a pan-Pacific restaurant called Monsoon a few months ago. He's pretty sure someone on staff is ripping him off."

"Theft in a restaurant? No, you must be kidding." I was well aware of how often restaurateurs got robbed blind by their employees. "Give him my number and I'll see what I can do."

Sunday, 9:12 pm

After dinner at Shane's place, I made the rounds of the blocks near the Eaton Centre. A crazed old gummer, wearing a white terry cloth robe and misshapen top hat, and holding a crucifix made out of tinfoil, was standing on a crate while warning passers-by about the pending day of reckoning. I wondered if the aluminum wrap interfered with the telepathic messages being sent to him from homicidal zombies in New Jersey. I flashed him a peace sign as I passed. He curtsied and then spat at me. I fleetingly contemplated the symbolism of the moment, but came up empty.

A gaggle of kids in faded jeans were playing hacky-sack in Dundas Square. They hardly stopped playing long enough to look at Macy's photo. I talked to anyone and everyone who looked to be in Macy's age group, but scored exactly zero. My feet were getting sore from all the walking. The pool halls and coffee shops I popped into didn't net me so much as a nibble, but there was no reason to expect that they would have. It was safe to assume that Macy didn't have a lot of cash, so she wasn't likely to be anyplace that cost money.

A few of the punks hanging out in front of the Evergreen Centre for Youth were borderline helpful.

"I know for sure I seen her around here a coupla days ago," said a guy in a hoodie. He passed the photo to the freckle-faced girl standing next to him.

"Yeah, for sure, it was yesterday," she said. The girl looked about fifteen years old, and about six months pregnant.

"She asked about places to hang out, you know, the scene."

"I'm flattered you think I'm hip enough to know the scene, but I haven't got a clue what you mean." There is nothing more humbling than vocalizing one's unhipness. If I were going to spend much more time talking to the under-twenty crowd, I'd have to bone up on current slang. An Urban Dictionary tutorial might be in order.

"She asked about scoring some Clarity," said Preggers.

"Clarity?" it was anything but clear to me.

"You know, Adam, the Love Drug, E."

Ah yes, E. Ecstasy, the latest drug to capture the attention of teenaged morons. Methylenedioxymethamphetamine – short form: MDMA, which explains the street name "Adam." I'm unsure what would explain the nickname "Clarity," but I sensed I'd have to actually try the drug to understand, and I'm just not that dedicated to my job.

"And where might she find that?" I asked.

"Where can't you find it is a better question," said Hoodie. He had me there.

"Well, if you see her, give me a call," I said as I dug in my purse for one of my business cards. Preggers pocketed my number. "When are you due?" I asked her.

"He's s'posed to pop out on December twenty-fifth. He's gonna be a boy."

"I'm very happy for you," I said. Actually, I wasn't. Call me old fashioned, but I think there should be a checklist before people are allowed to reproduce. Finishing high school would be the first parental criterion. A fixed address would be number two. "Have you chosen a name yet?"

"I'm gonna name him Noel, like, you know, for Christmas?"

"That's a good choice," I said.

"Yeah, you think so? I think so too, but what if he

doesn't come exactly on Christmas Day? Would Noel still be a good name?"

"Well, if he comes out on December twenty-sixth, you could think about calling him Rocky."

"Uh, maybe…" she said.

I admit the Boxing Day reference is rather oblique.

"Here," I said, passing her twenty bucks. "Grab a bite. You're eating for two."

Searching for someone is no fun. You walk and walk, and talk and talk, and most of it ends up being for naught. It occurred to me that perhaps I should try to beef up the corporate background checking side of my business. Missing persons cases are a drag at any time, but they would suck a lot more once winter comes around and the sidewalks are piled high with dirty snow.

I continued trucking north along Yonge Street towards Wellesley. Now that the sun had long since set, I kicked myself for not being bright enough to bring along a jacket. It had gotten a bit chilly, and while my Ramones T-shirt is cool, it's anything but warm.

I didn't expect much from this 'hood, but there are a few small parks off Yonge where kids hang out sometimes, and I wasn't too far from Jessica's apartment. I could let myself into her place if I wanted to borrow a jacket or go pee. At the risk of making generalizations, Yonge and Carlton is pretty much the edge of the gay neighbourhood. I had little expectation of finding the not-so-sweet-sixteen Macy here, but you never know.

A group of teenaged guys was sprawled out on the patch of lawn near Buddies in Bad Times Theatre. I could smell the dope as I approached them.

"Yo, guys, anyone interested in helping me out?" I asked.

"Maybe. What's up?"

"I'm looking for my little sister. She took off from Peterborough a while ago. Her name's Macy. You see, our mom was in a really bad car accident. Things don't look so good. I think Macy should at least know what happened, you know, in case she wants to visit our mom or something."

"Don't know no one named Macy," said a guy in camouflage pants and a dirty white wife-beater. It was obvious by his demeanour that he was intent on being seen as Mr. Tough Guy, but his bare arms were covered in goosebumps and he was shivering from the cold. Too tough to put on a jacket. Idiot.

"Look at the picture. She might be using a street name, you know?" I waved the pics at them, but they scarcely gave them a glance.

Forward ho. Onward and upwards. Off to my next dead end.

The little park off Church Street north of Wellesley was another known hangout for teens and druggies. It was also reputed to be a little more hard-core. There was a wino passed out in a pool of vomit. Nice. I treaded carefully, not just because of the puke, but also because it wasn't unheard of to find used condoms or syringes around here. Quite unfortunately, a friend's dog had died after accidentally ingesting a needle that was lying among the blades of grass the pooch had decided to munch on. I thought briefly about the dog, a gorgeous golden retriever, and got angry, but had no one to direct the anger at. This generation of druggies was every bit as culpable for the dog's death as the one before them and the one that would follow. Drugs really piss me off, drug dealers even more so.

The park should have been reasonably well-lit, but someone had smashed out the bulbs in three of the streetlamps. A bunch of slackers in grubby clothes and miscellaneous chains were huffing glue on a bench at the far end of the park, where it was especially dark. Nice. It was probably ill-advised to approach them, but I don't always do the smart thing. Like not wearing a jacket. I was really starting to feel cold, and decided I'd call it a night after this.

"Any of you guys know a chick named Macy?"

One guy shrugged his shoulders. The two girls sitting next to him just giggled.

"Even if we did, why would we tell you?" said another.

I tossed twenty dollars at the guy who had shrugged. "No hassles, no worries. I just want to be sure she's safe."

Shrugger pocketed the money. "I seen her a couple days ago. I think Friday. She took off with some guys to go to a rave."

"Where was the rave?" I asked.

"Cherry Beach –"

"Shut the fuck up, man. You shouldn't be telling her this shit," said the guy on the end.

"What the fuck difference does it make?" said Shrugger.

"No worries," I said. "Everyone knows about the raves at Cherry Beach. I've been to a few myself."

"Yeah, right."

"Years ago. Know the guys she went with?" I asked Shrugger.

"One's called Shank. He don't come around here much. Hangs mostly around Queen and Bathurst."

"You're awesome, dude. Thanks."

Monday, October 1, 12:25 am

Instead of going back to my house in Riverdale, I walked the few short blocks to Jessica's. I was too lazy to go back to the east end, and I liked the idea of temporarily having my own space.

Her apartment is kind of small, but very cozy. The front door opens on to a small foyer from which you can pretty much see the whole apartment. There's a little galley kitchen on the left, a bathroom on the right. Straight ahead, there's a living room on the left and her bedroom to the right. The bedroom door was open and I could see Bella curled up on the bed. She let out a throaty mewl and pawed at her ears.

I kicked off my shoes, and poured myself a glass of white zinfandel from a Tetra Pak I found in the door of the fridge. I flicked on the television and stretched out on the paisley couch. Wrapping myself up in an old patchwork quilt, I sipped my wine while I channel surfed. Bella pawed her way in from the bedroom, and hoisted her twenty pounds of fur up onto the couch. She turned herself into a fluffy white foot warmer, purred softly a few times and then started to lick herself. Hell, if I could do that, I'd never leave the house.

Even though it was pretty late, I was wide awake, at least mentally. The runaway teen was on my mind. I'd been a bit of a rebel during my youth, but I'd never done anything to cause Dad sleepless nights. Grey hairs, sure, but I would never have crossed certain lines. Most drugs were on the wrong side of that line, although I confess to smoking a joint or two back in the day…but I didn't inhale. It's the chemical and synthetic stuff that makes me grind my teeth. So often, the synthesized drugs are a one-way ticket to Hell.

I wondered what was going through Macy's mind. Probably not much, if she was huffing glue or popping meth.

I hoped some mindless television would lull me into Neverland, and push the troubled teen from my hyperactive cerebellum. *Boring sci-fi movie. Infomercial. Infomercial. Cheesy sitcom rerun. Sports. Another infomercial.* I was just about nod off when something on the local news grabbed my attention and I sat up for a closer look. The news anchor cut to earlier footage from a crime scene. The on-the-scene reporter was standing in front of an area cordoned off by yellow police tape. A body had been discovered early Sunday morning in Toronto's Port Lands. It was the mention of a black leather kilt on a deceased man that caught my attention. I cranked up the volume.

Early this morning, a dog walker in the Port Lands area, south of Lakeshore and Leslie, discovered a body police are now calling Toronto's fortieth homicide this year. Thirty-eight-year-old Ian Dooley of High Park was found face down at the water's edge, the two bullet holes in his back indicating foul play.

At the time Dooley's body was discovered, he was wearing nothing but a leather kilt, and a pair of leather army boots. His abandoned pickup truck was found illegally parked a few blocks away in Leslieville. Authorities called to remove the vehicle became suspicious when they noticed what they believed to be weapons in the back of the truck. Further investigation led to the identification of the body.

Police have begun tracing the victim's final hours and have determined that what they thought were weapons were actually equipment used the previous night at a fetish party held at The Stealth Lounge above The Pilot Tavern in Toronto's Yorkville neighbourhood. Police continue their investigation and say they are pursuing several leads.

Holy crap.

My life is anything but normal. I take on casual work when it comes my way. I investigate freaky cases. I get whack jobs as clients. But until yesterday, I'd never been to an S&M party and I'd never really known a murder victim. Not that I knew Ian Dooley well. In fact, I didn't know him at all. However, the last time I'd seen Ian Dooley, he'd been very much alive. And now he wasn't.

Shit. I had a whole new incentive to return Ian's BlackBerry, but obviously not to its rightful owner. The cops would want it now as evidence, of a sort. Oh dear. I was too tired to do anything about it for the moment. Besides, the homicide dicks were probably sleeping right now, just as I should be. I could take care of it in the morning.

Although it's not decor I'd ever choose, Jessica's bedroom is very calming. It's a large square room. To the right of the bedroom door is a huge walk-in closet, and straight ahead is a four-poster bed with a pale rose Laura Ashley floral print. The bedroom is just a bit too girly-girl and fifi for me. I couldn't imagine a guy feeling comfortable having sex in this room. Hell, I couldn't even picture a guy getting it up in here, but maybe that's just me. I thought wallpaper in general was pretty much out of style, but all four walls of Jessica's room are covered in textured floral paper. The window is covered in frilly curtains with a valance that matches the wallpaper. The dresser and night tables are whitewashed faux French Provincial covered with lacy doilies, dainty knick-knacks, framed photos, and scented candles.

I threw my clothes on the floor and borrowed one of Jessica's T-shirts to sleep in. Her bed was comfortable, and the bedroom was soothingly dark and very quiet. Up here on the twelfth floor, I couldn't hear any of the noise or traffic from the street below.

I should have drifted right off to a deep sleep, but I didn't. Images of leather and people spanking each other, and bullet wounds, and bodies on the beach, and runaway girls kept me tossing and turning for quite a while.

Then, somewhere around 5:30, I awoke from a bad dream. Not a nightmare exactly, but unsettling and rather disturbing. I dreamed I was a Jersey cow, languishing in a sunny green pasture until a throng of cloaked and hooded people came along and tore the leather flesh right from my bovine body with their bare hands. After each strip of flesh was torn, a new one immediately grew, which they also tore off. I mooed and grazed while they skinned me alive.

It took a while to drift back to sleep.

Monday,
9:00 am

The ringing phone on Jessica's night table jolted me out of my reverie and into semi-consciousness.

"Yo, sis, sorry to wake you," Shane said.

"Ugmmpth. This better be important. What time is it?"

"Some cops called here a few minutes ago. They want to talk to you. Something about a dead guy by the waterfront and that fetish party you worked at the other night."

"I had a feeling I'd be hearing from the boys in blue."

"I'm not even going to ask," Shane said, "but I wanted to give you a head's up. I figured you were at Jessica's and gave the cops her number."

"Thanks. I think."

There was no point trying to get back to sleep, so I dragged myself out of bed and into the bathroom, where I promptly tripped over Bella and the damn litter box. I kicked the mess aside and jumped into the shower. I stood under an icy cold stream until I felt clear-headed and semi-human. As I was towelling off, Jessica's phone rang again.

"May I please speak with Sasha Jackson," said a woman with a no-nonsense voice.

"This is Sasha."

"I'm Detective Wright. I'm with the Homicide department. I'd like to speak with you this morning if you have some time."

The "if you have some time" bit was tacked on at the end out of politeness. Cops never call with passive requests. For them my schedule this morning was wide open, even if it wasn't.

"I'm staying at a friend's place downtown. Apartment-sitting. Or actually cat-sitting." I made a mental note to fill Bella's food dish. "I'm at 29 Wood Street, just off Yonge."

"We'll be there in about twenty minutes." Detective Wright said.

"I'm on the twelfth floor, apartment 1202."

A soon as I hung up the phone, I did a whirling dervish routine to get dried and dressed. I threw my hair into a ponytail and quickly plundered through Jessica's closet. I put on a pair of her dark blue Lulu Lemon yoga pants and a long-sleeved T-shirt from The Gap. Each was a little bit baggy on me, but I didn't want to put on yesterday's grunge wear again. I didn't have a toothbrush in my bag, so I swigged a mouthful of Listerine.

Then I ran into the kitchen and threw down a scoop of cat food for Bella, and put on a pot of java for the arrival of Metro's Finest.

I had next to no time to snoop through Ian's BlackBerry and make note of whatever was worth noting. I'm not sure why I did this, but it was more or less automatic. Gut instinct and general nosiness maybe? Knee jerk sleuthing? An autopilot reaction to hearing about a crime? More likely it was partly because I sort of knew the victim, but it's also my nature to take whatever info comes my way. My entire career is based on knowing things that other people don't.

Damn. I kicked myself for not being more of a snoop last night. The cops were due in about five minutes. I jotted down names and numbers for the last few calls on Ian's BlackBerry. *Mimi. Scott T. Tricia Lado. Wendi. Robin.* I wondered if that was a guy or a girl. *Justin. Justin again. Wendi again. Lisa Gardiner. Mimi again. Paul Avignon.* If I were smarter than a fifth grader, I'd have copied or swiped the SIM card. Alas, I didn't think of that until much later. Damn.

The stored photos tab included folders called *Jamaica, Wendi, and Birthday.* I had already peeked at the *Jamaica* and *Birthday* folders when I had discovered the phone. I had assumed – wrongly – that the Wendi folder contained more pictures of the same kid, but I couldn't have been more wrong. The *Birthday* pictures showed a pudgy little dark-haired girl, maybe four years old, wearing a party hat and opening presents. The *Jamaica* photos were typical holiday beach shots: sunsets, seashores, and scenery.

The *Wendi* files were probably related to the Wendi

on his callers list. The pictures in this file were a bit of a shocker. There were five pictures, each a bit grainy and somewhat fuzzy, but there was no doubt the pictures showed a naked woman doing things that made even me blush. The first picture showed a dark-haired young woman giving oral sex to a very well-endowed man. The next two were full frontal shots of her lying on a bearskin rug, legs spread, fingers exploring, grinning from ear to ear. The last two photos of Wendi showed her on all fours, with one guy keeping her busy in front, while another kept her busy from behind. *Yikes.* For some reason I couldn't explain, I was sure these pictures had nothing to do with the fetish scene. Although these were pretty X-rated, there were no toys and no leather or chains in any of the images, just straight-up, raw sex. If I ever met Wendi, I'd be embarrassed to talk to her. Too much information.

I was about to poke through Ian's text messages again when an authoritative rap on the door made me jump. I shoved the BlackBerry and my notepad in a kitchen drawer and answered the door.

"So what can you tell us about this fetish party?" Detective Wright was clearly in charge. Her partner, a lanky Italian guy with buck teeth, didn't say anything after introducing himself. I think he just came along for the ride. He stroked Bella behind the ears a few times, and then just sat there looking useless.

"It was a pretty weird bunch, but except for the overall strangeness of the whole evening, I really didn't see anything unusual."

"Were there any conflicts? Any confrontations?"

She furrowed her brow as she jotted notes on a little pad. Detective Wright looked like she followed the police force guidebook to a tee. Her posture was pickle-up-her-butt straight, her pants had knife-edge creases, and her red hair cropped so short it was almost a crew cut. She seemed like the kind of person who wouldn't find a whoopee cushion very funny. I think they're hilarious.

"Nothing that I was aware of. People did their kinky role-playing, and spanked or whipped each other, but it was a pretty…um…festive atmosphere," I said.

"Did anyone, male or female, seem to zero in on Ian?" Detective Wright asked.

"I don't think so. I mean, he was the guy who had arranged the party. He made the rounds talking with just about everyone. Actually, there was one couple who tried to get in, but the doorman escorted them out."

I'd almost forgotten about the trailer trash couple who were thrown out after the broad had a deliberate wardrobe malfunction. Could anyone be pissed off about not being on the guest list to kill someone? Seems unlikely, but human nature's unpredictable.

"Do you have their names? Did they try to come back?"

"I don't think so. You'd have to ask Moose."

"What about the woman he left with? Minerva?" Wright asked.

"I don't know what to say. She got there pretty late, around eleven o'clock, or maybe just after eleven? I think she and Ian were pretty much together from that point on. They were definitely the last to leave. She helped him take some of the, uh, toys down to his truck. They couldn't take everything with them that night, so Ian said he'd pick up the rest of the, um, gear the next day."

"We've already sent some of our guys down to the bar to pick up the rest of the props."

"Have you spoken to Minerva?" I asked.

"Yes. Her name is actually Mimi Westlake. She ID'd the body."

"Oh." Hadn't some of the recent calls on Ian's cell phone been to or from someone named Mimi? Hmmm. "Apparently, many of the folks who are into this scene use a role-playing name," Wright said. "I see…" I said with as much import as I could muster, which was about zero.

"She says they were at her condo, at Yonge and St. Clair, until a bit before six a.m. Security cameras show Dooley getting into the elevator around that time. There's footage showing him exiting the building via the lobby alone. Then nothing else. At around quarter to nine, a dog walker found the victim's body facedown at the water's edge in the Port Area. Coroner thinks he was dead about two hours when he was found. And here we are."

"Holy shit."

"Did anyone in the crowd seem particularly intoxicated? Did you notice anyone using drugs?"

"If there were any drugs there, then I sure as hell didn't know it. Booze yes, but nothing excessive. Apparently people in that lifestyle aren't really into getting wasted. You want to keep your wits about you when you're going to whip someone." The other cop, whose name was Detective Buccheri, looked down at his shoes. He seemed a tad uncomfortable and I sensed he had some first-hand experience in this world. I wondered if he'd be a whipper or a whippee?

"Guess that makes sense. I wouldn't want to be spanked by someone who was too drunk to know what he was doing," Detective Wright said.

"Do you want some more coffee?" I offered. I'd been hurried, and the pot I'd brewed was pretty weak.

"Thanks, but we're almost done here."

"Excuse me a sec, while I top mine up." Bella followed me into the kitchen. I filled my mug and wished I could spike it with a hefty shot of brandy. Alas, this was definitely not happy hour.

"I have something for you," I said, passing the cell phone to Detective Wright. "This is Ian's."

"I was wondering when you'd tell us about it." Her eyes narrowed, her body stiffened, and her face grew all stern and stony. I immediately felt guilty – of what, who knows, but there you go. Body language speaks volumes, and authority figures or people in positions of power used to really intimidate me. I think the word for this is "powernoia." Now, I usually try to circumvent the brass, at least when I'm not trying to manipulate them. Manipulation is infinitely more fun, but often gets me into trouble.

"Somehow, I ended up with it at the end of the night. Ian left some of his things behind the bar, where Jessica and I stored our purses. Maybe it fell out of his jean jacket pocket or something. At the end of the night, I just thought it was mine. I don't know. Same model, see?" I held my BlackBerry out for her to compare.

"You should have turned it over to us immediately."

"I didn't even realize I had it until yesterday afternoon. And I didn't even realize Ian was dead, until late last night. I just thought he'd misplaced it. I left a message at his home number asking him to call me."

"Yes, we heard your message. All right. We'll look into this. What about your colleague Jessica?"

"I'm sure you can reach her on her cell, but there's a bit of a time difference. She's on vacation right now. She flew to England last night for a family reunion."

"That's no problem. We can get someone overseas to take her statement."

"Have you talked to Moose? The doorman who worked the fetish party?" I asked. "His real name's John Porfirio."

"We're seeing him next."

Monday, 11:33 am

I called Jessica's cell but got her voice mail. Then I called Moose, and told him to expect a visit from Metro's Finest.

"The cops already phoned to say they're on their way," he said.

"Hmmm. Well, call me back after the cops leave, and we can compare inquisitions."

"Will do."

I was still in slo-mo, so I made another pot of coffee, a strong one this time, and a fried egg sandwich with lots of ketchup. I'm shameless enough to take advantage of connections and the inside track whenever I can, so I called my friend Mark Houghton, a cop on the Toronto Police force. Straight to voicemail. Damn. I left a message asking that he call me as soon as possible. Then I made another fried egg sandwich. I had no pressing reason to rush off anywhere. I wasn't planning to search for Macy again until much later in the day.

I flipped on Jessica's computer. Her music library left much to be desired. Dance music. Soft rock. Top 40 AM radio tunes. I set the player on shuffle. *Taylor Dane, Taylor Swift, Lady Gaga, Shakira, Katy Perry, Celine Dion.* Ugh. The computer seemed to be a fan of pop music by female solo artists. Despite my background as a singer, and despite my futile attempt to forge a career in the music business, I'm not really into contemporary chanteuses. Give me Mavis Staples or Bettye LaVette or Marianne Faithfull, or even the late, great Amy Winehouse any day, instead of the honey-drenched songbirds currently chirping in department stores and elevators all over North America.

I was curious about the S&M world. I'm not exactly a virgin, but I've never before had any reason to learn much about the lifestyle. Apparently, the abbreviation for what I was looking into was BDSM, which is a catch-all term for bondage and discipline, dominance and submission, and sadism and masochism. Seems to me the acronym should have had six letters, not four. My starting point for the fetish tutorial was Wikipedia, which has a fairly comprehensive article on the S&M world, including its history, which dates back longer than you'd imagine. Apparently the Ancient Egyptians were really into bondage. Not much of a stretch, if you think about mummies; and it's easy enough to picture Cleopatra as a dom. Betcha won't find info like that in Encyclopaedia Britannica.

Next, I Googled fetish clubs and came up with links for groups in Canada, the States, and Europe. *Fetish Scene. Sin City. Torture Gardens.* I saw subcategories for foot fetishes, female dominance groups, dungeons, and swingers' clubs. Google Groups has listings for leather clubs from coast to coast, and for groups devoted to just about every specialized fetish you could imagine. There were even groups for different demographics, if you will: age, race, income. One group sounded rather elitist. I visualized a leather-clad horde of Ivy League Yuppie kinksters trading stock tips while spanking each other.

As I surfed the Internet, I bypassed several links to X-rated videos, PVC attire, and tried to ignore pop-up ads for fetish equipment and sex toys of every size, shape, and description. Some of them looked lethal. And I'd definitely have to clear the cookies and history from Jessica's computer…or maybe not. Instead, I bookmarked several sites, and pinned the raunchiest ones to her start-up menu.

After getting the basic background, I clicked on the Bound for Glory website. Turns out the group took their name from a downtown Toronto store that sells leather apparel and fetish supplies. The Bound for Glory social group's website had a page listing upcoming events; Saturday's party at The Stealth Lounge was the last event listed. There were links to swingers' clubs, to paid escorts, and to clothing-optional vacation spots.

Not surprisingly, there were links related to public health, planned parenthood, and to confidential help for people with STDs. I also found tabs to classified ads, which mostly meant personals. *Women Seeking… Men Seeking…Couples Seeking…Bi Seeking…Dom Seeking…Sub Seeking…Octopus seeking….* And there was a buy-and-sell section, although second-hand fetish gear strikes me as a bad idea.

Moose called just as I was about to respond to an ad from a guy who wanted to be someone's slave. Damn, I was *this close* to finding someone to do my laundry for me.

"What'd they want to know?" I asked Moose.

"Probably the exact same things they asked you. Any drugs, any fights, any drunkenness," he said. "I didn't really have much to tell them."

"Me neither. I didn't see anything Saturday night that would have given me a hint the poor guy would be dead a few hours later."

"It's pretty freaky," he said.

"What about that that trashy couple where the woman who flashed her boobs? They seemed pretty pissed off."

"They were just idiots. I saw them flag down a taxi just after I showed them out."

"Hmmm."

The remainder of our conversation consisted of surprise at what had happened, a bit of speculation, and a lot of unanswered questions.

Monday, 2:46 pm

I had to get back to my dad's place to get a change of clothes. Jessica's glorified gym wear was better than my frayed jeans and soup-stained shirt, but I felt a bit weird wearing her clothes, even though as teens we had regularly raided each other's closets. Besides, apartment sitting didn't mean assuming her identity, even though I had added her name and email address to a number of swingers' club newsletters. Also, I needed to brush my teeth. If I had thought ahead last night, I'd have packed a bag and brought it with me.

When I left Jessica's place, I should have headed straight for the College Street subway station, but instead I took a detour up Yonge Street, past the crew of hot construction guys working at the end of Jessica's street. Although spitting distance from Yonge and Bloor, the city's main intersection and home to some of the most expensive real estate in Toronto, the blocks on Yonge Street south of Bloor comprise one of the tackiest areas of the city. On both sides of Yonge Street, there are cheque-cashing places, head shops, dollar stores, discount shoe stores, and souvenir shops offering a variety of phallic CN Tower mementos, most of which are made in China. Peppered in among the bargain bins and tattoo parlours are a number of "adult novelty" stores.

I found myself standing in front of the Bound for Glory fetish leather shop. I guess I had subliminally planned to come here all along. I felt like an idiot as soon as I walked into the store. I couldn't have looked more out of place in my All American Girl workout wear. I'm rarely accused of being straitlaced, but compared to the other customers, I seemed like a tittering Montessori mom. If only they knew. Well, not really, but I am rather fond of my collection of satin and lace lingerie. So is Derek.

However, my frocks-for-fucking seem kind of Girl Scoutish compared to the displays at Bound for Glory. Their PVC and leatherwear was in a different league from my slinky negligees and flirty little thongs. Everything in here was hard-core. The clothing racks had garments and accessories that were studded and spiked, and some items had buckles and zippers and clasps in places that would cause pain if you moved too quickly or inhaled too deeply. I saw a lot of the apparel that people had been wearing the other night, face masks and chaps, plus some things that looked like they belonged on the set of a vampire movie. *Collars and cuffs and capes, oh my.*

"Those can be customized to your exact measurements," said a clerk with several metal rings through his bottom lip, as I examined a leather bustier. The leather was supple, like butter, and it had satin laces up the front. "We give free alterations." His tongue stud clicked as he spoke.

"No thanks, I'm just looking." I wondered if Derek would like to see me in something like this.

"Lemme know if ya wanna try something on," he

said with a pained smile on his face. I imagine his oral piercings limited his range of facial expressions.

"Sure," I said. I glanced at the price tag and just about fell over. One doesn't participate in the S&M lifestyle if they're on a budget. Even if I wanted to be a dominatrix, I couldn't really afford it.

Monday, 6:03 pm

Dad pulled into the driveway just a few minutes after I got home.

"Well, hello there, lovely daughter of mine. How nice to see you," Dad said in a sing-song sarcastic voice. It's amazing that we could live in the same house, and, because of our schedules and Dad's frequent travels, we can at times go for days without actually seeing each other.

"I'm broke, so I came home." Dad shot me a look as he reached into his back pocket. "Kidding!" I said. "But I'm glad you're here. I have a new case to tell you about."

"Would you like to tell me about it over a pizza? I'm starving. I forgot to have lunch."

"How can a person forget to eat? I understand being too busy to eat, but you've got time on your hands."

"I'll have you know today was very busy." Dad picked up the phone as he spoke to me. "I spent the afternoon training some new players for my blackjack team." Believe it or not, my dad – a retired math professor – is now a professional card counter. "I have a new shuffle tracking theory I'm eager to try in Vegas."

"Of course. Win lots and get me a pony for my birthday, okay?" Dad was staring absently at the phone in his hand. "The pizza place is number three on the speed dial, Dad."

"Right. Thanks. Are you going to whine if I get anchovies on it?"

"He who pays for the pie decides what's on it," I said.

"I'll get double cheese to mask the fishy taste for you."

Then why not omit the anchovies altogether, I thought, but I kept it to myself. I took the cribbage board off the shelf above the fridge and grabbed two cans of beer. I passed Dad a can, and parked myself on a kitchen chair. I aimlessly shuffled the deck of cards as Dad drove the order-taker nuts. The mathematician in him makes ordering a pizza much more complicated than it needs to be.

"The coupon I got with my last order offers two mediums for the price of one, but only with three toppings. Is that three toppings altogether, or three on each pizza?" A pause. "And how much extra is it for additional toppings?" Another pause. "I see. Does double cheese count as one extra item or two?"

I shuffled some more.

"What about the coupon in today's paper? It says I can get an extra-large for $19.99 and a second extra large for half price?" He tapped at a calculator as he spoke.

I took a swig of my Coors Light.

"It works out to be cheaper per slice if I get the extra-large. Can we get a side order of your crispy chicken wings with that? What sizes do they come in?" Silence. "How many wings can two people eat? With pizza? No, thirty's too many. I don't know if I'm that hungry." He tapped some more on the calculator and jotted some numbers down on the scratch pad beside the phone. "Okay then, a dozen. Barbecue sauce for the wings. What about a box of your wedgie fries? How much are those?" Another pause.

"Dad, don't forget to ask for a side of hot sauce for me," I interrupted. He ignored me.

"I can get the wedgie fries for free with an order of thirty wings or more? Do the wings freeze well if we have leftovers?" Another pause. I felt sorry for the person on the other end of the phone. "I'd like to get a side order of hot sauce too, please. It's not extra, is it?" Sometimes I'm embarrassed to admit he's my father. "And lots of napkins please." There was a whole package of napkins in the kitchen pantry. "Yes, I'll be paying cash."

I was almost finished my beer, so I grabbed another.

Dad finally ended the call. For no other person is ordering a pizza such an ordeal.

"It'll be here in thirty minutes," he said.

"It took you almost that long to order it. Anyhow, that should give us enough time for a game of cribbage." We cut the deck to see who'd deal first. He pulled a five to my Queen. "Here you go," I said, handing the deck to him.

"So what's happening in the world of detection?" Dad asked me as he dealt the first hand.

"I'm looking for a runaway. A sixteen-year-old girl who is slowly breaking her parents' heart."

"Thank God you made it through your teen years relatively easily. You were pretty rebellious, but never stupid. I used to worry that you'd have a hard time without a mother around."

"Can't miss what I never had."

"I suppose that's true," Dad said.

My mother took off when I was about two years old and Shane was just starting nursery school. I don't remember my mother at all, and for some reason I've never been very curious about her. As far as I know, she joined some freaky fundamentalist religious group, and is now a "plural wife" or "sister wife" to some bible-thumping misogynist on the West Coast. My lack of curiosity about the woman who gave me life is contrary to my usually nosy self. I mean, really, look what I do for a living. No doubt, denial plays a part in this.

The pizza arrived just as we finished the last hand. Dad beat me by three points.

"Go ahead and deal the next game," Dad said. "I'll get out the plates and cutlery. Want another beer?"

"Nope. Two's my limit. I have to work later tonight. Grab me a can of Coke."

Monday,
9:45 pm

I was in grungy attire once again, perhaps more convincingly this time. I was wearing the exact same outfit as yesterday and it was wrinkled after being left in a heap on Jessica's floor last night. Just after nine o'clock, I walked north from my house on Carlaw to Danforth Avenue. It was just a short walk from there to the subway. Along the way, I passed Omega Fitness, the gym where I've had a membership for the last two years. I waved at the gym as I walked by. I hadn't darkened its doorway in about five or six weeks. I've either got to start working out, or cancel my membership, I thought. The monthly fees come out of my account whether I've been going or not, and walking past the gym hardly counts as a workout.

The subway ride from Pape station to Bathurst was quick. I hate the subway, but in the late evening, it's usually not too crowded, so I can deal with it. I cranked up the volume on my iPod and zoned out to the songs I'd recently downloaded. Little Feat's "Dixie Chicken." Damn, Lowell George up and died way before his time. They were on the cusp of greatness, when the heart and soul of the band kicked the bucket. Up next was "The Night They Drove Old Dixie Down" by The Band, arguably Canada's greatest musical export, and a group I never tire of listening to. I'd give anything to be able to simultaneously sing and play drums as Levon Helm does, although it must be noted that he's the token American in The Band. When I hopped off the train at Bathurst station, Bob Dylan was asking me how does it feel. If he'd been at all interested in my answer, I'd have said that I was feeling all right, Bob.

Bathurst and Bloor is an interesting part of the city. To the east, the area is a favourite among students from the University of Toronto. There are some wonderfully divey bars with cheap draft beer and live music. To the west, it's more or less Koreatown, with one restaurant after another offering homemade kimchi and bibimbap. At the intersection of Bloor and Bathurst stands one of Toronto's best known retail establishments: Honest Ed's. Honest Ed's is the standard bearer among discount retail outlets, and takes up most of a city block. Try as one might, the place is impossible to ignore. The corner it sits on is garishly illuminated by bright bulbs and flashy colours that bring to mind a carnival. And the windows all have corny slogans in them, touting the rock-bottom prices of Honest Ed's wares. *Come In and Get Lost!* and *Honest Ed's a freak! He has bargains coming out of his ears!* and *Honest Ed attracts squirrels. At these prices, they think he's nuts!* I don't think I've ever met a Torontonian who shops here, but every tourist to Toronto makes a point of popping into Honest Ed's.

I ignored the bargains and hiked towards the hip Gen-X bars and teenager hangouts. I knew this area would likely be a waste of time. Macy clearly wasn't legal drinking age, but there were some coffee shops and diners where punks sometimes hang out. Now and then, depending on what band is playing, some bars are open to all ages, and serve alcohol only to those with wristbands indicating age of majority. As if that's effective.

Lee's Palace, an edgy bar with a wonderful cartoon graffiti frontage, was my first stop. I felt a bit weird walking in there. Many, many moons ago, in another lifetime, my band had played a few gigs here. We actually got booed one time, the last time we gigged there. Some assholes had thrown beer at us, so we had walked offstage halfway through the first set. It wasn't a pleasant memory.

Pauper's Pub, The James Joyce, and Insomnia Cafe all yielded naught. After more than an hour of walking and talking, my feet were sore and I was getting cranky. Luckily, I caught a break at my next pit stop, The Purple Door. The irony is that I almost didn't go in there. The Purple Door is a neat-looking Bohemian restaurant and coffee shop, with a huge back patio surrounded by ivy-covered walls. They have about two hundred kinds of herbal tea, they carry only craft brewed beers, and their rather eclectic menu is dirt cheap. The Purple Door has been shut down several times by Toronto Public Health. Customers have complained of seeing cockroaches with chutzpah casually crawl across tables, and health inspectors have found mouse feces in the kitchen. Every time it reopens, the university crowd is lured back in by the very low prices. Clearly the establishment cuts corners on sanitation and food safety, and passes the savings, along with a side order of salmonella, on to their customers.

"Yeah, she's been around a few nights the last while," said a pair of girls with electric blue hair who were drinking bubble tea on the crowded back patio. In my opinion, it was too cold to sit outside, but the courtyard is the only place smokers can puff away. Inside, the restaurant was almost empty.

"Any idea where she is now?" I asked, sticking Macy's photo back in my purse.

"Try down across from what used to be the Reverb. Last time I saw your girl, she was with Shank, and he always scores around Bathurst and Queen. Never lets anyone else work that corner."

"Do I want to know who or what a Shank is?"

"He's hard, man, but he's cool. Him and Macy are together, at least for now. Shank's tough to pin down."

"Sounds like he's hot and he knows it," I said.

"Oh yeah. Tall guy, olive-like skin. Gorgeous face and a ton of long, black hair. Good looking, but really edgy, you know? Not a pretty boy."

"So what does Shank do?"

"Nothing really. He asks people for spare change in front of that building down there, you know some church or whatever, on the north corner."

"You mean the building that used to be a bank?" I asked.

"I guess so. How should I know what it used to be?"

"Good point. I think the place you're talking about is now a native centre or something."

"Yeah, that's the place. Shank's usually around there when he's not partying."

"You rock. The next bubble tea is on me." I tossed a twenty at the girls and walked to the streetcar stop. I'm sure my use of the term "you rock" underlined just how dated and uncool I really am, but I could live with that. If being up on urban slang meant saying "sick" instead of "cool," then I guess I'll have to resign myself to not being plugged in. Maybe next time I'll say "groovy" or "23 skidoo."

Bathurst and Queen is another interesting Toronto intersection. On the edge of the place people mean when they say "Queen West," the blocks to the west of Spadina have a different feel than the blocks to the east. Around Bathurst, there's a certain *je ne sais quoi*. A massive early morning fire a couple of years ago gutted most of the block between Portland and Bathurst streets. Duke's Cycle, National Sound, Suspect Video, and a number of other neighbourhood faves were all destroyed. At some point, a developer was bound to put up condos on what was once a trendy urban strip.

The southeast corner of Bathurst and Queen was once the home of a bar that was variously known as The Big Bop, Reverb, or Holy Joe's. My band had played there in the late nineties and we'd had a few good gigs there. No one had booed us or soaked us in beer. Until a couple months ago, the building stood vacant. Now a developer had snapped up this lot as well, and was set to build another "funky" glass and red brick monstrosity that would no doubt be advertised as "lofts" and would sell for very fancy prices. Across the street stood Healey's, another former bar formerly featuring live music, another place Mick, the guys, and I had played a few times. The neon sign above Healey's door was dark, and there was a *For Lease* sign in the window. I find it a tad depressing that so many of my touchstones and teenage party references are now prefaced by the phrase "used to be…" As Mr. Zimmerman was currently croaking into my iPod, *the times they are a-changing.* Yes, indeed they are.

The corner that I was interested in was on the northwest side. By day, the former bank now housed St. Christopher House, an adult drop-in centre. I'm not sure what exactly it's all about, but I think they provide counselling and job search assistance to Native Canadians and homeless people. The centre keeps standard office hours, so in the evenings street people and stragglers hang out on the centre's wide front steps. This is where I found Macy and Shank. They were sitting on the lowest step, asking passers-by to throw some coins into the empty coffee cup Shank proffered.

Macy looked dirty, unkempt, and probably stoned, but she was safe and in one piece. Technically.

"I'll give you bills, not coins, if I can talk to Macy for a few minutes," I said to Shank. He was indeed good-looking, or would have been if he hadn't been such a scrubby, dishevelled street kid.

"How do you know my name?" Macy asked.

I passed Shank a twenty dollar bill. "There's another twenty for you, Macy, if we can talk privately for a few minutes."

Macy looked nervously at Shank. His head hardly moved, but he indicated for her to go with me. "Stay where I can see you," he said.

Macy and I walked to the far end of the drop-in centre and sat next to each other on the sidewalk. It was cold on my ass.

I gave Macy the once over. She was a bit glassy eyed, so I figured she was high, but on what, I wasn't sure. She was dressed the part of a punky little brat with a hate-on for the whole world. A red and black tapestry skirt that could have been the window covering in a Santa Fe brothel, a red T-shirt under a drab green army surplus jacket with the sleeves cut off, and red and black striped leggings with runs in them. Her bare arms had some fresh looking scabs on them. The earlier references I'd heard about cutting appeared to be true.

Macy had a few fresh slices on the inside of her forearms. God, I wanted to smack her.

I handed Macy my business card.

"A private detective," she sneered. "What the hell's going on?"

"Your parents hired me." She made a move, like the conversation was over, so I grabbed her shoulder. Shank was watching us, but he didn't get up from his panhandling perch. "It won't kill you to give me five minutes of your time. Here's the twenty." Macy grabbed the money and stuck it in her shoe.

"Why'd they hire a detective?" she asked.

"Are you serious? They're worried sick about the daughter they haven't seen or heard from in a month." I had taken out my cell phone and was dialling the number for Mr. and Mrs. Edquist. "All you have to do is tell them you're alive and well, and in Toronto," I said, handing my cell phone to Little Red Riding with Hoods.

"No fucking way! They're going to come after me and take me back to Peterborough. I'm choked and strangled and suffocating there! No fucking way I'm going back, and you can't make me." The last line turned her tone from defiant to whiny.

"Look, your folks are back in Peterborough now. Even if they got in their car right this minute, they couldn't possibly get here in less than an hour and a half. That gives you an advantage. My job was to find you and to tell them that you're safe and sound, even though I don't think you are."

"I can take care of myself just fine."

"Where have you been sleeping?"

"Here and there. Couch surfing."

I didn't say anything for a moment. I was too angry. This little snot was breaking her parents' hearts. She had no idea how good she had it, and she was choosing to throw it all away and scrounge on the streets like an abandoned mutt.

"Even if you don't talk to them, Macy, I'm still going to tell them that I found you, and where I found you, and they'll come back here to look for you. They'll be poking around here and Cherry Beach and the Eaton Centre and they'll eventually find you. Plus I'll be around to help them."

Macy gave me a sneer, a dirty look, and a pouty face all at once. I held back a rather pressing urge to shake her. I felt so sorry for Mom and Pop.

"Please, Macy, just talk to them for a minute. Let them know you're alive, and you can do whatever the hell you want after that. Trust me. Giving in to me on this is the easiest thing for you. If you won't talk to them now, I'm going to be on your ass until you do. Think how much fun it would be having me show up at a rave, when you and your friends are all adding new slices to your forearms."

"Go fuck yourself."

I really should think about getting a new job.

"I've got all the time in the world to fuck myself while making your life uncomfortable. Your parents would happily pay to have me following you."

"All right, all right, fuck it. I'll talk to them, but then just leave me alone."

It was almost midnight. I knew I'd be waking the Edquists, but they likely weren't sleeping very restfully anyway. "Harold?" I said when Mr. Edquist picked up. "I've found Macy."

"Oh, thank God, thank God. Where is she? Is she okay?"

"I'll let her tell you herself." I passed the phone to Macy and took a couple of steps back from her. I stood far enough away to give her a sense of privacy, sort of, but close enough to catch her if she decided to take off with my phone.

"Thank you," I said two minutes later when Macy passed the phone back to me. "Here's another twenty. For God's sake, get something to eat. And keep my number. If you change your mind and want some help, call me. Anytime, day or night."

Macy took the money without saying a word, and then slinked back over to Shank and his sidewalk shakedown.

Tuesday, October 2, 9:40 am

I short-changed myself on sleep once again, and was up and at my office early Tuesday morning. I was anxious to wrap up the file on the runaway. It was a less than satisfying feeling to send a final report to Mom and Pop Edquist. The girl was alive and she was safe and sound, in the loosest interpretation of the phrase. But knowing that would only give her parents a sliver of peace of mind.

I was starting to write up my invoice when I decided that my work for the Edquists would be pro bono. It hadn't really taken that much of my time, nor had it cost me very much cash, about $150, not a huge sum in the grand scheme of things. I considered it good karma. Besides, I felt sorry for the parents – they seemed like such nice people – and I could safely predict their troubles with Macy were just beginning. I'd write up a report and send it this afternoon. I had just wadded up their invoice to shoot it into the wastebasket when the electronic *brrring brrring brrring* of the phone on my desk startled me. I missed the basket by several inches.

"Hey gorgeous. I only have a minute, but I wanted to hear your voice." Ah, Derek. I promptly forgot all about runaways and panhandlers on Queen Street and fetish parties and waterfront murders and invoices, and let myself be distracted by lust.

"How's the trial going?" I asked. I know he could hear the smile in my voice. How could a phone call from some guy have such an effect on me?

"Better than I could have hoped. We might even wrap up early."

"Oooh, that would be great. I'm dying to see you. It would be nice to spend Thanksgiving together." Thanksgiving in Canada is always the second Monday in October, so it was just a few days away.

We quickly gave each other the highlights of the last few days: his trial, my runaway, the weather in Timmins (where Derek was), the fetish party, the murder, and my exploration of the S&M world.

"A leather what?" he asked.

"Bustier. You know, a merry widow, a corset. It was kind of sexy."

"Well, just promise me you won't go shopping without me," he said.

"Deal."

"I'll call you again as soon as I get a chance."

I sighed and smiled after I hung up. I had a few butterflies in my belly and a tingly sensation a bit lower.

Another *brrring brrring* snapped me out of my wet daydream.

"Sasha? It's Phyllis Edquist."

"Hi there. I was just thinking of you."

"I'm calling to inform you that Harold and I have discussed things, and we're going to refuse to pay your invoice."

The invoice I hadn't sent yet? The invoice I'd just tossed onto the floor next to the trash?

"Excuse me?" I asked.

"We're not happy with your results. Simply determining Macy's location on one particular night is not acceptable. We want our daughter to come home."

No good deed goes unpunished.

"You realize that I can't make her go home, don't you?" I said. "Nobody can make her go home if she doesn't want to. Not even the cops."

"Well, our intention when we hired you, our goal when we spent all that time in Toronto was to make sure Macy comes home. She's still living on the streets. She's still running around with God knows who. I'm sorry, but that just isn't good enough."

What to do, what to do? I was pissed that the Edquists were in effect screwing me out of my bill, and out of my chance to comp my bill and do something generous for people who deserve it.

"I don't know what to say. I could drag her home, or I could tell you where to find her and you and Harry could drag her home. Or a team of cops could throw her ass into the back of a cruiser and drag her home. And you know what? She'd just run away again."

The conversation went on like this for a few more minutes, and eventually Mrs. Edquist hung up on me.

Damn.

I was still stewing over Mrs. Edquist's call when my phone rang yet again.

"May I please speak with Sasha Jackson?" I didn't recognize the man's voice, but I swear, if aardvarks could talk, this is exactly what they'd sound like.

"This is Sasha."

"My name's Hugh Vanderhoof. I'm the owner of The Pilot Tavern."

After what I'd seen on the news over the last couple of days, I was less than surprised to hear from him.

"Ah yes, Hugh. We've met once or twice."

"Obviously through Jessica, though I'm sorry to say I can't quite place you." I guess my hotness rating is much lower than I'd care to admit if Hugh couldn't picture me. "In a lot of ways, I'm the wrong type of person to own a bar. I hide out in the office all morning and I'm never there in the evenings when the after work crowd comes in. There are a lot of regulars I've never even met, and even some of the night staff. I've got to get out of the office more and talk with customers. I really should."

"Well, if it ain't broke...and the staff and night managers are great..." I said, just to fill the air.

I knew exactly why Hugh had called me, but I'd long ago learned it's best to let potential clients take their time when initiating contact with me.

"I got your number from Jessica. I called her last night, forgetting about the time difference in England. And the jet lag. I think I woke her up. Anyhow, she called me back just now. She had her statement taken by a cop in London."

"Uh huh..."

"I trust you've seen the news," Hugh said.

"You're calling me about the story of the dead guy found Sunday morning in the Port Lands," I said with all the delicacy of a thirteen-year-old boy farting in church.

"Yes. The murder of Ian Dooley, who was last seen at a fetish party at my bar, and where you bartended."

"We'd better talk in person. Can you meet me at my office?"

Tuesday, 11:25 am

"Jessica, what the hell is going on?" I asked as soon as Jess picked up the transatlantic call.

"Man, the roaming charges are going to kill me. Let me call you back from a land line."

"Okay. I'm at my office."

She phoned back right away.

"Hugh just called me," I said. "He's on his way here, so I can't talk long. He said you've spoken to the police over there?"

"I'll have you know that here in jolly old England, we call them 'bobbies,'" Jessica said in a voice that even a Cockney would ridicule.

"Whatever. Spare me the British accent. You sound like a constipated Camilla Parker Bowles."

"If you were sleeping with a warthog like Prince Charles, you'd sound pretty miserable too. Anyhow, yeah, I had to give a statement to one of the local cops. I signed it, he faxed it, and could you please tell me what the hell is going on?"

I gave Jessica a thumbnail sketch of the last couple of days.

"My God. Poor guy. I suppose it would be inappropriate to say he went out with a bang?"

"Only a little."

"So if Hugh called you, I assume he's looking to engage your services?" Jessica asked.

"We'll see. I'll keep you posted."

"Is everything okay at my apartment? How's Bella?"

"Bella's fine. She eats, sleeps, sheds, and pees. What else do cats do?"

I pulled up a new Internet window and typed in the web address for an online radio station that played Motown and R&B from back in the days when R&B meant what it should. I hummed along with Sam Cooke while I checked my email. I deleted a bunch of spam while listening to the smooth soul sounds of Al Green. I ignored an offer for a new credit card, while not ignoring a Sly and the Family Stone hit. Ah, this is more my style, and beats the hell out of Britney Spears and other Kewpie Doll Pop Tarts on the Charts on Jessica's iTunes.

I read through a hilarious email from an old friend, while Marvin Gaye lulled me into my happy place. My friend Breanna is spending six months backpacking through Central and South America. This week's email was from Panama, and in the email she described the surprising events that unfolded after several Balboa beers. The incident involved some exuberant howler monkeys, a banana tree, the Panama Canal, and a hostile cross-dressing sidewalk souvenir vendor. Breanna said something about only needing three stitches and the doctor didn't think she'd have much of a scar. She ended the letter by asking me if I'd like to hook up with her on her travels. I love to travel, but a voyage with Breanna has *potential international incident* written all over it.

After I had read all the emails worth opening, I searched some local news websites for updates on the Ian Dooley murder. Sure enough, there were several more mentions of the man who had died as a result of foul play after a party at The Stealth Lounge. And sure enough, each and every story referenced the fact he had last been seen at kinky sex party before being spanked into the great hereafter.

I was loudly crooning about the dock of the bay when Hugh arrived.

"The police haven't said much yet, but the fetish party at my bar has been mentioned in every news update. The negative publicity is going to ruin the bar," Hugh said.

Hugh Vanderhoof was sitting across from my desk,

his hands folded on his lap. I was trying to get a feel for him, but nothing jumped out at me. His clothes were middle of the road, a pair of black chinos and a grey shirt with a button-down collar; he had rolled the sleeves up past the elbows. Hugh was clean-shaven, with brown eyes and hair. Neither handsome, nor homely. About five feet ten and maybe about 160 pounds. He could easily be nicknamed "Composite Man." I scarcely knew Hugh, but by all accounts he was pleasant, soft spoken, and mild-mannered. Basically an innocuous, inoffensive, and rather forgettable guy. Owning a bar seemed an odd vocation for him. But given my own checkered past, who am I to make snap judgements? Then again, snap judgements are an asset in my profession.

"I've already talked to the cops," I said. "It's not like Dooley was killed at your bar, or even in front of the premises. Ian left with some chick who looked like Elvira Mistress of the Dark. I told the cops that. And the news reporters all say he spent the night with her, until six in the morning or something. The police confirm this."

"Yes. 'Mistress Minerva.'" Hugh held up his fingers in quotation marks as he said this. "She gave a rather candid interview to one of the tabloid papers." He passed me a copy of today's *Toronto Sun*. Somehow, despite all my cyber surfing, I hadn't seen this story. Minerva's newspaper photograph wasn't very flattering. The woman I recalled from Saturday night was much more attractive. The caption was less than flattering as well. It said "*I Gave Ian His Final Whipping.*" Oh dear. "And of course, right there in the same story, The Pilot and The Stealth Lounge are mentioned several times."

"It says right here that he was killed at the waterfront early Sunday morning, nowhere near The Pilot or The Stealth. Give it a few days, and it'll all blow over, at least where you're concerned."

"Until it's all wrapped up, The Pilot Tavern and The Stealth Lounge will be mentioned in connection with the…incident every time it's on the news. I really don't want to be associated with this."

"Then perhaps you shouldn't have rented the party room to this group." It wasn't very nice of me to say this, but at times my mouth works completely independent from my brain.

"In hindsight, you may be right," he said.

"I hope you don't take offense at this, but you don't really seem like the kind of guy who would own a bar, especially a bar that rents space to an S&M group."

"No offense taken. Owning a bar was never my dream. I wanted to be a doctor."

"That's quite a stretch. How'd you end up owning The Pilot?"

"It's been in the family for three generations now. My grandfather established it back in the forties after he returned from the war. He called it The Pilot as a tribute to aviators in the Second World War."

"I've always wondered where the place got its name."

"Grandpa ran The Pilot until his feet and back gave out on him, and then my father took over. Dad was only in his forties when he stepped in, and I was in my teens. I figured he'd be running it for another twenty years at least. Dad absolutely loved the place. Most of what it is today is thanks to him. He was the one who had the idea of renovating the second floor and turning it into a private party room. He was the one who designed the rooftop patio. Dad loved people, and he liked to build things. The bar had always been successful, but he really made it grow."

"He sounds like a neat guy."

"Then my dad was killed in a car accident when I was in my second year of university."

"That sucks. Sorry to hear it."

"Thanks. It was rough. My mother was a mess, it was so unexpected. I had no choice but to step in, and here I am, thirteen years later, still wishing I had gone to medical school."

There was an awkward pause for a moment. Neither of us knew what to say next.

"Anyhow, so what about the fetish party and Ian's murder?" I asked.

"This Bound for Glory group rented The Stealth Lounge once before. It was no problem and we made a lot of money off the event. Heck, we make money just off the rental fee. Besides, the people at the party didn't do anything illegal."

"I second that, and that's what I told the cops," I said.

"I'm sure you did, but still, I have a feeling the liquor licensing board will be breathing down my neck."

"I didn't see anything happening that was a violation of the liquor act, or even violations of municipal bylaws. The whole night was way too weird and kinky, and probably at least a few of the people who were there need therapy, but I honestly didn't see anything that was a legal no-no."

"The liquor board can make my life difficult if they want to. They can nail me for anything, if they put their minds to it, whether it's over-serving or being over capacity or not checking ID."

"Moose kept a close eye on ID, and I can guarantee no one was served to the point of intoxication. Most people just had one or two drinks. Apparently, people in this lifestyle like to stay in control."

"I guess that's what I'd want if I were playing those kinds of games. Anyhow. I know the police are investigating, but their priority is solving the case, and my priority is the bar and its reputation. I haven't heard from my insurance company yet, but I expect my premiums are about to go up."

"Ugh, don't get me started on insurance companies." I'd recently sorted out a claim with my insurer. My old office had been ransacked when I'd worked on what I've since nicknamed the Bride and Doom murder case this summer. The insurance company had eventually settled my claim, but not before making me jump through hoops. My new office, at Church and Front Streets – just around the corner from the St. Lawrence Market – was nice enough, but rather basic and strictly functional. I had bought some new office furniture from IKEA, and had given the space a fresh coat of paint, but I still need-ed to give it a personal touch. The plants I'd brought in a month or so ago had died a slow and painful death from neglect. Maybe I should hang some pictures on the walls. A *Chippendales* calendar might be good.

"I'd like to hire you. Perhaps you can help me clear up my involvement in this more quickly than the police can."

A little part of me thought Hugh was overreacting, but I'm not one to talk someone out of paying me a potentially healthy fee. I told him my rates, and we shook hands to confirm my latest case.

Tuesday, 12:20 pm

Once again, I was walking around aimlessly, completely lost in thought. I was so knee-deep in trying to figure out how to approach the Ian Dooley murder that I was unaware that I'd walked against a red light right into a busy intersection.

"Watch where you're going, stupid bitch."

Some people are so rude. I gave the driver the finger, even though I was in the wrong.

I had vague notions of who I should see and who I needed to talk to. Unfortunately, reaching people proved to be a challenge. I had time to kill before my appointment with Mimi-Minerva. I sat on a park bench on King Street and worked my way through the list of people I had copied from Ian's BlackBerry. Tricia Lado: a chirpy outgoing message saying she was sorry to have missed my call, and please leave a number. Paul: no answer, and after eight rings, no machine picked up. In the twenty-first century this is weird, but probably not unheard of. Wendi: An automated recording from a computer invited me to leave a message. Lisa Gardiner:

a teenaged voice said "Can I get her to call you back?"
I was about to try the number for Justin when someone
actually called me.

Ahhhh, like an oasis in the desert, Officer Mark
Houghton finally returning my call from yesterday.

"Please tell me you're fully clothed?" he said.

"I am wearing jeans, a red shirt, and I have shoes on
both feet. How's that?"

"Good, I guess, but it would have been more fun
picturing you running around topless in Forest Hill."

"You can always dream." Mark was referring to my
last big case, one in which I'd rapidly shed my top and
exposed my upper body to some stunned residents of
a quiet upper-crust neighbourhood. It wasn't one of
my proudest moments, but I'd caught a cold-blooded
killer, so the ends justified the semi-naked means. "Do
you have time for a coffee?"

"Not much, but I can squeeze in about half an hour,"
Mark said.

"There's a Second Cup at King and Jarvis. I'll be
there in five minutes."

"On my way."

"I'm starting to see a pattern with you, Sasha," Mark
said. He seemed a bit harried today, but still looked
rather handsome. I'm not really one for a man in
uniform, but at six foot four and built like a brick
shithouse, Officer Mark Houghton looked every bit
the alpha male. Yummy, but he's no Derek.

I innocently looked up from my caramel, mocha,
foamy, sweet, frappa crappa caffeinated beverage.

"Can't an old friend get together with you just for the sake of catching up?"

I was saying "old friend" in the loosest sense of the term. Mark had been a high school fling, a brief one, as adolescent romances are wont to be. We had reconnected a couple of years ago when I was taking my Private Investigator course at Sheridan College. Bryan Bessner, my favourite professor, had invited Officer Houghton to be a guest speaker. Houghton had talked about surveillance techniques while I slid lower into my seat in the front row. I had really hoped he wouldn't recognize me, but of course he had.

He commandeered me after the class and stole me away for a drink. It was the first time I'd seen Mark since he'd ungraciously dumped me back in the days when I was an insecure teenager. I'm still a bit insecure at times, but now I hide it beneath a layer of chutzpah and the occasional bratty comment.

The conversation was a bit awkward at that first reunion, but since then something of a professional friendship has formed.

"An old friend certainly could, but I always seem to hear from you when there's a new murder in the headlines."

"Ian Dooley. The guy who was found down by the Port Lands after a wild night at a fetish party."

"Aha!" Mark banged a fist on the edge of our table. A bit of coffee splashed over the lip of his cup. "I knew it." He used a paper napkin to wipe up the spill. "What's your involvement?"

"The owner of the bar, Hugh Vanderhoof, has hired

me to try to speed things along. He's worried about bad publicity, soaring insurance premiums, and keeping his liquor licence." I had expected the question, and had already decided to be almost forthright with Mark, at least as to who my new client is. However, I didn't see any reason yet to mention to Mark that I'd bartended at the fetish party. Besides, he'd probably find out soon enough, if he didn't know already.

"The bar's role in all of this is kind of peripheral. It'll die down," he said.

"I agree, but try telling that to Hugh."

"Besides, the press coverage may even be good for business. As they say, there's no such thing as bad publicity."

"You're probably right, but Hugh feels otherwise. Anyhow, what can you tell me about the crime?" I asked.

"Guy took two shots from behind."

"That's such a gutless way to kill someone. If you're going to kill a person, you should at least have the *cojones* to look them in they eye when you do it."

"Um, yeah. Anyway, first shot entered his heart, second his lung. He would have been dead even if he'd been rushed to a hospital right away. Both shots were at close range."

"And the gun?"

"My guess is several months from now some kids playing on the beach will find it. Most likely it was flung into Lake Ontario. Evidence techs are combing the scene but *nada* so far regarding the weapon."

"I see. What about the truck? How did it get to Leslieville?"

"I thought that would have been your first question." Mark took a sip of his coffee. "Theory one is that he drove there, and then walked to the Port Lands, and was the victim of a random crime."

"Not terribly plausible. Wasn't he getting it on with Minerva until the wee hours of the morning?" I asked.

"Exactly. What guy gets laid all night and then goes for a morning stroll by himself? And Port Lands isn't exactly scenic."

Mark was right about that. Toronto has some nice stretches of waterfront. Ashbridge's Bay and Scarborough Bluffs in the east end are lovely, and Harbourfront, at the base of downtown, is pretty and vibrant, especially in summertime. But the Port Lands is something of a waterfront wasteland. Located at the mouth of the erstwhile marshy Don River delta, the Port Lands' *raison d'être* over the years had mainly been industrial. There was movement afoot recently to revitalize the area and make it more recreational, but other than some bike paths and the Leslie Spit, the area is still generally abandoned. It would be my last choice for a Sunday morning post-coital stroll.

"So, then what's theory two?" I asked.

"A whole lot of things. The truck was moved maybe. A carjacking gone wrong maybe. The killer had an accomplice maybe. Someone followed him maybe. He was brought there by force by persons unknown maybe. Maybe some combination of the above."

"Could you narrow it down a bit for me, Mark?"

"Well, here's what's not in the news reports. When the crime tech guys connected the truck to him, they took a careful look at everything about it, in it, and so on. The thing they noticed first was that the driver's seat was pretty far forward."

"Ian Dooley was well over six feet tall," I said.

"He was six feet two and three-quarter inches. Whoever last drove the truck was a shortie, probably five foot two to five foot four. That guess is based on the seat position and the angles of the rear-view mirrors."

"Interesting. But the newspapers all say he left alone. There was security video footage showing him leaving Minerva's, I mean Mimi's, place early Sunday morning."

"My guess is that he was ambushed on his way home. The question is why and by who?"

"You mean 'by whom' not 'who.' You need the objective form after a preposition," I said.

"Why do I continue to return your calls? You're such a pain in the ass."

"It comes naturally."

"I know," Mark said.

"I know you checked the truck for prints and evidence and everything else, but what about the victim's home?"

"Naturally, we've had a look through it. We checked the last number dialled on his phone. Played the messages on his answering machine. Your message about having his BlackBerry was on there."

"Ah. So you know what my interest in this is then."

"And your involvement."

"I wasn't exactly involved."

"You know what I mean. And you're going to be a royal pain in the ass now, aren't you?"

"Yup."

"Anyhow, we took a look through his belongings Monday afternoon, and talked to the other tenants in his building."

"Is it a high-rise? What street is he on?"

"I can't give you his address, but I suspect you'll find it out sooner or later anyway. Ian lives, or lived, across the street from High Park. He's in a house that's been converted to three apartments. We talked to the couple who live in the apartment above him and they didn't have much to say. He was quiet, never caused any fuss. According to them, Ian was the one who kept the yard and the driveway looking nice. Cut the grass, shovelled the snow. That stuff."

"Any other neighbours?" I asked.

"There's a single guy who lives in the basement apartment, but he only moved in about a month or so ago. A graduate student at York University. Told us that he never said much more than 'good morning' to the late Mr. Dooley."

"Was there anything interesting inside the apartment?"

"Not really. A lot of fetish gear. Remember, he's the victim here, not the suspect. The cops are more interested in the crime scene and the truck than in Ian's place. By all counts, it was random, wrong place, wrong time. And if that's the case, it's unlikely there's anything in his apartment that will help to connect Ian to an unknown killer."

"Hmmm."

What Mark was saying made a certain amount of sense, but I still had a feeling that Ian's killing wasn't just a random act of violence. I couldn't help but think that someone from the fetish scene had taken rough play just a bit too far.

Tuesday, 2:12 pm

Next on my agenda was a visit to Mimi-Minerva's studio. Although she lives in a condo uptown, her workspace is in the east end of downtown, just past the Distillery District. I figured that the *Mimi the Sculptor* person I was meeting with today would probably be quite different from *Minerva the Dominatrix* of Saturday night.

I was wrong.

Mimi was dressed in black from head to toe. Her appearance was a little scary, but she turned out to be very warm and laid-back. Her clothes were layered – a tapered black satin shirt under a black velvet vest, and some kind of black mesh covering over that. Her shirt was pretty snug, and the top couple of buttons had been left undone. The bottomless cleavage peeking through made me feel very inadequate. Her outfit was accented with a billowy black sheer scarf that draped down her legs, which were covered in black tights, accentuated by a wide black leather belt. She had about seventeen bangles dangling from each wrist, and they too were black. Shoes, nail polish, earrings, eyeliner, eye shadow, necklaces, hair accessories, all black black black.

I hadn't noticed it the other day, but she had a little diamond stud piercing her nose, and it was the only thing that gave her face any colour. I also noticed that she was about five foot seven, not that I suspected her of any involvement in Ian's death. I just can't help noticing things.

"What do you think of this piece? It's called *Carbon Footprint #4*," Mimi said.

A whole bunch of copper wires had been bound together and twisted into the shape of a tree, about eight feet tall. Instead of leaves, the branches had several pieces of gold-painted footwear hanging from them.

"Wow. Incredible." I hoped my voice sounded sincere, and in a sense I was sincere, if you take "incredible" to mean "unbelievable." I truly couldn't believe that a bunch of shoes on a wire tree would be considered art by anyone with two working eyes. Or even one.

I walked around the piece and noticed a fuzzy bedroom slipper, a Nike Air Jordan, a run-of-the-mill pump, a couple of mismatched sandals, a rubber rain boot, two different loafers, a child's sneaker, three or four Crocs, and a couple of brogues. All had been spray painted in the exact same shade of metallic gold paint.

"What do you notice about them?" Mimi asked.

"A variety of styles?" I guessed.

"Yes, but look again."

I did another lap around the shoe-tree sculpture. I knew I wasn't getting it. "They're all different sizes?"

"Yes, but that's not the main point. Each of those is a right shoe."

"Okay, and…?"

"I collect them along the highway. Any highway, driving from here to wherever, but these ones are all from a trip around Northern Ontario last fall. Have you ever noticed that on roads to nowhere, out in the middle of nowhere, you'll often see a random shoe lying on the shoulder or in a ditch?"

"Yeah…"

"Whenever I see them, I stop the car and pick them up. This piece is the fourth instalment in my *Carbon Footprint* series."

"Okay…"

"When I first started collecting roadside shoes, I had no idea what I was going to do with them. They just seemed interesting to have. But then I noticed that random footwear is almost always on the right side of the road, the passenger side."

"I suppose…"

"And nine times out of ten, the shoe that has fallen off is the right one. It's hardly ever the left one. I imagine someone sitting in the passenger seat, with the seat tilted back, and his or her feet propped up on the edge of the open window. The sculpture symbolizes society's choice to drive everywhere instead of walking. And once one shoe is lost, walking isn't as much of an option, at least not a comfortable one. The sculpture symbolizes waste and litter and our disregard for the environment."

"I see," I said. Actually, I didn't, but how else could I have replied?

"The other pieces in the collection follow the same format, but the shoes are painted different colours. I chose gold for this one it reminds me of the fall colours on the trees I saw during that trip."

"That's pretty cool," I said. Not really, I thought.

"I've already got a commission for piece number five. I haven't even started it yet, and already the buyer has contracted to pay $20,000 for it. Go figure."

"Jesus Murphy. Maybe I should have gone to art college."

"I got lucky. Right medium, right time, right message. Anyhow, this isn't what you're here for. I don't plan to do any more work today, so I'm going to have a beer. Want one?"

"Absolutely."

She grabbed a couple cans of Guinness from a mini fridge in the corner of the studio.

"Sorry, I don't have any glasses."

"Not to worry," I said, licking some creamy brown beer foam from my upper lip. "So, I saw you at the party Saturday night, and I've seen the papers. I need to know more about Ian. What can you tell me?"

"The cops asked the same question. Where do I start?"

"How about the basics? Bio stuff. The story in the paper said he worked construction."

"Yeah. He did a bit of everything. I never really talked to him much about what he did for a living, frankly I found it quite boring. I think he did some roofing, drywall, that kind of stuff."

"Know who he worked for?"

"Some guy named Scott. No idea what his last name is," Mimi said.

I recalled that there was a Scott on Ian's caller list. "Without getting into details, I would have been interested in talking to you even without the story in the newspaper."

"Why's that?"

"Let's just say, I know the names of some of the people Ian last spoke to on his cell. I assume some of them were at the party, since the calls were from Saturday. Any one of these people could potentially help in finding his killer. Or maybe not. Or maybe one of them is the killer."

"I hope not."

"Me too. Anyhow, I have no idea who any of these people are. You name was one of the last calls on his phone. Scott's was another."

"I see. So this is how a detective detects."

"Pretty much. Somebody out there knows something. People don't just get offed because they took someone's parking spot. Any idea who Robin is?" I asked.

"Robin Stanhope?"

"I guess. I don't know the last name. I don't even know if that's a guy or a girl."

"There was a Robin at the party. Some old cowboy was playing with her."

"You mean the chick who was down on her hands and knees being whipped? Giddy-up?"

"That's Robin, but her scene name is Alexa," Mimi said.

Okay, so that was two people from the callers list. I probably wouldn't get much out of talking to either of them, but what the hell. Scott and Robin were now on my to-do list.

"What about Tricia Lado, Lisa Gardiner, and someone named Wendi?" I asked.

"No idea who Wendi is. Lisa is part of the fetish scene, but she wasn't there Saturday night. Tricia is an ex-girlfriend. Ian and her have a kid."

"Oh?" The pictures on the BlackBerry of the little girl's birthday party made sense now. "Is Tricia a friendly or hostile ex?"

"Pretty friendly, I think. Ian never said much about her. All I know is he saw his daughter on alternate weekends, so you could forget about playing when he was in daddy mode."

"How old is his daughter? What's her name?"

"I forget her name. She's just young, maybe around three or four. You gotta keep in mind, my relationship with Ian wasn't much about talking. We kept things pretty much to the bedroom."

"I'm starting to get the picture. Tell me more about the parties and the lifestyle. Why did he host them at a bar? Wouldn't someone's home have been easier? More private?"

"How to explain this... Well, it's hard to get a good party going at a private home. First of all, who wants to host it? It's a lot of work, a lot of mess. You'd probably be worried about things getting broken if people play a bit rough. And there's the space issue too. You get at least sixty or seventy people at each event. Someone would have to have a pretty big house to host a party like this."

"I see your point, but isn't a bar just a little too open, too public for some people?"

"Yes, and no. It's not like just anyone can walk in off the street." I was reminded of the unwelcome loser couple Moose had tossed out. "Ian rented the room for a private party and people had to be on the guest list to get in. As for being in a semi-public place, well, that's actually a turn on for a lot of people in the lifestyle. Exhibiting and watching, it can really give you a rush."

"I think I saw just about every kind of kink and fetish the other night, but I didn't see anything, um, I didn't notice much... What I mean is, all the S&M stuff just seemed like foreplay. Does anyone ever actually get laid, or what?"

"Some do, but for a lot of us, it's the control or punishment that matters. Treating some guy like your slave can be a real turn on."

"Okay." I really don't get it. I couldn't picture treating Derek like a slave. I'd lose all respect for him if he turned into an obsequious little puppy. "Any chance you know Justin or Paul? Could they be a couple of the slaves from the other night?"

"If it's who I'm thinking of, Paul is Paul Avignon, and he's not a slave at all. Total dom. He was the guy who had a leash and a dog collar around his girlfriend's neck. The redhead. No idea who she is; Saturday's the first time I've seen her. Her name might be Cindy."

"I don't know if that matters, at least I don't think she does, if she's new to the scene. What about Justin?'

"I'm pretty sure Justin was the guy in the tight red underwear. Do you remember the guy with the crown and sceptre?"

"Uh huh," I nodded.

"I think he calls himself King Arthur or something stupid like that when he's on the scene. I have no idea if he's dom or sub. I kinda think he's neither, he's more of an exhibitionist."

Ooohhh, the throbbing bulge in the red briefs. *Eeee-ww*, the warm credit card.

"You might think I'm a bit of a bitch for saying this, but you don't seem particularly heartbroken over Ian's death," I said.

"This is really hard to explain. Ian and I played together often, quite a few times in fact, but only in the last three or four months or so. I met him in May or June, I guess. Actually, I had met him before then, but this summer is when we started to play together. I never let him sleep over, though. It was pretty much a physical relationship, and not much else. Besides, a lot of people in this lifestyle draw a definite line between their regular weekday selves and their fetish selves. That's why a lot of people use a fake name when they're on the scene."

"To protect their anonymity and reputations," I said.

"Partly that. But it's also a control thing. *This is who I am in my regular life; this is who I am in my fantasy life.* Never the twain shall meet."

"Hmmm. Interesting."

"You don't know much about the fetish lifestyle do you? Or about S&M?"

"Not a clue. Sorry, I'm not judging or anything, but it just doesn't do it for me."

"Well, some people get a lot more into their roles than others. I'm a pretty hard-core dominant, and Ian was a full-on submissive. He was basically my slave. One of the reasons I never got to know him very well is because I hardly ever let him talk. I just didn't give him permission to speak."

"Hell, that sounds perfect. I'd love to be able to shut up some of the men in my life," I said.

"Ian liked to be punished. I'd whip the hell out of him, until he was whimpering halfway between agony and ecstasy. Most of the time he was on his knees, and most of the time he was handcuffed. He loved to be paddled."

"Looks like someone punished him permanently on Sunday morning. Can you think of anyone in the fetish world who had it in for him? A jealous lover or an ex? Maybe a lovers' triangle?"

"The cops asked me the same thing. I really can't think of anyone. There are a lot of unwritten rules in the community, and there's a lot you just have to accept, like sharing partners and stuff like that."

"Uh-huh…"

"As long as the boundaries are respected, people are cool. I don't know of anyone he might have pissed off, and I never heard of him crossing the line. It's possible, and maybe I just don't know about it. You should talk to his ex, Tricia," she said.

"I will."

"It might be worthwhile to talk to Lisa Gardiner as well. She wasn't there on Saturday, but I know she and Ian played together for a while."

"Will do."

"I'll definitely miss my sessions with Ian. He was a lot of fun and we were really in sync."

"Will you go to the funeral?" I asked.

"Probably. When is it?"

"I dunno. I thought maybe you could tell me."

Tuesday, 4:02 pm

Back at my office, I was once again trying to chase down the leads from the names on Ian's caller list. There was still no answer at the numbers I had for Tricia or Wendi, but Lisa said she'd be home all evening if I wanted to drop by. I was just about to dial Robin's number when she called me.

"I got your message from before, but honestly, I never have a moment to myself." Robin Stanhope sounded very harried, and the high-pitched screaming and whiny *Mommmm-y-y-y-y* in the background explained why. "My boys are three, five, and six. Do you have kids?"

"No," I said.

"Want some? Even one of them? Even for a few hours?"

"I'll pass."

"I swear to God, all three were quiet, eyes glued to the television, so I thought it was a good time to call you. I know all three of the little buggers will be quiet again as soon as I get off the phone."

"Listen, if now's not a good time, could we talk later?"

"Why don't you drop by the house this evening? After the kids go to bed. Around nine?"

"Sure, what's your address?"

"Actually, better make it closer to nine thirty. Their dad's still out of town, and they put up more of a fuss when he's not around."

Next I called Scott, and this time he picked up on the first ring. Turns out that Scott Allen Tomlin is the sole proprietor of SAT Construction *We Specialize in Renovations and Residential Construction.* For the last three years, Ian had worked as a general contractor for Mr. Tomlin.

"I don't really know what to tell you. I told the cops everything already, which wasn't much. Ian worked for me. He was reliable and did good work," Scott said.

"You were one of the last people who called him."

"Yeah, I needed people to work some overtime on Sunday. Ian said he wasn't available. No big deal. He worked overtime lots before and came through for me whenever he could."

"I don't think I need to know anything about his professional life. My gut tells me it's not related," I said. "What about socially? You must have known him at least a bit, outside of work."

"Not really. I usually have at least six or seven different projects on the go at any one time. I have more than twenty people who regularly work for me, like electricians, plumbers, and painters and everything in between. I don't go to every job site every day. I see the guys a lot, but don't really hang out and chat with them, ya know?"

"Oh. Well, there must have been a couple of people who worked with him more than others."

"Rodrigo and Phil are working on a home reno in Leaside with him. They'd be your best bets."

He gave me their numbers.

"Actually, why don't you just tell me where the job is and I'll drop by?" Something told me that contractors and renovators might not drop everything to answer the phone, especially if they were hanging off the side of a roof or doing a scroll saw tango. Scott gave me the address and I bid him adieu. A visit to Leaside was on the agenda for tomorrow.

Paul Avignon answered on the second ring. I remembered that Paul of the Master and Slave Dog Leash Duo was probably about five-nine, five-ten. I didn't think he could have been the driver of Ian's truck, so he wasn't one of my suspects per se, but I hoped he'd be helpful for insight into the victim.

"Actually, we met at the fetish party," I said after introducing myself. "I was one of the bartenders. The one with blond hair." There was no point in withholding the fact that I'd seen all these people in their role-playing mode. In fact, I thought it could be advantageous if the people on my hit list knew that I'd met them – however briefly – the other night.

"So you're a bartender and a private investigator?"

"Well, I'm not really a bartender. Jessica's been working at The Pilot and The Stealth for a few years. They were short-staffed that weekend, so she asked if I'd be willing to help out for the night." I didn't bother to tell Paul that they were short-staffed because the rest of the staff had refused to work the *sticks and stones may break my bones but whips and chains excite me* event. When the manager had been making the weekly work schedule, a number of bartenders had suddenly caught a case of twenty-four-hour religion, and had turned down the shift because it conflicted with their spiritual beliefs. "My full-time job is working investigations. I'm self-employed. The owner of The Pilot asked me to look into things."

"I see."

I asked Paul about spurned lovers or jealous exes, but he had no secrets, or wasn't revealing them if he had any. It can be hard to tell about a person over the phone, but my gut told me Paul was being straight with me.

I asked about people who were friends or enemies of Ian's.

"The cops asked me the same questions. I told them I have no idea who might have wanted to see Ian dead. He was a good guy," Paul said. "My birthday's tomorrow, so me and Cindy were celebrating early. We were just there for a good time."

"Well, happy birthday."

"Thanks."

Next up, I called Justin – King Arthur, he of the skimpy red underwear. He answered on the third ring.

"I'd be happy to chat with you. What say we meet for a drink? I know a place where they make great martinis."

"Sounds good, as long as I don't end up wearing it," I said.

"Know where Bartholomew's is?"

I'd never been there, but I knew its reputation for great steaks and for being Mecca for the Bay Street junior crowd who couldn't yet afford Bymark, Canoe, or Harbour Sixty.

"Sure, by Commerce Court, right?"

"How long will it take you to get there?" Justin asked.

"I'll be there in ten."

"Perfect. I'll be sitting at the bar."

Justin was at a high-topped table in the bar area. He looked damned attractive in a tailored suit and tie. I'd learned when we spoke earlier that he's a stockbroker with one of the firms that another of my clients, Mr. Belham, frequently does business with. Two women in serious-looking business suits were sitting with him, glancing frequently at their BlackBerrys as they sipped their glasses of happy hour vino. Justin made eye contact with me as I was handing my red suede jacket to the girl working the coat check.

"Hey gorgeous." Justin got up and excused himself from his two companions. "Can I buy you a drink?"

"I'll have whatever you're having."

I followed Justin over to an empty table by the window.

"Cheers," Justin said, but I could barely hear him over the noise. We clinked our martini glasses. Mine was delicious, made with premium gin, and served icy cold. I plucked an olive from the glass and popped it in my mouth. Although I wasn't in my scummy punk clothing today, I was a little underdressed for Bartholomew's. My Lucky Brand jeans and red cashmere scoop neck sweater weren't quite on par with the A-list crowd dressed in designer power suits.

"I'm glad to have a chance to chat with you again," Justin said. "You were by far the sexiest woman at the party the other night."

"Uh, thanks…"

I'm not sure how much of a compliment that was, given the yardstick against which I was being measured. I wouldn't be bereft of modesty in saying that I know I'm a helluva lot more attractive than the feather boa-draped cellulite queen or some of the other leather and latex ladies who had been at the Spank Me, Shank Me soiree.

"Ever thought of trying out the scene? I picture you as a dominatrix. You seem the type who wants to be in control. I'd be happy to bring you to the next party, if you're interested." If there was no Derek, and if I didn't already know about Justin's kinky sexual preferences, I would have been flattered and might have said yes to an actual date with him. His smile was almost disarming, his movements easy and assured. On looks, he's the kind of guy I'd jump in a heartbeat.

"I don't think there's going to be a next party. The organizer is dead, remember?"

"I realize that, but there are other groups besides Bound for Glory. I heard about something this coming weekend, in the Beaches. Would you like to join me?"

"I…uh. Thanks. I'm not…" Saved by the bell. I don't think I've ever been so happy to hear the electronic chirping of my cellphone. "Sorry, I have to take this. I'm on a case." I looked at call display. Unknown number. Hmmm.

"Sasha? It's me, Macy, from the other night?"

"Yes, yes. Hi Macy. Good to hear from you. What's up?"

"Nothing really. I just wanted to see if I'd get you at this number."

"Of course. That's why I gave it to you. Are you all right? Where are you?"

"I'm just hanging. Maybe I'll call you later. You sound busy."

"I'm not. Hold on, is something wrong?"

"No, it's okay. Bye."

"Wait, don't hang up –" But I was talking to the dial tone.

"What was that all about?" asked Justin as I stuck the phone back in my bag.

"Nothing. Just a case I wrapped up recently. Anyhow, I wanted to talk to you about Ian." I gave Justin a quick explanation of my involvement. "Your name and number showed on his callers list. As I recall, you talked to him twice on Saturday."

"Sorry to disappoint you, but my reasons for calling him the first time were pretty mundane. I asked him about the dress code and the cover charge. Some parties insist on leatherwear for all guests."

"I see."

"I called him back to ask if he was expecting many single women at the party. At the last party, there were slightly more men there than women. Of course, a couple of the women were happy about that. I saw one woman who had three guys at her beck and call, but I'm not into teams," Justin said.

"Can you think of anyone who had a grudge against Ian?" I asked.

"Nothing springs to mind. I didn't know Ian well, but I chatted with him for a while at parties. He seemed like a typical down-east guy. Laid back, good sense of humour. Pretty much Joe Average."

"That's what everyone keeps saying, but then who would want Joe Average dead?"

Tuesday,
7:30 pm

I hopped on the subway and then transferred to a streetcar to get to Little Italy and the home of Lisa Gardiner. The post-war red brick houses on the blocks around Euclid, Grace, and Palmerston had several election signs showing support for Ricardo Rocco. I'm neutral on, or in agreement with, most of Rocco's political platforms, with the exception of his idea of building a tunnel to downtown, which was exponentially stupid. But I have to say, his Tony Soprano styled ad campaign is a bit creepy, and more than a little ill-advised. His Godfather ads seemed to offend many Italians and to alienate other voters, pretty much guaranteeing that Rocco should just *fuhgeddaboudit* and drop out of the race.

Lisa's little bungalow looked charming from the outside. The tiny front yard was framed with sunflowers, black-eyed Susans, pots of bright purple mums, and bright yellow and orange asters. Lisa, a middle-aged academic with bifocals, wearing a heavy

Aran sweater, was outside plucking the odd dead leaf or browned flower petal from her radiant autumnal garden. I noticed she was kind of short, maybe five foot four or five foot five, possibly the right height to have driven Ian's pickup truck.

"I'm not shaking hands these days. I'm just getting over a bitch of a bout with the flu," she said after introducing herself. The poor old gal sounded pretty stuffed up.

"That sucks. Hope you're feeling better."

"Meh. This too shall pass," she shrugged. "What can I do for you?"

I gave her a thumbnail sketch of what I do for a living and why I was visiting her.

"Ian and I had a few sessions, but we just weren't that compatible," Lisa sniffled.

"He called you Saturday afternoon."

"Yeah, he was hoping I'd come to the party, he had some guy he wanted to hook me up with. I think his name was Arthur." I tried to picture this scholarly looking dame with the naughty man-candy I'd just left. Nope, couldn't see it. "I was just too damn sick to go." She sneezed, as if to emphasize the point.

"Can you think of anyone Ian might have pissed off? Did he cross the lines with anyone in the fetish scene?"

"Hell no. The cops asked me the same thing. Remember, he was the organizer for this group. Most people were keen to stay on his good side. His parties are fantastic. Were fantastic. Pissing Ian off or getting into a pissing contest with him would be stupid for anyone who wanted to play in his sandbox."

"Of course."

My gut told me she had nothing to do with Ian's murder.

"Is there anyone you can think of that I should talk to?" I asked.

"Not really, but let me think about it. My head's feeling really fuzzy right now." I gave her my card and trusted she'd call if she had anything for me.

After my visit with Lisa, I took a bus north to the Bloor-Danforth subway line, then changed to the northbound train at Yonge and Bloor. I got off at Lawrence station, and walked two blocks to the residence of Robin Stanhope. This mostly white and affluent part of the city had fewer election signs on the lawns than in Lisa's 'hood. Of those who used their front yards to expose their political leanings, very few were in favour of the Italian Stallion. The signs around here seemed evenly split between Cooperman, the political gadfly whose only consistency was his tendency to flip-flop – depending on which direction the wind was blowing – and Shane's fave, Nealson, the guy whose run for City Hall seemed preordained, if not quite a slam dunk. Fortunately, there were almost no signs for the three-hundred-pound, do-nut-snarfing, sub-literate, right-wing troglodyte – the only candidate whose victory would make me want to self-immolate in front of a library.

Robin Stanhope's house was a lovely Tudor set back from the road. There was a newer-looking addition above the garage, and the driveway was covered in interlocking brick that turned off into a path to the front door. There was a white Range Rover parked in the driveway, with a dark oil spot beneath it. Anyone walking past the house could tell youngsters lived there. Even though it was early October, the front yard was already decorated for Halloween. There were ghosts hanging from the trees, synthetic spider webs, a cardboard tombstone, and jack-o'-lanterns cut outs in the windows. Some of the All Hallows' Eve characters had chains draped over their figures. I wondered if those were the same chains Mommy used when she wanted to play rough?

It was about twenty-five after nine when I rang the bell.

"Come in, come in," Robin said, flashing me a welcome smile.

She took my jacket and then led me to a seat at a table in a gourmand's wet dream of a kitchen. I'm not one for cooking, but even I could see that the black and white kitchen held the best and newest of everything.

"My treat to myself, and sometimes the only thing that gets me through the day, is a glass of wine at night once the boys are in bed. Care to join me?"

"Happily."

Robin chatted while she poured us each a fishbowl sized glass of Shiraz. "I love all three of my little devils, but Christ on crutches, they're a handful sometimes."

I pictured Jesus in a cast.

"What are their names?" I asked.

"The oldest is Levy, the middle guy is Liam, and the baby of the bunch is Lucas. They're holy terrors sometimes. It takes a lot of energy to keep up with them, that's why I cut loose whenever I can."

"And by cutting loose you mean going to Ian's parties." I said.

"Exactly. But I don't get to go very often. Every two or three months, I guess. You see, I do this in secret. My husband doesn't know anything about it, and I don't ever want him to find out. He wouldn't understand. Jeremy is a wonderful man and a terrific father, but he is boring as hell in the bedroom. I can only go to the parties when he's out of town on a business trip."

"I see."

"And even if he's away, I still need to figure out what to do with the three amigos. Once in a while I can talk my sister or my mother into giving me some 'me' time and the boys will do a sleepover at Grandma's or Auntie Cheryl's."

"So when Daddy's away, Mommy gets to play," I said.

"Yes. I've built a pretty good life. Or, I should say we have. Jeremy is a wonderful man, and very successful."

"But something's missing?"

"I love my husband and love my kids. We have a nice home here, and lovely cottage in Muskoka. All the material things. I really don't have anything to complain about."

"Maybe it's all too easy?"

"I don't know. I had a job before we got married. I was a columnist for *Trixie* magazine. I really enjoyed it. I covered fashions primarily and went to lots of shows, met lots of designers. You wouldn't believe the swag I got. Fashion merchandisers give out all kinds of freebies in hopes of getting a good plug in a women's magazine. I have sixteen brand new designer handbags, all sitting in my bedroom closet. Not one of them has ever been used even once."

"So, let me guess, you traded in handbags for diaper bags?"

"You've got it. I went back to work for a while when Levy was about six months old. It was just too hard to manage a job and a baby, even with a nanny. So I resigned and had two more kids."

"Do you think you'll go back to work when they're older?"

"I'd like to, but it won't be easy. When you're out of the loop for a while, especially in something as competitive as a fashion magazine, it can be hard to break back in."

"So, the fetish parties…?"

"They're the only thing in life these days that gives me a rush."

At about five foot five, Robin should have been a person of interest to me, at least as a potential driver of Ian's truck. However, she seemed to have too much at stake – the house, the kids, the marriage, and the release she gets from fetish parties – for her to have been involved in Ian's death. I couldn't see a motive here. But that was the problem. So far, I couldn't see a motive anywhere.

As I walked away, I started humming "The Ballad of Lucy Jordan."

Tuesday,
10:44 pm

At Jessica's place I was immediately greeted by the stench of fresh cat piss. Even though Bella's litter box is in the bathroom, the smell permeated the whole apartment. I scooped the clumps into a green plastic bag and immediately dumped the bag down the communal garbage chute in the hall. Bella wrapped herself around my legs when I came back in. I think she expected praise for the performance of her bodily functions.

"Bella, you're cute and fluffy, but damn, you stink." Bella didn't reply. I filled her water bowl and then helped myself to another glass of wine from the Tetra Pak in Jessica's fridge. I was too tired and lazy to go home again tonight, but at least I'd thought ahead and had left a few changes of clothes and some toiletries at her place.

I was more than a bit curious about the legalities of sex clubs. Thanks to my last big case, I'm now something of an expert on commercial sex, but this was a very different animal. Luckily, the Criminal Code of Canada is available online. And luckily, Jessica has high-speed Internet. Her music selection sucks, but her computer set-up is much better than the antique in Dad's den at home, or the bargain-bin clone model I have at my office.

Parts V and VII of the Criminal Code were of interest

to me: Sexual Offences and Disorderly Houses. Section 159 *Anal Intercourse.* Section 160 *Bestiality.* Section 162 *Voyeurism.* Section 163 *Corrupting Morals.* Section 167 *Immoral Theatrical Performance.* Section 210 *Bawdy Houses.* Section 212 *Procuring.* And, of course, there were sections on pornography and sexual exploitation and minors. It was rather dry reading. *Section this, subsection that.* Eventually, I found what I was looking for.

In a 7–2 decision released in December 2005, the Supreme Court of Canada determined that because they are consensual and no money is exchanged, swingers and fetish clubs aren't a legal no-no. The issue that had been before the courts was one of indecency, and, not surprisingly, right-wing family action and religious groups had been up in arms at the decision. The ruling overturned two earlier court decisions, and ultimately determined that sex clubs do not harm society in general.

A number of sanctimonious Bible-thumping groups had sounded off online about the ruling. A Google search about the ruling called up as many web pages in favour of the legal update as those that renounced it. An online Catholic newsletter slammed sex clubs as homes for perverts and shameless conduct. *Let he who is without sin….* I wondered what the newsletter would have said if they'd seen what I'd seen the other night? Surely none of it was any worse than the activities the Vatican had covered up. And everything I'd seen had been consensual. Hypocrisy is anything but finite.

My next homework assignment was to learn more about booze laws in Ontario. The *Liquor Licence Act* told me all I needed to know about the sale and service of alcohol in a public place. There were more than twenty sections on licences and permits, including sections on conditions and renewal of licences, special permits, and compliance. Chapter 61 was all about offences, and Chapter 62 was all about regulations. Then there were sections on municipal bylaws, and a section specific to Toronto. There was enough legalese here to make me wonder why anyone would ever want to open an establishment with booze for sale.

A quick look at the *Provincial Offences Act* filled in a few more blanks, but it was even drier reading than the pages about alcohol. Most of the provincial stuff had to do with procedures, traffic violations, sentencing, and search warrants. After surfing the Net for a good long while, I now knew more about Ontario's rules for *wining, dining, and sixty-nining* than I ever wanted to. Nevertheless, I still planned to visit my contact at the liquor board tomorrow.

Wednesday, October 3, 12:11 am

Derek called just as I was shutting down the computer. My eyes were blurry after staring at the screen for so long.

"How's the trial going?" I asked.

"Basically, it's a long exercise in frustration. Whatever I thought before about wrapping up early was a fantasy."

"But it's Thanksgiving weekend. Surely the judge will pause things until everyone gets back to work on Tuesday?"

"That's another problem. I really should stop by to see my folks sometime this weekend. They're only a couple of hours from here. I can drive from Timmins to their place in about two hours. It would be at least another six or seven hours from there to Toronto, and then I'd have to turn around and drive back eight or nine hours to get back to court."

"That really sucks. What kind of a judge keeps a trial hanging in the air over a holiday weekend?" I asked.

"At this point, it's up to the jury, not the judge. Even if I'm not stuck here for the weekend, I still can't get back to Toronto right away. My parents and a side trip to North Bay."

"Hmmm. I guess we'll wait and see how things unfold."

"Trust me, I'm dying to see you too. Anyhow, what's happening in the private eye world?"

"I'm proud to say that I have a new client." I gave Derek the details – such as they were – of my latest case.

"I can see why Hugh hired you, although it probably wasn't necessary."

"Agreed, but he gave me a retainer, so I'm on the case."

"Any hunches yet?"

"Not really, but I have a lot of leads to check. His ex, his co-workers, other guests at the fetish party."

"Who have you talked to so far?" Derek asked.

"Well, his playmate, Mimi or Minerva, is pretty cool. She's the one who filled me in on the cast of characters. Mimi's an artist and makes a ton of money selling spray-painted old shoes on copper wire trees." I described the pieces I had seen and the prices Mimi had mentioned.

"And I spent three years in law school…"

"Yes, but darling, would you understand the deep, profound symbolism of abandoned roadside footwear?"

"You have a point."

"Anyhow, Mark, you know, my friend the cop? He gave me the inside scoop." I told Derek about the position of driver's seat and mirrors in Ian's truck, and the theory that Ian had been followed or ambushed, and that the murderer probably hadn't acted alone.

"So what does your gut tell you?"

"My instinct says the murder is unrelated to the fetish scene, but that would be the most obvious assumption. By the way, if you want to know anything at all about bondage and S&M and laws on swinger's clubs, just give me a call. I'm now an expert on them."

"And I spent three years in law school..."

As we wrapped up the quotidian part of the conversation, our talk turned to us and our budding relationship. We were each missing the other terribly, which was tough. What this really means is we were both really horny. Aside from hyperactive hormones, the whole relationship was wonderful and scary for me at the same time. Derek is the first guy I've fallen for since my tumultuous relationship with Mick. The Mick years were fast and furious, passionate and poisonous, and because we were band mates, it was hard to make a break from him. After one too many roller-coaster rides, I'd quit the band and Mick for good.

Eventually, the call with Derek took on a naughtier tone. That could be blamed on the headiness of a new romance, but it was more likely the fault of raging, frustrated pheromones. We ended up having phone sex. I can honestly say, it was the first time I've ever had phone sex when a) I wasn't getting paid for it, and b) I wasn't faking a damn thing.

It took me a long while to fall asleep.

Wednesday,
10:11 am

I took the subway and then a streetcar to Queen West at Spadina. I could have walked, as it wasn't really that far from Jessica's place, only about half an hour's walk, but I was feeling lazy. Besides, it was cooler today, and the sky threatened rain.

Mission number one this morning was a visit with Ian's ex, Tricia Lado. I'd learned that Ms. Lado is the owner of Serendipity, a store specializing in artisan jewellery. I walked into a dimly lit shop, with lots of candles, no customers, and the pleasing smell of vanilla incense.

"May I help you?" said a girl with honey blond hair styled in a flattering pixie cut. It would be odd to describe a human being as long, but that's exactly what I thought of the girl standing before me. At about five foot nine, she and I were roughly the same height, but she was lean and sinewy, only about 110 pounds, to my 125. Her voice sounded sort of like the person I'd spoken with earlier on the phone.

"Yes, is Tricia here?"

"I'm Tricia. What can I do for you?"

"Are you the Tricia who is Ian's ex-girlfriend?"

"Ah, you must be Sasha. Nice to meet you. Yes, I'm Tricia." I was a tad surprised at this. Ian Dooley's death notice had listed his age at thirty-eight, and this girl was in her early twenties at the most.

"Yes. Is there someplace we can talk privately?"

"We can talk here. I'll just lock the door and flip the sign to Closed."

"So, you're Ian's ex?" Might as well start with the obvious. I had pictured Ian's ex as someone in her early to mid-thirties.

"Yes and no," Tricia replied. "It's a long story."

"I've got all the time in the world. Start from the beginning," I said.

"Well, here's the *Reader's Digest* version of things, pretty much exactly what I told to the police when they came around. I guess you could say I was a spoiled little rich kid with a rebellious streak."

"Uh huh…keep going." After my recent experience with Macy, I could sort of guess where this story might end up, only if Tricia came from money, as she had indicated, hers was likely to be the designer version of the Edquists' drama.

"Are you familiar with a fast food joint called The Perogy Hut?"

"Oh yeah. I've pigged out there many times. The cheddar and bacon perogies smothered in sour cream are one of my favourite hangover foods."

"Mine too, although I haven't been hungover in ages. Being mom to a four-year-old really cuts into the partying."

"I can only imagine." No I couldn't, not really. Maybe I just hadn't met the right guy yet, or maybe my biological clock hadn't begun to tick, but being a mom seems like something that only happens to *other* people.

"There are fourteen Perogy Hut stores, located in food courts of shopping malls around Toronto. My dad owns them all."

"So the family dough is in dumplings. Interesting."

"Dad's a bit of an entrepreneur. The perogy business is just one of his ventures. Dad also owns Bronzeskin Tanning salons, and a limousine service, with a fleet of a dozen cars. They mostly get booked for weddings and prom nights and stuff. It's kind of a seasonal biz."

"I think I may have puked in one of your limos on my high school grad night." From what I remembered, grad night amongst myself and my cohorts had included pretty dresses, corsages, and the ill-advised combination of rum, vodka, grape juice, and jalapeno poppers. Lindsey, who was in one of her religious modes then, didn't consume any booze and was the only one who didn't spend the tail end of the evening bowing to the porcelain queen. Linds had taken great joy in waking everyone up at 7:30 the next morning.

"You and everyone else who finishes high school.

Dad's also into real estate. Nothing major, it's not like he's Donald Trump and owns a high-rise or an office tower. But he does own seven or eight apartment houses that he rents out."

"It's kind of neat that he's so diverse. He sounds like a smart man."

"Yeah, I guess. But it's also part and parcel of that whole immigrant mentality thing."

Tricia was giving me way more background than I needed for my case, but the tale had me intrigued. Surely to Pete she had a point and telling me the family saga wasn't gratuitous.

"The family now goes by the surname 'Lado', but when Dad first came here he was Kasper Ladowski. He calls himself Karl now. Dad's family immigrated here from Poland a few years after the Second World War. He was about eight years old – the baby of the family – when they arrived. His two sisters were in their late teens. Anyhow, his family was very poor, and Dad was teased a lot because of his accent, the way he dressed, and all that. I think he'll go ballistic if he ever hears another Polish joke. Anyhow, no one in the family spoke English. Dad's parents did menial jobs, and worked day and night."

"This is a pretty typical post-war immigration story."

"Yeah, so years later, Dad is financially secure, relatively successful, yadda yadda yadda. He takes great care of my grandparents, paid off their mortgage, and he's very generous with my aunts."

"So there's a happy ending. The hard working immigrant achieves the American dream and all that," I said.

"More or less. But it wasn't very smooth for a while. I was an asshole as a teenager. I rebelled at everything I could. I hung around a pretty rough crowd. I did every drug I could get my hands on, and did them all repeatedly. A bored, spoiled teenager who had everything handed to her and was too much of a jackass to appreciate it."

Tricia told the story as matter-of-factly as if she were describing what she had eaten for lunch.

"So, when and how did a baby come into this story?" I asked.

"Drugs weren't a lot of fun after a while, so I turned to sex. That's how I met Ian. I was already pretty promiscuous anyway, but I hadn't really experimented. I was only into straightforward fucking at that point. I met Ian at a party and he introduced me to the fetish scene."

"Oh, no, the rest of the story is coming right at me, just like a train wreck."

"You guessed it. I started hanging out with the bondage crowd. I had a blast playing the games, I never took it too seriously. For me, it was just shits and giggles. Another way to rebel and piss off my parents. Ian and I had been fucking for about two months when I discovered I was pregnant. I was just a few months shy of turning eighteen. So that's the story."

"Wow. So what happened between you and Ian? I mean, obviously he was involved with your daughter, so things worked out okay?"

"I straightened out pretty quick when I learned I was expecting a child. Gave up partying and drugs."

"You didn't really have a choice there."

"Exactly. It was one thing to fuck myself up, but another thing altogether to mess with a kid who wasn't even born yet. Anyhow, Ian wasn't thrilled about becoming a dad, but he wasn't really against it either. I think initially his only fear was being tied down to one woman. I made it clear to him that we were through. I wasn't expecting him to put a ring on my finger or anything."

"So you stayed on friendly terms and shared the parenting."

"More or less. Thank God my parents are able to help me out. Dad didn't want his grandchild to live in some flophouse, so he set me up in my apartment in High Park, it's actually in one of the triplexes he owns. A couple months later a place down the road became available, and he gave that apartment to Ian so that Kayla could be close to both parents."

"You're very lucky," I said.

"Don't I know it. Now, at least. When Kayla was a little over two, Dad financed this store for me. He owns it, really. But I'm here almost every day, and I design a lot of the pieces."

"I noticed some nice turquoise bracelets out front. You made them?"

"Nope. I specialize in earrings, but I do some necklaces as well. I take in other jewellery on consignment from local artists."

"Well…" I was at a loss what to ask next. There were so many questions, but I had no clue which ones were important and which ones were barking up the wrong tree.

Tricia steered me back on course.

"I suppose you're wondering about Ian's funeral," she said.

Actually, I wasn't. It hadn't even crossed my mind, but I nodded. "What are the plans?"

"We can't do anything until the coroner releases the body, which should happen by the end of the week."

"Then what?"

"You know Ian was from Nova Scotia."

"Not really. I definitely noticed the East Coast accent though."

"He was from Sydney Mines, Nova Scotia. On Cape Breton Island. His family is all down east, so that's where he'll be buried. His mom is just a wreck. I talked to her last night."

"I can imagine."

"So, when the coroner gives his okay, the body will be flown there for burial. We'll do a memorial service here in a couple of weeks. I'm kind of the default planner for that, and I don't want to do it until the dust settles. There's too much going on right now."

"I'd love to have a look around Ian's place. It may not tell me anything, but you never know."

"The cops have already checked it out. They didn't find anything useful."

"That may be true, but I'm not necessarily looking for the same things as they are. Keep in mind, this is one more crime on a list of crimes the cops have to solve. And their client is everyone and nobody at once. In my case, I'm working for the owner of the bar where Ian hosted a party the night before he was killed. The cops and I aren't exactly working at cross purposes, but we have different incentives," I said.

"I wouldn't feel right giving you the key, but I can go there with you after work, if you want," Tricia said. She wrote down the address on the back of a cash register receipt.

"Awesome. I'll meet you out front. What time?"

"I'll see you there at seven."

Wednesday, 11:54 am

I realize that the police have far greater powers and far greater resources than I do, so I decided to pursue the angles they were likely to ignore. It isn't as if the cops and I are partners in the Dooley case, but I'd be able to keep up with them one way or another. Most likely by sweet-talking Mark Houghton.

The cops were no doubt combing through the names on the guest list and tracing Ian's last movements, so I began by exploring the liquor board angle. I knew the liquor board would probably be useless in solving the murder, but they could be a good source in terms of finding out where things might lead, or from whence pressure might come, and I was sure they could provide some interesting background about The Pilot. Actually, I was just being nosy about the bar and my client. I mostly believed Hugh's reason for hiring me, but not entirely. He was spending money unnecessarily by retaining my services. Although I'm not the highest-priced investigator in town, I do charge a helluva lot more than minimum wage. My gut told me that most bar owners would let the police do their jobs, and save the bar's profits for something else.

"Yes, both of them on dark rye with lots of mustard, please," I said to the clerk at Moishe's, my favourite deli.

"You want fries or coleslaw?" asked the over-the-hill woman behind the counter. She had a rather dour expression on her face, but then if I looked like her, I'd be less than effervescent too. Someone had clearly stolen both of her eyebrows, and replaced them with pencilled-in semicircles in a shade of burned sienna not found in nature.

"Both, please. And a few pickles. I'll take a couple Cokes, too, please."

She packed up the smoked meat sandwiches, and I headed off to the liquor board's office on Lake Shore Boulevard to offer a deli bribe to my friend who works there. Eleanor Gluckstein is actually a neighbour of my ex-boyfriend Mick, but I've often been known to appropriate alliances as needed.

"Okay, now that we've stuffed ourselves, you may as well tell me what you're looking for," said Eleanor, wiping a few crumbs from her chin.

"What makes you think I came here for something?" I asked with feigned defensiveness. "Can't I just visit my friend for lunch?"

"Sasha, why the hell would anyone want to spend their lunch hour in a bland government office with no windows?"

"So, you don't believe I just wanted to spend quality time with you?"

"I have a feeling this is about The Pilot Tavern and the guy who was killed after the kinky sex party there the other night, right?"

"Well, since you brought it up, what can you tell me about The Pilot Tavern and The Stealth Lounge above it?"

Eleanor took a manila file folder out of her desk drawer. "I pulled this out right after you called. I knew you'd be poking into it."

"I'm nothing if not transparent."

Eleanor held the file at arm's length. "About eighteen months ago, The Pilot Tavern was fined for overcrowding." Eleanor was looking at the hardcopy file. It seemed silly to me that the liquor board still relied so heavily on paper.

"That's not too big a deal, is it?" I asked.

"The biggest concern with overcrowding, of course, is that it poses a safety hazard in the event of a fire or other emergency." She was squinting as she read.

"Girlfriend, don't you think it's time to get reading glasses?"

"I know, I know. I just don't want to yet. They'll make me feel old." Eleanor continued, "Anyhow, about the overcrowding thing, as long as nothing calamitous occurs, it's not exactly a mortal sin. Pay a fine, get a slap on the wrist and that's that. Let's see, what else is there…" Eleanor flipped through a few more pages.

"Hmmm. About six months after this, the bar was given a hefty fine for serving a minor in The Stealth Lounge. That's a big no-no."

"They didn't lose their licence for that? Or get a suspension?" I asked.

"No. Turns out the minor had some really good fake ID and the cop who did the bust was almost fooled by it himself." She leafed through a few more pages. "The bar appealed it, and the ruling was reversed. The staff were able to show that they had made a reasonable and responsible attempt not to serve alcohol to anyone under the age of majority."

"Yeah, and…?"

"Basically, bartenders and waitresses are not meant to be experts on forged identification."

"Hmmm. I see. Interesting."

"That's about it, amiga. Damn, there's mustard on my sleeve. I'll be right back." Eleanor headed to the washroom to try to get rid of the yellow blob on her blouse, and I took advantage of her absence to poke through the file.

There really wasn't much else to see. Eleanor had already given me all the dirt. The annual licensing fees were due again in February. They had applied for and had received a special permit allowing extended hours of service during the Toronto International Film Festival that had wound up just a few weeks ago. Like most bars in downtown Toronto, the Film Fest was practically a license to print money. All the establishments near the cinemas where premieres were held raked in tons of cash from the glitterati during the maple syrup version of the Cannes festival here in Hollywood North.

I heard footsteps in the hallway and quickly closed the file and put it back on Eleanor's desk. Nothing ventured, nothing gained.

Wednesday, 1:44 pm

Next on the agenda was a trip to Leaside to chat with Ian's co-workers. I stopped at a newsstand on my way to the subway so I'd have something to read on my journey. I bought the new issues of *Rolling Stone* and *Mother Jones*, and picked up a free copy of *Now* magazine. I used to plan my social life around the live music listings in *Now*. In fact, for many years my life revolved around seeing my band's gigs being mentioned in those listings. As I headed to the subway, I briefly lamented the fact that my crazy work schedule has been keeping me out of the music loop lately. Maybe this weekend I'd make a point of seeing some live shows. It would be fun to check out the music scene with Derek. I hoped his trial would wrap up and he'd come back soon. I was really missing him, and I was getting rather sexually frustrated, especially given all the horny allusions tied to this case.

I was just about to take the stairs down to the subway entrance when my phone rang. If the call had come about a minute later, I wouldn't have received it, as our fair transit system is stuck in the middle ages. A significant percentage of the subway system is devoid of cyber service, but hey, maybe we'll get a tunnel to downtown. That would be progress, baby. Not.

"I know it's last minute, but do you want to join me for a late lunch?" asked Lindsey.

"I just had a feast from Moishe's, but I'll tag along and watch you eat if you want," I said.

"Sure. Where are you now?"

"I'm just outside Union station, and I eventually have to make my way up to Leaside."

"I'm feeling Greek today. I have a craving for sou-vlaki."

"You do realize that's grilled meat, don't you? And may I remind you that you're Hindu?" Lindsey's real name is Lakshmi. Her family had migrated to Canada from Sri Lanka when she was just a little girl. Although the family observes strict Hindu customs at home, Lakshmi/Lindsey eats whatever the hell she pleases when her parents aren't around. Being engaged to a chef makes it easy.

"I'm beyond redemption. How about taking the subway to Penelope's on the Danforth, and I'll drive you to Leaside afterwards?" There are times it feels like Lindsey's my personal chauffeur.

"I'm on my way."

Penelope's, a standby neighbourhood restaurant on the Danforth, isn't too far from my home, a place I hadn't seen much of in the last few days. Penelope's specializes in Greek food and is the go-to place for ouzo and saganaki. *Opa!* I happen to hate the place, but Lindsey likes it, and since I wasn't planning to eat, I was in no position to argue.

It had clouded over a bit while I was having lunch with Eleanor, and by the time I exited the subway at

Broadview station, the sky was very overcast. I was glad I'd be able to mooch a ride from Lindsey, since it looked for sure like it would rain soon, and I, of course, didn't have an umbrella.

Lindsey was already at a table in the dining room when I arrived. At 2:15 on a Wednesday afternoon, the place was fairly quiet. The hostess led me to Lindsey's table, where I sat, completely ignored by the wait staff for the next ten minutes.

"Oh, someone's joined you," said the waitress to Lindsey, as she set down a plate piled high with two skewers of charred pork souvlaki, a heap of saffron rice, lemon roasted potatoes, Greek salad, tzatziki, and a mini-loaf of sesame crusted bread. Just the starch in the meal would have killed me.

"This looks fantastic," Lindsey said as she placed her napkin on her lap.

"I didn't see you come in," the waitress said to me.

I bit back a sarcastic comment and ordered a glass of red wine. After the deli lunch, I didn't have room for a beer, and my usual sweet and creamy cocktails wouldn't taste right given that I could still taste the garlicky pickles I'd had with lunch.

"Before we start talking about the murder, I've been meaning to ask you about the runaway girl," Lindsey said between mouthfuls.

"Macy. I found her Monday night, down around Queen and Bathurst."

"Wow, congrats! That was quick. Her parents must be so relieved."

"Not exactly." I told Lindsey about my unpaid and

uninvoiced bill to them and about being fired for unsatisfactory results.

"Shit. I'm not saying I agree with how they treated you, but I can kind of see their point. They're worried about their kid and they took it out on you."

"I guess so. Anyhow, Macy called me yesterday, but didn't say why she called. The kid is something of a fuck-up, but technically she's alive and well, though for how long I don't know."

"What do you mean?"

"Well, there's the drugs, of course. I suspect she's using crystal meth. She sure as hell seemed stoned when I saw her, but the more disturbing thing about her than the drugs was this business about cutting herself."

"What?"

"It's something that some screwed-up teens are into. Seems to be more common among goths and punks, and a group called 'emos', as in emotion."

"So what's the cutting all about?" Lindsey asked.

"Well, for one thing, it's about control, but let's face it, it's got to be a cry for help or to get attention. The kids who do this cut themselves in a place where the marks will show, like on their forearms. They get into self-mutilation as a way to express anger or depression."

"Seems to me it'd be easier to see a doctor or a shrink."

"The kids who do this don't think they need help. The whole point is that they feel it's a kind of control. Autonomy, if you will. Some kids get addicted to it and look forward to doing their next cut. They say it's a rush."

"I don't get the link between pleasure and pain. Really, I don't," Lindsey said. "I still cry when I go to the dentist, even though Dr. Sylvestri is kinda hot."

"Cutting yourself is not exactly about pleasure, it's more about control. If you think about it, in some ways it's like the whole fetish thing. The S&M world and control. That's all about pain too, giving and receiving," I said.

"In any case, pain's not really my cup of tea. I could maybe handle a playful little smack on the ass, but –"

"Uh, too much information. Getting a bad visual. I do not need to picture you and my brother in bed."

"Sorry. Sometimes I forget you're related. Anyhow, what about your guy who was murdered?"

"I have a feeling the murder is unrelated to the bondage and domination world, but I could be wrong. That wouldn't exactly be a first…."

"What other reason could there be?"

"That's the problem. If it's separate from kinky sex, then it must be random, and I can't get my head around that. There's no logical explanation for Ian to have been in Leslieville or the Port Lands on Sunday morning. His partner, Minerva, lives at Yonge and St. Clair. Ian lived in the west end, near High Park. He wouldn't have driven south-east to go home."

"Have you talked to everyone whose number was on his cellphone?" Lindsey asked.

"Most of them. I haven't been able to connect with someone named Wendi yet, but I've talked with pretty much everyone else. The only other lead for now is to meet with his co-workers this afternoon, which is why you're driving me to Leaside." One of these days,

I really should get a driver's licence. In my last major case, I had "borrowed" Dad's car a couple of times, and it's a miracle I didn't turn it into an accordion. It's a little embarrassing to be in my thirties and frequently mooching rides from friends. Besides, how cool can a sleuth possibly look getting on a bus? "Then later to-night, his ex, or as they say, his 'Baby Mama' is going to give me an escorted tour of Ian's former dwelling."

Wednesday, 3:38 pm

Plumber butt is never a good thing. Two simultaneous versions of plumber butt is even worse. The guys working on the house in Leaside needed to learn about a wonderful and practical fashion accessory called a belt. Rodrigo and Phil, who were up on ladders doing something with the eavestroughs on this house, were literally giving me a crack of a smile. The song "Moon River" popped into my head.

"Hey guys, can you take a break for a moment and chat with me?" I called up to them.

"Give us a minute. We're kind of in the middle of something."

I had no idea what they were doing, so I paced the sidewalk for a few minutes, humming "Fly Me to the Moon," and tapping out the beat on my thigh as I dawdled along in front of the house.

I noticed that this street seemed to have a greater quantity of election signs than the streets around my neighbourhood, or Lisa's or Robin's. Residents appeared to be divided among all the leading mayoral candidates, but there seemed to be slightly more signs in favour of Tim Nealson. His slogan was *Change for the Better*, which is something I agree with in any situation, not just in politics, but it doesn't strike me as a particularly zingy political slogan. I hoped he'd be charismatic and get me fired up when I saw him at the dinner at Shane's tomorrow night. Based on what I'd seen so far, I expected little more than bumper-sticker political posturing. Mind you, the other candidates' campaigns, with the exception of the Mafioso Mayor-hopeful, were equally banal. I wished some politician would run a campaign saying "I only lie now and then, and I won't rip you off for very much." He or she would most certainly earn my respect, if not my vote.

The dark-skinned guy I assumed to be Rodrigo hopped off the ladder first.

"Whassup?" he asked.

"My name's Sasha Jackson. I'm investigating the death of your co-worker Ian Dooley."

"Oh yeah, Scott said you was gonna come around."

Phil hiked up his trousers as he walked over to join us. He had a few years and quite a few pounds on Rodrigo, and seemed to be more winded from whatever home improvement task they were doing.

"I'm still pretty freakin' stunned by the news," Phil said, panting a little.

"Yes," I said. "I guess the murder came as quite a shock."

"No no, I don't mean that. I mean, yeah, the murder kind of floored me, but what I meant is all the freakin' kinky sex?" Phil said.

"Yeah, like, we had no idea. Sounds like Ian was pretty wild. I wouldna guessed he was into that stuff, man, spanking and whipping. It's crazy," Rodrigo said.

"You mean neither of you knew about his fetish life? S&M? Nothing?" I asked.

"Unh unh. He bragged about getting laid lots, but I always thought he was shitting us," said Phil.

"Wow. That kind of voids most of the questions I was going to ask you. What about his work life? Did he have any enemies on the job? Any clients he seriously pissed off?" I couldn't picture bad renovations as a motive for murder, although friends who have lived through home remodelling may beg to differ.

"Nah. Ian done mostly finishing stuff, like walls and floors. He done good work."

So my trek up to Leaside was a waste of time. I hadn't expected to glean much, but I had hoped to get slightly more than zero from the journey. I stuck the buds in my ears and cranked up my iPod. The first song up was Van Morrison's "Moondance."

Too bad I hadn't asked Lindsey to wait for me. Now I was going to have to spend about forty-five minutes making the return trip on the bus and subway, and the whole interview with Phil and Rodrigo had lasted less than five minutes. Not a good ratio of time versus results.

Wednesday, 7:00 pm

I stood in front of what was once an old house at 256 Geoffrey Street, at the corner of Parkside Drive. It was still nice-looking, but as it was no longer a single-family dwelling, it seemed less impressive. I hoped Tricia would show up soon, as it had just begun to rain lightly.

Geoffrey Street ends at Parkside Drive, and the other side of the road is the edge of High Park. Even though the old home in front of which I stood had been subdivided into three apartments, it still had some of its 19th-century charm. The tenants obviously took some pride in keeping the grounds and common areas neat and tidy. Garbage cans were neatly stacked and lidded, and recycling bins were pushed off to the side of the double driveway.

"Hope you weren't waiting too long," Tricia said, catching her breath. "My afternoon spun right out of control. The shop was busier this afternoon than usual, especially on a Wednesday of all days, and I was late getting home, and then Kayla wouldn't eat her dinner. She pitched an absolute fit and threw her plate of mashed potatoes at the wall. She's normally a good eater, but she likes to kick up a fuss at exactly the wrong moments."

"Hell, I have some ex-boyfriends who do that," I said.

"Let's go in before we get any wetter."

My first impression of Ian's apartment was that it gave no hint of his sexual proclivities. It was a basic two-bedroom apartment, taking up the main floor of the house. The front foyer had a full bathroom to the left, closets and a laundry room to the right, and faced onto an open kitchen. Beyond the kitchen was a big square room that doubled as both a living room and a dining room. The apartment was fairly tidy, if not super clean. The furnishings were plain and in good shape, but clearly not much thought or effort had been put into decorating most of the apartment. The living room and kitchen were all boring shades of beige, as was the bathroom. It reminded me of the generic decor in a hotel room.

"I don't know why, but I always expect the homes of single guys to be a mess," I said to Tricia.

"I can see why you'd think that, and it's true for a lot of the guys I've dated. I don't mind if the guy's place is a bit untidy, but if it's a pigsty, that's a deal breaker." I'd been impressed the first time I'd gone to Derek's condo, and not just because of the amazing sex. His place was tidy and comfortably stylish, but not so anal that I couldn't throw my clothes in a heap on the floor.

"I'm with you on that." I poked my head into the fridge. I wasn't likely to find a smoking gun in there, but it's my habit to look at everything, every time.

No one had gotten around to cleaning out fridge yet. There was a row of Capri Sun drink boxes, three opened packages of sandwich meats, milk, cheese, several bottles of hot sauces, a full carton of eggs, and some leftover spaghetti in a Tupperware dish, plus some overripe fruit and wilted veggies in the crisper. The door of the fridge was covered with "artwork" by his daughter Kayla. I think it's safe to say that, thus far, the little girl is a student of Surrealism. The crayon depictions of three-legged animals, trapezoid houses, and flying trees ignored traditional colours, perspectives and dimensions.

Tricia followed me as I went into the living room. I didn't expect to find anything X-rated in the rooms his daughter had access to. Four-year-old kids get into things. I doubted Kayla would have known what nipple clamps and handcuffs were all about, but it would be embarrassing if she used Daddy's leather bullwhip as a jump rope.

The south side of the living room held a wall-to-wall built-in shelving unit, with space for a giant flat-screen television dead centre, with a DVD player and a VCR beneath it. Something told me that Ian had designed and built the unit himself. The shelves to the left of the TV seemed to have been designated "kid stuff." There were stuffed animals on one shelf, the complete works of Dr. Seuss on another, the bottom shelf held bins filled with miscellaneous toys, like My Little Pony and Strawberry Shortcake figurines, crayons and colouring books, a few jigsaw puzzles, Fisher-Price this and Leapfrog that, plus a host of glittery pink fluffy things to amuse a four-year-old girl.

"I see that Kayla's a fan of Dora the Explorer," I said as I thumbed through a row of DVDs on an upper shelf. "And of Barney, and Magic School Bus." There was also a bunch of DVDs for Fred Penner, the Care Bears, and, of course, a whole whack of Sesame Street stuff.

"Trust me, sometimes a DVD player is a parent's best friend. I throw in a video for Kayla while I'm making dinner or doing housework. I don't even notice the soundtracks from the kiddie shows and cartoons anymore. It's like they're white noise," said Tricia.

"Good thing. I swear to God, if I had kids, and I had to listen to Barney singing "I Love You," I'd probably kill someone," I said. And I'd almost certainly go mental if I had to hear Kermit the Frog doing "Rainbow Connection," or listen to Big Bird doing the alphabet, even though I'd loved both of them when I was a kid.

"At times though, I think I should be stricter about the television. Everything aimed at kids these days is just thinly disguised half-hour commercials. It's a bit worrisome, but what can you do?"

"I don't know. Give them a cardboard box and tell them to use their imaginations?"

"That only keeps them occupied for so long. Then they come screaming at you."

"Hmmm."

The shelf on the other side of the television looked like it was Ian's turf. There were dozens of music CDs on the middle shelf. Ian's tastes ran to classic rock and some heavy metal. *The Best of George Thorogood* (in my opinion, it should have been called the worst of George Thorogood, if there's one artist I can't stand, that's the one). AC/DC's *Back in Black* (who doesn't have that?). Creedence Clearwater Revival's *Greatest Hits* (I can't think of one song of theirs that I'd want to have on my iPod). About a dozen Metallica CDs. I like to head-bang now and then, but Metallica's not among my faves, although their version of "Whiskey in the Jar" is a lot of head-banging fun. Ian even had a few audio cassettes, but I didn't see a tape player on which to play any of them. There were several issues of *Sport Illustrated* on the next shelf, and the bottom shelf seemed to be a place to shove work stuff. A yellow hardhat and a dirty pair of steel-toed boots were shoved in there, plus a few pairs of thick socks, a pair of leather work gloves and a red metal toolbox. The top shelf held a few sci-fi paperbacks. Asimov and Bradbury, of course, plus some Robert Sawyer. The books took up only about half the shelf space; the other end of the shelf had a few VHS videos with handwritten stickers labelling them *Disney*.

"You know I want to see his bedroom, right?" I asked.

"Yeah, no problem."

On the other side of the main room were doors to two bedrooms. The smaller of the two belonged to Kayla. It was a typical little girl's room all done up in pink. Ian had obviously put some effort into his daughter's surroundings, even if he hadn't bothered doing much to dress up the rest of the home. I gave Kayla's room nothing but a brief glance. I had no reason to expect to find anything in here.

Tricia followed me into the master suite. Ian's bedroom set looked like a Sears special, with matching night tables on either side of a queen-sized bed. The same beige broadloom that covered the living room floor carried into the bedroom as well, although the rest of the room was painted in dull shades of masculine grey. The bed hadn't been made on the last day of Ian's life, and the grey striped sheets were in a tangled mess near the foot of the bed. The bedroom window was covered by vertical blinds, angled to keep out sunlight. I noticed the window was open about half an inch, but I didn't mention it. It surprised me that the cops had missed this, but occasionally luck is on my side. I knew I'd likely want to make an unaccompanied return visit to Ian's home, and it's always been my preference to make illegal entries as easy on myself as possible.

A corner of Ian's bedroom had been set aside as a de facto office. There was a cheap, "ready to assemble" particleboard desk with a computer and printer on it, a cork board above it, and some drawers beneath the desk.

"If I hope to get any clues as to who killed Ian, I'm going to have to poke through his things. You understand that, right? I'm not trying to be nosy for the sake of being nosy."

"I don't really care what you look at, so long as it's fast. I left Kayla with my neighbour, but I'm going to have to get her soon. Bedtime's eight o'clock and I still need to give her a bath. She still has clumps of mashed potato in her hair."

"I'll try to be quick."

Tricia left the bedroom, and parked herself on the sofa in front of the TV. I could hear Alex Trebek offering pompous commentary to *Jeopardy* contestants.

I poked through Ian's bedroom closet rather quickly. As Mark Houghton had told me, there were a bunch of shirts and pants hanging there, of course, but one side of the closet was dedicated to fetish stuff. There were at least a dozen pieces of leather clothing and gear. Seeing his kinky ensembles hanging there kind of gave me the creeps. Mostly, I wondered how clean it was. I made short work of the closet and then rifled through the chest of drawers opposite the bed. Nothing of interest in it.

However, the bulletin board above the desk intrigued me. There were several recent newspaper clippings tacked onto it. All the clippings had something to do with Tim Nealson's mayoral campaign. I shuffled through them, some tacks had three or four clippings pegged up one in front of another.

Nealson to speak at the Board of Trade.

Tim Nealson and wife Gwendolyn feeding the homeless at Westminster United Church.

Tim Nealson to appear at all candidates debate.

Hell, if Ian were still alive, I'd sit him down with Shane and the two of them could jointly sing the praises of mayoral hopeful Tim Nealson.

The drawers below the desk held several more pieces on Tim Nealson. There was a biographical article from a September issue of *Maclean's* magazine. There was an interview in this month's issue of *Toronto Life*. It was a puff piece, complete with lots of pictures of Tim and Gwendolyn looking casual in their garden, businesslike in his office, and friendly at some local sporting event. The missus seemed the perfect fit for an up-and-coming politician. She was a petite blond, stylishly dressed, and seemed content to stand in his spotlight. I couldn't imagine hitching my wagon to someone else's star. That probably explains why I've never even dreamed of getting married. I'd miss my freedom, and, to me, the idea of becoming "Mrs. So and So" and losing my own identity would be akin to suicide.

The more I dug through Ian's desk, the more I started to wonder about stalker potential.

Wednesday, 8:51 pm

It was a short walk from Ian's place over to Ronces-valles, where I was lucky enough to catch a streetcar right away. I hopped off the 504 at the corner of King and Bathurst. It was only a short jaunt north from there to Queen Street. I was making this pit stop along my way because I was curious as to Macy's whereabouts, and figured it wouldn't kill me to take a quick look. I was more than a little perturbed by her call yesterday. And more than a little worried, even though my case file on her was now closed. I zigzagged up and down the same streets as I had before, but saw no sign of Macy or Shank. After pointlessly pounding the pavement, I hiked over to Kensington Market to try my luck there.

The rain had stopped for the moment, but it was still pretty soggy outside. I doubted there'd be much street life, but you never know. The top end of Augusta Avenue has some really nice restaurants, but they're way out of Macy's price range. Supermarket, an urban hipster place with Thai food and blaring electronic music, had a cluster of Gap-clad yuppies smoking out front. My mouth watered when I walked past El Trompo. It was already closed for the evening, or I'd have ducked in for some tacos el pastor and a margarita or two.

Towards the end of the street, just past a bar called Amadeu's, sits Bellevue Square, which some people also call Denison Square. No matter what it's called, it's nothing special. A favourite hangout for the counter-culture, it's an easy place to buy, sell, or consume drugs, or to drink out of a paper bag.

With an amazing disregard for common sense, I approached a throng of riff-raff who were teasing a German shepherd. Cage the Elephant was cranking out from a clunky old boom box on the ground beside them. I thought perhaps someone should cage this gaggle of stragglers and knock some sense into them. None of them seemed to notice that everything was wet and that the rain was likely to start again any minute. Dummies.

"How's it going?" I asked the guy holding the leash. He took a swig from his can of Molson Golden.

One of his friends tossed a small broken branch in the air. The dog leaped for it, but his owner pulled him back. The dog started barking.

"Shut up, Duke." The dog barked a little louder. "It goes," Molson said to me. "Do I know you?"

"Doubt it. I don't usually hang out here. I'm looking for my little sister." I passed him Macy's photo. "She ran away from home. I don't want to make her go back or anything, I just want to be sure she's okay."

"I mighta seen her around, you know, but I dunno." He drained his can, then belched and reached into a duffel bag for another beer.

"Yo, fix me up," said the guy who was tossing the sticks. He crushed his empty can against his forehead, and then tossed it under the park bench. How very macho and oh-so-cool. Molson passed another ale to him. "You want one?" he asked me.

"Thanks, but I'm good for now. Anyone else recognize her?" I asked. They all shook their heads after looking at the picture.

All in a night's work.

After about an hour of damp walking and talking, I decided to take a break.

"Hey Sasha," said a long-haired dude as soon as I walked in to Graffiti's. I knew him from my bar band days, but I had no clue what his name was. I remembered that he plays bass in a rockabilly band.

"How ya been? I haven't seen you in ages." For the life of me, his name wouldn't come to mind.

"Can I buy you a drink?"

A struggling musician offering to buy someone a drink? Unheard of. I had to say yes.

"A quick one. I'm kind of working tonight." The bartender passed me a pint of wheat beer.

Drinking draught beer from a heavy glass mug in a licensed establishment is classier than swilling canned beer out of a duffel bag in the park, but given I was at Graffiti's, this was only marginally so.

Long Hair asked about my current situation. I gave his a brief outline of the last couple years of my resume, and I got the lowdown on his recent musical misadventures.

"Wow, what a change. An investigator. Do you still have time for music? Any gigs coming up?"

"Nope. I quit the band a while ago. There's too much competition in the music biz, and we weren't going anywhere."

We chatted a while longer and I still couldn't remember Long Hair's name. I had another half-pint with him as he filled me in on some of the people we both knew from the bar band circuit.

"I heard Ogilvie has given up bars and now mostly does weddings," I said. Ogilvie had tried just about every genre available on the local scene: jazz, rock, country, blues. A talented bass player, he might have made it big someday if he hadn't been such an asshole. In the music industry, like just about anywhere else, it pays to have friends in high places and people who were willing to do you a favour.

"That didn't work out too well. Turns out, he did two weddings in a row where he'd slept with the bride once upon a time. The groom at the second wedding didn't find this very amusing and broke all his fingers on both hands."

"That seems a little extreme," I said.

"You know, you should jam with me and the boys some night. Maybe we could try to get a few gigs somewhere? A chick singer's always good. Gives us a chance to do some new material. You and Smith would probably sound good together," he said.

"Thanks, but I'll pass. I'm more interested in drumming than singing these days. I got a new drum set a while ago. Mapex. They're really nice." I hadn't had much chance to play them in the last few days, and I was jonesing for a chance to smash away on them and blow off steam.

"Don't say no yet. Think about it."

"Listen, if I don't get back to work now, I'm not going to get anything done. Let's do this again sometime," I said, and gave Long Hair one of my cards.

The rain had started up again, but only lightly. I held a copy of *Now* over my head as I made one last quick trek up Augusta and then across Nassau. Not one of the water-repellent little punks I came across along the way recognized the picture of Macy. Or, if they did, they weren't saying so. I hoped she was sleeping somewhere safe and dry tonight. I walked north on Spadina, and then hopped on the 506 streetcar.

Thursday, October 4, 9:32 am

I walked quickly from Jessica's place to my office. The skies were dull and grey, and threatened more rain. Even though there were two umbrellas in Jessica's front closet, I wasn't bright enough to bring one with me. Sometimes I wonder how I manage to get myself dressed in the mornings. Luckily the rain held off as I made my way down to Church and Front.

There was really no solid reason to go to the office instead of staying at Jessica's place. Anything I wanted to do here, I could have done there, and it may have been easier at her place, since her computer is much better than mine. But sometimes being in my office helps me think. Popping in once in a while also justifies the monthly rent.

When I sat at my desk, I discovered I had a bit of a problem awaiting me. Well, not really a problem. Or, if it was a problem, this was a good one to have. For the first time since I started my investigations biz, I found myself having to turn down business. My voicemail had not one, not two, but three calls from prospective new clients. Things were looking up for Sasha Jackson Investigations. Who woulda thunk it a year ago? Hell, who woulda thunk it last month or last week?

The first call was from Mr. Belham, the horny old money manager who had given me a break when I'd started out. He wanted me to do a corporate background check, and such cases are my bread and butter. I could count on Belham for a file about every six weeks.

The second call was a husband who suspected his better half was cheating.

The third call was from Percy Wiggins, the restaurant owner Shane had mentioned. Unfortunately, as a one-person operation, there was no way I could take on three new cases at once, especially on top of a murder case.

The wayward wife was an easy case to refuse. I suggested the client call Marko Krebs, a guy I'd gone to college with who relishes cases of cheating wives. I think deep down, Marko is a peeping Tom, and would probably spy on straying spouses for free, especially if there was a good chance of catching them *in flagrante delicto.* Or, as he says, *in flagrante delicious.* Ick.

The corporate background check for Mr. Belham

was a definite yes. Easy money, and a loyal client, even though I know Belham is a dirty old man in private.

"Good morning, sir," I said when Mr. Belham came on the line. Quite unwillingly, I pictured him naked. During the Hispanic Hooker Case, I'd accidentally learned all the secrets of Belham's sex life. Too much info, but my brain simply would not let me erase the images of him being straddled by a copper-haired Celtic nympho for hire.

"Well hello, Sasha. How has life been treating you?"

We exchanged a few pleasantries before he got to the reason for his call.

"I'm recruiting a new Investment Manager. Would you be able to check into the work histories of the two candidates I have under consideration?"

"I'd love to, but I can't get on it until early next week. Monday's a holiday, so I guess I could start on Tuesday. Does that work for you?"

"Certainly. That would be fine. I will email their resumes to you."

"Perfect. I'll get back to you when I have something."

Next up was a call to Percy. As it was a referral from Shane, there was no way I could turn him down.

"Hi Sasha. Thanks for getting back to me so quickly," Percy said.

"No problem. Shane said you think someone is pilfering from your restaurant?"

"I hate to think so, but it looks that way."

"We should probably have a chat face to face," I said.

"Can you come to the restaurant somewhere around mid-afternoon? I won't be able to talk while the lunch rush is on."

"How about three?"

"Great. See you then," Percy said as I hung up.

I next turned my energies to the wannabe mayor. My gut told me that poking into the life and times of Tim Nealson would be either very boring or very unpleasant. So far, it was proving to be the former. Regardless, my gut told me that I needed to learn why the late and probably not great Ian was so obsessed with our wannabe mayor.

Nealson's was a white-bread existence. Toronto born and raised. Middle- to upper-middle-class upbringing. Lived here all his life, save two years in grad school, and one year doing contract work in Vancouver. Bachelor's degree in Economics from the University of Toronto. Master's degree in Public Administration from Carleton University. He had attended grad school after the brief hiatus during which he had worked for the Ministry of Natural Resources in British Columbia. Since completing his Master's degree, Tim has mainly worked for the Ontario government and at City Hall. His jobs have taken on greater and greater responsibilities over the years. He worked for a couple of years in the City's budget office, he had done a brief stint as the Communications Director for the Ministry of Health, and he worked as the campaign manager for the runner-up in Toronto's mayoral race eight years ago. Most recently, he had been working at the Toronto Commerce Development Board.

Hmmm. A nice resume, but nothing more than a whole lot of bupkus in terms of my current case.

Time to call in some favours. Or to put myself in

debt owing favours to whoever might be in a position to help me.

"Dawn, can you meet me for lunch? My treat." Dawn Valentini is a lovely woman, a militant lesbian, a fan of Irish step dancing, and a fervent Civil War buff. She had once told me that she spends every vacation dressing in period costumes and re-enacting battle scenes in Charleston, Atlanta, Richmond, and elsewhere among the rebel states. I couldn't picture her in the hooped skirts of Scarlett O'Hara's days, but I had no trouble visualizing Dawn with a musket.

Dawn also happens to be a reporter for the *Toronto Sun*, and her beat is downtown Toronto.

"What's in it for me?" she asked. That's what I love about Dawn. She never even pretends to be anything she's not. A competitive bulldog of a reporter, she would do whatever she could for a scoop. The buying and selling of information is all in a day's work for her.

"An exclusive, if my current case unfolds as I think it might?"

"Talk to me."

"Local politics," I said, hoping that would be enough of a lure.

"My butt doesn't leave my chair for an unknown. Who?"

"Tim Nealson," I said.

"Meet me at Cafe Victoria on The Esplanade at noon."

Thursday,
12:10 pm

"I haven't really got much to tell you. As with any public figure, there have been occasional rumours, but in Tim Nealson's case, even those are pretty tame. No Chappaquiddicks, or bike courier manslaughters, or Lewinskys, or Germans with cash-stuffed envelopes in his past. Arnold Schwarzenegger he ain't." Dawn lit another cigarette off the butt of the one she was just finishing. In my opinion, it was a tad too cool to be sitting on a patio, and the ornery October skies looked like they would open up any minute. The disgruntled waiter serving us seemed to side with me. He was abrupt to the point of being snotty, as if he wanted to punish us for making him serve a table outside. We were on the patio so Dawn could chain smoke. I suspect she wakes up hourly throughout the night in order to feed her nicotine addiction. I wondered how she managed nicotine cravings when she was at the office.

"Keep going. Give me whatever you've got," I said.

"It's a rather dull story. Bloated expense accounts. He was able to justify most of them, even a receipt for a six-dollar chocolate chip muffin. A lot of parking tickets and a couple of speeding tickets. A few embarrassing moments in university. He and a bunch of classmates mooned the visiting team at a Varsity football game."

"I doubt his ass is very interesting. What about gambling, drugs, booze, or sex with a hermaphrodite midget or an albino ostrich? C'mon, there's gotta be something. Nobody is that squeaky clean."

Our waiter dropped off two steaming espressos, then took our lunch orders. I wasn't yet very hungry, so I just ordered a bowl of the soup du jour. Dawn settled on an order of fries and gravy.

"I see you're on a health kick."

"Food's not a priority right now. Not if I'm on the cusp of a scoop."

"It could turn out to be a scoop of nothingness, and I wouldn't say you're on the cusp exactly. This may take a while to unfold."

"Whatever. Anyhow, back to Tim Nealson. A few people were pissed at him for giving municipal contracts to a cousin. Nothing major, I think it was gardening or something with Parks and Rec. Watering the flower beds in front of City Hall maybe? It was a few years ago."

"That's pretty tame. What else?"

"If I recall correctly, he was part of a group rounded up for protesting at, let me see now, it was probably a protest over NAFTA or something. Nothing came of it. Again, university days."

"Something about him just doesn't feel right to me."

"Mind telling me why you think that?" Dawn asked, lighting yet another cigarette.

"It's related to a case I'm working on. No details or names, yet, but at the apartment of one of the people involved in this case, I found a thick file of clippings about Tim Nealson. All recent stuff, from each of the local papers. And there were a bunch of printouts from Nealson's website."

"This is very interesting. Keep going."

The waiter brought our food. Dawn squeezed a generous amount of ketchup on top of her fries and gravy, turning the plate into one of the most goopy, unappetizing, gelatinous red and brown things I've ever seen. I spooned a mouthful of potato-leek soup and was disappointed. The flavour was bland, the soup was barely tepid, and it had the consistency of Elmer's Glue. I pushed the bowl aside.

"There was a little bit of everything. Campaign ads, press photos of him and his wife, his official bio, a schedule of events and public appearances, interviews, position statements on everything. Some info about volunteering or donating to his campaign. Even an interview his wife gave to some chick publication. *Toronto Women's Herald* or whatever."

"And you want to know why this person is so interested in him," Dawn said.

"Yup."

"C'mon, Sasha, quid pro quo. Why are you fishing in this pond? What are you offering if I uncover some dirt? "

"I can promise you the sun and moon and stars. How's that for an offer?"

"Humph." Dawn finished her fries and waved to get the waiter's attention. "I don't think I heard you correctly. Didn't you say you'd give me an exclusive on a juicy story to unfold very soon? I'm pretty sure that's what you just said."

The waiter cleared our plates, and I ordered another espresso. Dawn lit another cigarette.

"You have to take me at my word. I'll give you the whole story. I promise. But nothing yet. I wish I could, but I just can't. It could screw everything up, or worse, I could be dead wrong and then I'd look like an idiot."

"Pride isn't something you have in abundance, my dear." Dawn blew smoke out of her nostrils. Given that I often share a cigar with Derek, I can't claim to be the conductor on the anti-tobacco bandwagon, but something about the two streams of smoke flowing out of her nose was quite repulsive.

"If I give you what I have so far, and I turn out to be wrong, you could get your ass sued for libel. I'll tell you everything I can ASAP, okay?"

"Deal. But you know that in the meantime, I'll be trolling for Tim Nealson chum." Two more streams of smoke.

"I was counting on that."

Thursday,
1:30 pm

Dawn had a meeting to get back to, but I didn't have any place special to be right now, so I moved to a table inside the restaurant and ordered my third espresso.

I grabbed the copy of today's paper that was lying on the empty table next to me.

My horoscope didn't make any grandiose promises about the day ahead. Apparently I would be rewarded by patience in the not too distant future. I flipped to the comics and was disappointed. None of them seem very funny anymore, except maybe *The Far Side*. God, I wish *Calvin and Hobbes* were still in syndication. I mulled over my latest case while sipping my drink and doing the daily crossword. I was trying to think of a landlocked African nation with six letters – Malawi? Uganda? Rwanda? – when my phone rang.

"Sasha? It's Hugh. Do you have a minute?"

"Sure do. What's up?" I started to write in "Lesotho," but then realized it has seven letters.

"Nothing. I just wanted to touch base, see if you had any news."

"Sorry Hugh. Too soon to tell." I pencilled in "Zambia" as I spoke. "I've talked with a number of people, but so far everything's cold. I'll let you know the minute I have something."

I hoped Hugh wouldn't turn out to be a pushy client, pestering me 24-7 for updates. So far, he hadn't. The world of detection moves very slowly, almost glacially, until all hell breaks loose and everything magically begins to happen at warp speed. The shift from low gear into overdrive could happen at any time during an investigation, except when you're expecting it. On more than one occasion, I'd made a routine visit, or talked with a seemingly useless source only to have things suddenly – and quite literally – blow up on me.

Nothing like that appeared to be on today's horizon. The only thing on my to-do list was to make a few calls. Any one of them could turn out to be a turning point in my investigation of Ian Dooley's murder, but I really didn't think so. I was just getting my toes wet in this case and I likely wouldn't recognize a clue if it bit me in the ass.

I called Mimi-Minerva, Scott Tomlin, Robin Stanhope, and all the other contacts I had. As far as any of them could tell me, Ian had little to no interest in politics, whether municipal, provincial, or federal.

"I doubt Ian ever even voted. Politics never interested him. Hell, I don't think he even read a newspaper regularly," said Tricia.

"About the only party Ian cared about was a fetish party," said Lisa Gardiner.

So what's up with all the news clippings I wondered? If Ian wasn't a diehard political fan, then why collect these? My gut told me it was related to stalking or something equally seedy and nefarious.

I wondered briefly about blackmail. If that were the case, what did Ian have on Tim Nealson? Dawn's research and my own hadn't come up with anything so secretive that it would be worth killing for. I wondered if perhaps I hadn't dug far enough into Nealson's background. I also wondered if digging into this a bit more would prove to be another great big waste of time, like much of my efforts around Macy had been.

I was also curious about the dirty pictures on Ian's phone. It struck me as odd that a guy who had access to as much kinky sex as Ian did would keep five poor-quality porn pictures on his cell.

I dialled the number for Officer Mark Houghton.

"Got a sec?"

"Not really. I'm knee-deep in something that's going to come to a head very soon," Mark said.

"I'll make it quick. Can you check into the history on Ian Dooley's cell phone?"

"As flattered as I am that you seem to want me as your full-time resource guy, you know I have a real job, don't you?"

"How about a steak dinner this weekend?"

"The Leafs are playing the Canadiens on Tuesday night. Tickets have been sold out since before they went on sale."

"I'll get the tickets. I desperately need a favour."

"You're shameless. I'll see what I can find out. What do you need? If I know you, there's something specific."

Mark was right about my being shameless. I'm happy to flirt and use feminine wiles to get what I want, but I really didn't want to lead Mark on. He's sort of been eyeing me ever since seeing my boobs at the end of the Hispanic Hooker case, but I have absolutely no romantic interest in him. Plus, I'm crazy about Derek. Damn, absence really does make the heart grow fonder…and the loins a bit more tingly…

"As a matter of fact, yes." I really wanted to know about the dirty pictures. "There are some smutty photos on the phone. Five that I saw, although perhaps there's more. They're in a folder called 'Wendi.' Can you tell if he's sent those pictures to anyone? And to whom?"

"Tall order, Sasha, but I'll try."

"Here's an even taller order. Could you get me copies of the pictures?"

"The tickets better be front row, centre ice."

"Will do," I said as I hung up. I'd have to call a ticket

scalper I know for the tickets, but since I'm anything but a hockey fan, I didn't bother calling right away.

Instead, I did a mental recap of the case so far.

A guy gets murdered after a fetish party. Did someone from the fetish world kill Ian?

The list of possible suspects, based on the people he talked to on his cellphone on Saturday, appeared to be a dead end.

Scott Tomlin, his boss, had no motive to want to kill Ian. His two co-workers at the renovation job didn't seem interested enough in Ian alive to want to see him dead.

The shoe-tree artist Mimi-Minerva also had no motive. It sounded like she had many more reasons to want to keep Ian alive, albeit handcuffed and ball-gagged. I wondered who her new playmate might be. I pictured her paddling King Arthur-Justin. Oooh, bad visual. Besides, she's too tall to have been the driver of Ian's truck.

Former sex partner Lisa Gardiner was sick with the flu when Ian was iced. Very unlikely she was involved, although her height is about right for the driver of Ian's truck. And the cops are leaning towards the murderer having an accomplice. Maybe it was Lisa, but probably not. I couldn't even speculate who she would have used as an accomplice if she were a suspect.

Paul Avignon and his red-haired playmate. No motive. I had noticed Paul and his dog-leash date at the party. Like all the other guests, they had chatted with Ian for a while, and the exchange had seemed friendly enough. Paul was too tall to drive the truck, but his girlfriend wasn't. I remembered that she had been kind of petite, several inches shorter than I am. But the two of them had been pretty much wrapped up in each other. As far as I could recall, they'd left the party a little earlier than most of the other guests.

I played back the mental tape of the fetish party. Spankings, and whippings, and people pretending to be cowboys or people wearing bizarre leather clothing and sleazy lingerie. Not one face stood out for any reason. No one had seemed angry or potentially violent, other than the pseudo-violent games that brought them all there in the first place. Ian had been affable and generally welcoming to everyone at the party. I remembered him high-fiving the guys, and greeting the ladies. It didn't seem to me that anyone there wished him dead.

So who killed him?

On the surface, the most obvious person would be his ex, Tricia, but she didn't fit, not at all, and anyway she was too tall to have driven the truck. Besides, she truly didn't seem to harbour any animosity towards Ian. Plus, Ian was the father of her kid. Whether Tricia liked him or not, the little girl would miss her father. Even if Tricia hated him, killing Ian would invite a whole new set of problems into her world, the first of these being a crying daughter who wants her daddy.

I had fleetingly thought at the beginning of this case that the murder might have had something to do with The Pilot and The Stealth Lounge, but nothing in my investigation thus far seemed to support that. If someone wanted to ruin Hugh and the bar, then the murder would have happened on site.

Could the murder really have been random? If so, how did the movement of the truck fit in? And if Ian really was killed in a random act of violence, then how would his killer ever be caught? With murder, it usually boils down to two things: money or relationships. If you shake the money tree long enough, something soon falls out. As for relationships, whether romantic or familial, those too unwind pretty quickly, as these murders are usually wrapped up in a thick blanket of emotion, and somebody always talks.

But random murders – as in wrong place, wrong time – are an investigator's nightmare. There is no connecting thread, there's no pattern, there's no inside source or trusted confidence, or skeletons in the closet. You have no idea if you're looking for a male or female suspect. You don't know if the suspect is local or nomadic. Even worse, with random killings you have no idea *why*. Was the victim chosen by location, or height, or eye colour, or accent? Had the victim been stalked, or was he or she just fatally unlucky?

My eyes were rolling into the back of my head as I considered all the permutations and combinations that could have led to Ian's unfortunate death.

Thursday,
3:05 pm

According to Percy, Monsoon was garnering amazing reviews, and had been since its grand opening a few months ago.

"The reviews have helped make this place one of

the hottest spots in town. We have reservations booked solid for the next six weeks," Percy said.

"Judging by the atmosphere, I can see why. The dining room is beautiful," I said.

The amber-hued dining room on Ossington was the perfect spot for a romantic tête-à-tête, or for a showy corporate dinner that pushed the boundaries of conspicuous consumption. Small waterfalls trickled in each corner, and a larger waterfall in the centre of the room created an atmosphere usually seen only in travel brochures for Tahiti. Guests ate mouth-watering, pan-Pacific, haute-cuisine delicacies in a setting that felt like a Gauguin painting. Attractive servers dressed in sleek black uniforms effortlessly tended to guests' needs, and they were all highly knowledgeable about wine selections. One reviewer had referred to Monsoon as a gastronomic nirvana.

"Even though we're busy as hell, the numbers aren't great. Our operating costs haven't changed since day one. Food and labour are what we expected, but profit is running at about fifteen percent and it should be about double that," Percy said.

"So, you think you're being ripped off."

"I'd love to be wrong about this, but what other explanation is there?" Percy wanted me to nose around after closing time and find out who was doing what and how. "Here's the key and the alarm code."

"Thanks. I'll start tomorrow night. What time does the place empty out?" I asked.

"Everyone should be gone by about midnight."

On my way home from Monsoon, I made a detour

down to Queen and Bathurst. It was still overcast and kind of chilly, but it hadn't yet started raining again. I was still a bit concerned about Macy. I wanted to take a quick look around the usual teen haunts, even though I didn't really have time to spend looking for her. I kept wondering about her call the other day. Earlier, I had phoned Mr. and Mrs. Edquist. They were rather cold towards me, but they did say they hadn't heard from her.

It was just after four o'clock, so the drop-in centre at Bathurst and Queen was still open. A cluster of First Nations youths were hanging around out front, minding their own business. There was no one else around, so I turned north and cut through the park on a short-cut to the market. Some teens were dribbling a basketball behind the school. Some skateboarders were trying to impress each other in the skateboard park off the currently ice-free outdoor hockey rink.

Once I got to the market, I saw a few of the same faces I'd seen when I initially began looking for Macy.

"Any word yet?" I asked Ink. I know the homemade tattoo guy recognized me, even though I wasn't wearing my faux grunge attire. His tattooed neck was red and puffy.

"Natch. How's yer mom?"

"Still hanging on. You still have my number?" "Dunno." he fumbled through his pockets and Twiggy shrugged.

I scribbled it out again on a scrap of paper from my purse. "I promise, there won't be any hassles. Just gimme a call if you see her." I handed them ten bucks and kept walking.

Thursday,
5:34 pm

I didn't have any dressy clothes at Jessica's place, and there was nothing I could have borrowed that would fit right. Her sweatshirts and yoga pants fit well enough, but the rest of her clothes are just a bit too loose on me, and since she's only about five foot five, most of her things are a bit short for me anyway. I swung by her place and made sure Bella had enough food and water. Then I hiked it home to Riverdale to the Jackson abode.

The house was quiet when I entered. As much as I enjoyed the peace and quiet and privacy at Jessica's, I found the silence at home mildly disappointing. I had time to kill before the political fundraising shindig, so I went downstairs to cut loose and clear my head, and to take advantage of the empty house.

When I first took up drumming, Dad had done his best to soundproof the basement. At first blush, that might have seemed like a thoughtful and generous thing for him to have done, but he'd done it for self-ish reasons. Whenever I get into full-scale drumming mode, I can make enough noise to shake birds from the trees.

I closed the door to the music room and put on a pair of headphones. For some reason, it seemed like a good idea to start off with Motown. The Contours and The Velvelettes got me warmed up. "Needle in a Haystack" pretty much summed up my recent search for Macy. After Detroit, I shifted to Chicago for some Albert Collins and The Icebreakers. "Don't Mistake Kindness for Weakness" isn't just a great tune, mistaking kindness for weakness is also an all-too-frequent strategic error. Next, I played along with Howlin' Wolf's "Killing Floor." My subconscious was no doubt making my song selections for me. When I got to New Orleans, it was Randy Newman's turn. "Bet No One Ever Hurt This Bad" from his debut album made me think of Ian Dooley and what his final moments must have been like. They surely must have hurt something fierce. I wondered what he thought when the first bullet hit him. I wondered if Ian would have even felt the second bullet.

As luridly enticing as the fetish stuff is, I was more intrigued by the possible political angle. I had no reason to think Ian was a rah-rah-rah political junkie. As reluctant as I was to go to the fundraiser at Shane's tonight, I recognized that it was fortuitous. I also recognized that I'd been grooving for over an hour on the drums, and I would have to hurry to get ready to go to Pastiche. I put down the drumsticks and went to my bedroom to try to figure out what to wear. I just about jumped out of my skin when I passed Dad in the kitchen.

"Shit, I thought no one else was home."

"I called out when you came in. I was in the back-yard."

"Sorry, Dad. I didn't even hear you. I've been playing for the last hour. Why didn't you let me know you were here? I could have stopped."

"No big deal. You like to play. I didn't want to interfere. Anyhow, I'm going to pass on tonight. I've got a headache thanks to you. That room isn't very soundproof, you know."

"Shit, Dad, I'm sorry. I really let it all out."

"It's all right. I'll lie down for a while and be fine."

"You're going to miss the dinner for Nealson. The tickets aren't refundable, you know."

"I don't care. It's a political fundraiser, right, so the ticket is still a tax deduction, whether I attend or not."

Dad gave me a sheepish smile. The light bulb went off above my head.

"Admit it, you're glad to have an excuse to bail out tonight. Damn, I was counting on your misery loving my company. I'm as excited about this event as I am about a pap test."

"Nice image. Why do you think I didn't tell you I was home? Like I said, thanks to you, I've got a headache, and there's just no way I can go out this evening. Please give my regrets to Shane and the others."

"You know you suck, right, Dad?"

"Yeah, but I'll be sucking at home in my favourite recliner while I watch the Leafs blow their first game of the season again this year."

He winked at me and gave me another shit-eating grin. Then he went into the family room and flipped on the television.

Wily old bugger.

Thursday,
8:05 pm

"It would be decidedly *uncool* to get shit-faced tonight, wouldn't it?" I whispered to Lindsey, as I drained my wine glass.

"Yes. That would be very wrong," Lindsey said.

The tables in Pastiche had been rearranged for tonight's political photo-op and cash grab. We were seated in groups of eight. Lindsey and I were knocking elbows with three campaign volunteers, plus one of Nealson's paid sycophants and the toady's wife. The only empty seat at our table was the one that was meant for Dad. I kind of wished that I'd come up with a migraine excuse before him. The evening promised to be long and painful, and I'd likely have a real migraine by the end of it.

The dinner conversation thus far felt like something between a live-action infomercial or the beatification ceremony for Tim Nealson. He actually seemed like an okay guy, and was rather handsome. Nealson had a firm jaw, sandy-brown hair with a slight wave to it, and was average height and build. It wasn't so much his looks one noticed, as the way in which he carried himself. He came across as confident and open, and his smile seemed genuine. His campaign slogan should have been *He Even Looks Like A Mayor.* At least the folks at central casting would think so. Nealson had come around to all the tables and thanked people for their support. We had just finished our appetizers, and had four more courses and probably as many mind-numbing speeches to get through. Unfortunately, I was still stone cold sober.

"If it were anybody but Shane, and if it weren't for my current case, there's no way in hell I'd stick around. This is *so* not my cup of tea."

"Would you rather be letting some leather-clad stud whip you?"

"Touché."

"How does your current case connect with this event anyway?" Lindsey asked discreetly.

"If I told you, I'd have to kill you."

"Whatever. At least you're dressed the part of the *femme fatale*. You look fantastic."

I'd been hurried getting ready. My hair was loose and tousled. It was too damp outside to even try styling it. I was in a plain violet sleeveless dress. It was simple, but fit me perfectly, and looked great with the amethyst pendant and matching earrings I was wearing. I wished Derek could have seen me. On most of our dates, other than the first one, we'd done something casual, so he hasn't yet really seen me all gussied up. Of course, I think he's perfectly happy to see me naked, which is how our dates usually end up.

Lindsey looked pretty hot herself. She has sunset skin and long, black hair, which were both set off nicely by the harvest yellow D&G suit she was wearing.

"I wish Derek were here. Mind you, if he had come, I wouldn't be wearing panties."

The serving staff cleared our appetizer plates and delivered a fish dish for the second course. I looked at the plate of sesame crusted tuna with wasabi and ginger in front of me, and held back the urge to shove the whole thing in my mouth at once.

"Damn, this is delicious, but I'm going to be stuffed soon. I had another late lunch today," Lindsey said.

"I more or less skipped lunch, so pass your leftovers my way. I'm hungry enough to eat a horse." The wallpaper paste soup that I hadn't really eaten with Dawn at Café Victoria was the only quasi food that had passed my lips all day.

"Will do. But only the food, this wine is too damn good to share."

Tonight's fundraiser was a $200 per person event featuring a five-course menu with wines paired to each course. The tuna was accompanied by a deliciously musky 2003 Pouilly-Fumé.

As people nibbled and sipped, one of several campaign workers got up in front of the dais to tout the many virtues of Tim Nealson. The speaker told the audience the top ten reasons why we should vote for Mr. Nealson. I think "he walks on water" was reason number two. I would have cheerfully become the campaign manager if the speaker had said Nealson can turn water into wine. My glass was empty.

Once diners had eaten all five courses and coffee had been served, the atmosphere lightened up and people mingled. I suddenly found myself sitting next to Gwendolyn Nealson. Up close she was really quite pretty. She was somewhere in her early forties, trim and petite, and very stylish in a Jackie O suit. Her right arm was in a sling, but no cast, and the sling was the same shade of teal as her suit. I'd seen a few pictures of Gwendolyn in various news articles, and the real woman looked just like the one in the photos; no need to airbrush. Even though I'd seen her face many times throughout this campaign, I couldn't help but think that I knew her from somewhere else too.

"I heard you were in a car accident a few days ago. How are you feeling now?" I asked. I didn't want to discuss the campaign anymore. I'd had enough of politics for one night.

"Oh, I'll be fine. It's just a nasty sprain. I'll only need this for a few weeks. It's my own damned fault. I should have been paying more attention." He voice had a pleasant lilt to it. She spoke softly but clearly, as if choosing her words very deliberately, and clipping them at the ends.

"How did the accident happen?" I asked.

"It was silly, really. I was driving on Lake Shore Boulevard, coming home from St. Lawrence Market. I was in a hurry because we had a community event that afternoon, and I wanted to make a salad." Unlike Kensington Market, which is a funky urban neighbourhood that happens to have several greengrocers and butchers in it, St. Lawrence Market actually is a market.

"But St. Lawrence Market isn't open on Sundays," I said. My office is a stone's throw from the market. I know for sure it isn't open on Sundays, and I've never understood why. It's a fantastic market with superior butcher shops, locally grown produce, and an interesting history. In the old days, the building now housing a farmers' market had at various times been the home of Toronto's City Hall, a police station, council chambers, and even a jail.

"I'm sorry, did I say St. Lawrence Market? I meant Kensington Market. Anyhow, I was driving home from Kensington Market in a rush to get things ready for the neighbourhood barbecue and I didn't check my mirror when I switched lanes. I should have paid more attention. The poor guy I hit was so upset. He was driving a new car. His first brand new car. But at least he's okay."

"That's too bad, but the insurance should cover it," I said.

There was a moment of uncomfortable silence. No one else was at our table, and neither of us knew what to say to the other. As a political wife, Gwendolyn seemed adept at spouting campaign one-liners or at echoing her husband's political platform, but she herself was no great shakes at small talk.

"Let me ask you an odd question, if I may." If nothing else, I could usually find ways to keep myself from getting bored.

"Certainly. Ask away," Gwendolyn said.

"Has Tim ever been threatened? Does it feel like his foray into public life has compromised personal safety in any way?"

"What a strange thing to ask. But off the top of my head, I'd say 'No.' Why?"

"Just wondering. Public figures seem like such targets these days. On the one hand, they want to be out and be seen. Talk to voters, meet people in the community. And so many politicians and celebrities use YouTube and Twitter to get the word out. Hell, even Queen Elizabeth has a Facebook page. Of course, the corollary to this is that Joe Q. Public knows every move a public person makes, where they'll be, when they'll be there."

"True, but what choice is there? You just have to keep your wits about you and use common sense."

"I guess so. I know you never want to alienate a fan or a supporter —"

"We'd be lost without all the people volunteering for us."

"I know that. What I mean is, I guess, only a loyal supporter would become a volunteer, but has Tim ever had a fan who's too loyal?"

"You're starting to scare me."

"Sorry, I don't mean to. It's just something I've wondered about. I'm an investigator. Maybe my line of work has turned me into a paranoid conspiracy theorist." There was another awkward moment of silence, until Lindsey sat down and joined us.

"So, Mrs. Nealson —" Lindsey said.

"Please, call me Gwendolyn."

"Right, okay. So, um, Gwendolyn, have you always been interested in local politics?" Lindsey didn't seem any more comfortable in this milieu than I did. I kept my mouth shut just for the fun of watching her squirm.

"I have been since I moved to Toronto. I met Tim in my first week here. Tim and politics are something of a package deal. For instance, do you know about his ideas for cutting waste at City Hall?" It sounded like Gwendolyn had memorized a campaign brochure. I politely nodded now and then, as I sipped my coffee.

"I understand he would like to contract out a number of municipal services," Lindsey said.

"Well," said Gwendolyn, "from a cost-benefit point of view, it doesn't make sense for certain services to be provided by city employees. Garbage collection, for example, could be done much more economically than it is now."

"Maybe. But if those garbage collectors weren't working for the city, where would they be working?" asked Lindsey.

"Presumably they'd be hired by the companies that bid on the contracts. The details are still in the works, but the point is that overpaid, unionized trash men wouldn't be eating up such a disproportionate amount of the city's operating budget."

This line of conversation made me want to swan dive into a dumpster. I excused myself from the table and went in search of more booze. My motto for this evening should have been that tacky T-shirt slogan *I drink to make other people more interesting.*

"Darling dearest Drew," I said to the bartender, "what would it take to get you to fill my coffee cup with some kind of alcohol? Any kind."

"That bad, huh?" replied Drew. "Pass it over."

Drew has been bartending at Shane's place ever since it opened. Normally, Drew's very creative with cock-tail ingredients and has quite the flair when it comes to preparation, but tonight he was discreet as he tilted a bottle of Baileys over my cup.

"It's all just so *rah-rah-rah.* Nealson seems like a good candidate, but if he gets elected, do you think he'll ac-tually do any of the things he promises?" I said this *sotto voce.* No one was around, but being overheard slagging politicos here and now would be embarrassing. I re-flected on all the news clippings I'd seen at Ian's place. I scanned the crowd, wondering if any one of them was a stalker or a threat to Nealson in any way. No one seemed unduly interested in him, at least not in any way that caused me concern.

"The chances of significant changes with Nealson are no better and no worse than with any of the other candidates," Drew said.

"You're probably right."

I wandered back to my table. Shane had popped out of the kitchen and was chatting with Gwendolyn and Lindsey.

"The lobster bisque we had here a couple of weeks ago was the best I've had since I was a kid. Nova Scotians do great things with lobster," said Gwendolyn.

"I'm glad you liked it," Shane said.

"And the rack of lamb tonight was superb. It reminded me of the dish I used to order whenever I went to the Beaver Club at the Queen Elizabeth." Gwendolyn was referring to the restaurant in one of the nicest hotels in Montreal, and not to a regal strip joint, but one could be forgiven for mistakenly assuming otherwise.

"That's probably because I was the chef there for a couple of years," Shane said. "When did you live in Montreal?"

"I moved there in my early twenties," Gwendolyn said.

"So just a couple of years ago." Oh barf. My brother the flatterer. Lindsey wasn't impressed with the comment either. I noticed her kick him under the table.

"You're too kind," Gwendolyn said.

"What made you move to Montreal?" I asked, as I drank the last of my Baileys. My cup doth not runneth over. My cup runneth out.

"Like everyone else who left the Maritimes back then. I needed to find work," Gwendolyn said.

They talked about the East Coast for a while, fishing and mining, and the lack of job opportunities in Nova Scotia. It was a common thing for able-bodied men and women from Nova Scotia, New Brunswick, Newfoundland, and Prince Edward Island to leave home and head to Canada's bigger cities in search of jobs. Manufacturing in Ontario, oil work in Alberta, logging out west, you name it. Just about any province has somewhat better job prospects than the precarious fishing and seasonal tourism economies of Atlantic Canada. Gwendolyn rather adeptly shifted the conversation to Toronto's economy and job market, and her husband's campaign platforms to keep both robust. I rather adeptly excused myself and slunk back to Drew and the plethora of potent potables at his disposal.

Thursday,
10:43 pm

Lindsey and I bid adieu to Shane, the Nealsons, and all the lackeys with whom we'd been making painful civic small talk.

"Let's grab a nightcap somewhere. Preferably in a place with live music. I need to get all that gung-ho campaign crap out of my head," I said.

"It was a little over the top, wasn't it?" Lindsey replied. "But it mattered to Shane. And I gave out about a dozen business cards. At least one of the couples I talked to sounded serious about listing their house for sale."

"Shameless opportunist."

"Guilty as charged. The whole political fundraising thing isn't my cup of tea either, but like I said before, it was good for networking."

"Wanna see who's playing at The Moon Dog?" I asked.

"Here comes a cab. Let's grab it."

I instructed the cabbie to take a circuitous route. We detoured through Kensington, and then got caught up in late-night traffic along Queen. I knew the odds were slim, but I kept my eyes peeled for Macy anyway.

Friday, October 5, 9:20 am

I usually resort to doing something stupid if I can't think of anything better to do. Plus, I learned long ago not to ignore my gut reactions. I needed to have another look inside Ian's apartment, and this time, I wanted to do so without Tricia acting as my chaperone.

There's also an increased likelihood of my doing something stupid when I'm hungover.

Lindsey and I had ended up going on quite a tear last night. The Moon Dog had been the first of several stops. And of several drinks. This morning my head felt like a hockey puck right after faceoff. I vaguely recalled flirting with a stodgy old British man in a pub somewhere, and giving a fake phone number to an oily *playah* at a club on Richmond Street. I'm not sure what else had happened or where we'd gone, and I'd just as soon not know. I think somewhere along the way, we'd done tequila shots with a group of chiropodists in town for their annual foot fungus and bunion convention. I had tried to convince one of the foot doctors that the active ingredient in Gold Bond medicated foot powder comes from agave cacti. Oh dear. I think the guy had licked my foot.

It wasn't even 9:30 yet, I'd had only about four or five hours of drunken sleep, and here I was on the 506 streetcar. I was en route to Ian's apartment, when my cellphone bleeped. Ahhh, Derek's number.

"So, are you still as horny as you said you were last night?"

"What?"

"You sounded ready to jump through the phone line and have your way with me. It was pretty sexy, even though I was half asleep."

"Huh?"

"You do know you called me last night, right? Or, actually, this morning, around three?"

Gulp. Not really, at least I didn't remember it until he mentioned it.

"So you thought I sounded sexy, did you?" I asked.

It was coming back to me now. I called him when I got back to Jessica's. I had described in vivid detail what I'd like to do with my mouth. Oh God.

"Not exactly sexy, but you sure sounded horny," he said.

"Last night got a bit out of control..."

I told him about the dinner and our shenanigans afterwards. My tummy did a little flip-flop when I mentioned what we had ingested. After such a rich and filling dinner, I shouldn't have had room for anything. Along with the wine and Baileys I'd consumed at Pastiche, I had sucked back a pint of Smithwick's, and a few ounces of single malt Scotch. And then the tequila. No wonder my head was pounding. I wondered how Lindsey was feeling.

"Sounds like it was fun. Listen, on another note, I doubt this trial is going to wrap up today."

"What does that mean?" I asked.

"It means I'm probably stuck here for the weekend. It all depends on how long the jury takes to reach a verdict."

"That sucks. It's Thanksgiving weekend."

"I know."

"Damn, I really miss you," I said.

"You made that very clear last night."

"You know I'm only interested in you for your body, right?"

"You made that clear last night too. Listen, I have to get going. I'm due in court soon," Derek said.

"Okay."

"I'll call you when I get a chance. Bye."

"I love you, bye."

Holy shit, WHAT did I just say? I didn't just say *you know what*, did I? Where did that come from? I stared at the phone, trying to see sound, as if by looking at it,

I could tell what Derek had heard. The call was over when I said it, right? He didn't hear me say *I LOVE YOU*, did he? He'd clicked off already, hadn't he? Oh, God, I hope so. Oh shit, oh shit, oh shit!

Lindsey, please pick up.

"I'm such a moron," I said when Lindsey answered.

"Yeah, it was pretty stupid to go on such a bender last night. It feels like there's a cactus or two growing inside my temples. I have to meet a client in less than an hour, and I'm still in bed."

"No, I'm not talking about being hungover, but I really do want to die. I want to crawl under a rock. I just told Derek I love him."

"You what? Woo-hoo! Did he say it first? Or did you say it, and he said it back?" she asked.

"It's not *woo-hoo*, it's *oh no*, and I don't know if he said it back. I said it first, by accident. I don't know what I was thinking. We were on the phone…"

There are those who might say I have commitment issues. And they'd be right. Crossing that invisible line from islands of carefree romance into "I love you" territory was not in my plans. Derek is special, he's sexy as hell, he's smart and he challenges me, and really rocks my world, but…

My cell bleeped to life again right after Lindsey and I finished talking. I looked at caller ID before answering. I was too embarrassed to talk with Derek right now.

Officer Mark Houghton's number showed on the display. I wondered briefly if he was calling because ESP or some kind of sixth sense had told him I was en route to High Park, with an ill-formed plan about entering Ian's apartment illegally.

"Well, good morning handsome," I said. Flirting often works to my benefit. "To what do I owe this call from the Finest of Metro's Finest?" Perhaps that was a little thick.

"Hey, Sasha. No need to suck up to me. If you had a hunch about the pictures, you were right," Mark Houghton said.

"Who did Ian send them to?" I asked.

"They were sent to someone named Wendi at 416-555-1212. Safe bet that Wendi is the girl in the picture."

"That's what I thought. But who is she? None of the people Ian's fetish circle seems to know anything about her," I said.

"I can't help you with that," Mark said.

"What would it take to get copies of the pictures from you?"

"I've already printed them. When can we meet so I can give them to you?"

"I'm tied up for the next couple of hours. How about lunch? My treat, as usual. Where do you want to meet me?"

"Since you're paying, I'll let you decide."

"How about The Pilot? I'm due to give an update to Hugh and might just as well do so in person."

When I got to Geoffrey Street, luck was on my side. No one had yet bothered to shut the window to Ian's bedroom, although a sealed window wouldn't have stopped me. I've been known to take chances more than once before, and windows could easily be broken.

So could hearts. Maybe I don't really have commitment issues. Maybe I'm just scared of being hurt. The scars from Mick had taken a long time to heal.

I was humming a Beatles song, only I substituted "bedroom" for "bathroom" when I landed rather gracelessly on the beige broadloom in Ian's bedroom. From this vantage point, I could tell he hadn't worried too much about vacuuming.

I wasn't especially interested in the bedroom, at least not for now. I headed into the living room for another look, and saw the exact same things I'd seen there the other day. My Little Pony and Dr. Seuss and Dora the Explorer on the left shelves. C.C.R. and *Sports Illustrated* and Disney videos on the other side. I saw a dark stain on the carpet in front of the couch that I hadn't noticed the other day. It wasn't fresh. It looked like grape juice or something. Whatever it was, it was dry.

The bathroom was tidy, but a far cry from spick and span. There was a ring around the bathtub, and the toilet had some nasty skid marks. Ugh.

A more thorough look through both the kitchen and Ian's bedroom yielded naught. I reread some of the Tim Nealson news clippings.

Ian seemed to have clipped just about everything written on Nealson in the last month. I noticed this time that on a couple of them, Ian had underlined or circled sentences giving information on where and when Tim would be speaking or campaigning. On September 22, a "Keeping Our City Green" symposium at The University Club. On September 25, he participated in a panel discussion about improving public transit. On October 1, he was scheduled for a debate hosted by

YYZ TV with the other mayoral candidates. The shindig at Shane's restaurant was also noted. Hmmm. Absolutely nobody and nothing had put me on high alert
last night. And I hadn't heard anything about threats or
other incidents at any of Nealson's public appearances.

I hadn't really looked in Kayla's room last time, and if
I had I would have struck gold sooner. Her room was
an explosion of pinks and lavenders. The walls, bed-
ding, and a throw rug were all done in the blinding
shades of bubble gum pink and cloying lilac that little
girls like. The colours made me nauseous, but that
could also have been attributed to my colossal hangover. There was a bin with toys at the foot of the neatly made bed. The dresser was filled with girly clothes
of more pink and mauve and some robin's egg blue.
Kayla's bedroom closet held very few of her clothes,
and much of the space had been turned into storage.
The under-used vacuum cleaner, a set of golf clubs,
and a winter snow shovel were propped up against the
back wall of the closet. There was a Barbie tricycle, an
old stroller, a kerosene lamp still in its box, and a pair
of bowling shoes. Junk. Stuff destined for a garage sale
some day.

The motherlode was on the top shelf of the closet. It held a collection of leftover stuff from when Ian
had painted the apartment. There was a folded dirty
drop cloth, sandpaper, a paint tray and some rollers,
and there were four old paint cans at the far end of the
shelf. Three of them had dried dribbles of pink and
pale purple paint along the edges of the can. The fourth
can had emerald green paint crusted around the rim. I

hadn't seen green anywhere in the apartment. I stood up on tiptoes to reach it.

Inside the can was green, all right, but cash, not paint.

"Holy shit," I said to the empty room, after I had counted all the money. There was $53,220 in mixed bills. Wow. Where did the money come from? How had the cops missed it? And thank God they had.

If you ever find 53K in an old paint can instead of a GIC or RSP, it's safe to assume the money came from a dirty or illegal source. But from whom or what? I dismissed the thought of drugs as soon as it came to me. Nothing, nobody, no one had even hinted that drugs were part of Ian's world.

Bribery maybe? If the money had anything to do with Nealson, that could be an explanation.

Blackmail? That seemed a likely possibility, but then what was the secret being hidden?

Had I missed something in Nealson's background? Was there something more sinister or more embarrassing than mooning people at a football game or protesting at a NAFTA rally? I felt there had to be a link between the fetish dude and the politico, but what the heck was it?

Once again, I wondered if I was completely off base. The smutty photos on Ian's BlackBerry came to mind. They might not have had anything to do with my case, but their existence struck me as odd. I wondered who the girl was and if she knew she was being photographed. My gut still told me these pictures were separate from the fetish scene Ian had been involved with. Damn, I wish I still had Ian's phone.

I fanned myself with the wad of cash and then folded it back into the can. I couldn't decide if it was smarter to take it with me for safe keeping, or to leave it here since it wasn't mine and I had no business touching it. I wondered if Tricia knew about it. I was amazed – and glad – that the cops had missed it.

Eventually, I put the can back on top of the shelf. Now that Ian was dead, someone just might come looking for it. Leaving the money there could be a lure. Taking it with me could turn me into a target. I shut the closet door and then made a hasty departure out through Ian's bedroom window.

Friday,
12:35 pm

When I got to The Pilot, the only seat I could find was halfway down the bar. The place was packed with the office lunch crowd and it was noisy as hell. My tender skull was still suffering greatly.

"Hey Masoud. Someone's going to join me shortly. Can I just have a glass of milk for now, please?"

Masoud, the bartender, gave me a puzzled look. "Milk? You mean a Brown Cow, right?" he said, reaching for the bottle of Kahlua.

"No booze, Masoud. I'm in the clutches of a five-alarm hangover. God hates me."

He set the glass of milk in front of me and I downed it, along with two Tylenols, in one long gulp. I glanced at the menu, though I needn't have bothered. I knew before coming here that I wanted a Patty Melt, one of The Pilot's signature dishes, and another one of my favourite hangover foods. It was a juicy hamburger patty served on toasted marble rye bread, smothered in caramelized onions, with gobs of cheddar cheese oozing out of it. The protein and grease were just what my aching, fragile body needed.

"Is Hugh upstairs in the office?" I asked.

"Yeah, why, have you got some news about the guy who was killed?"

"Sorry, darling, but that's classified information."

"Want me to get Hugh?"

"After lunch. It's too noisy to talk right now. Excuse me," I said as I reached for my ringing cell. Mark's number.

"It's hard to hear you. Gimme a sec." I walked up front and stood just outside the entrance. "What's up?"

"Hate to cancel at the last minute, Sasha, but something's come up," Mark said.

"Damn. I really wanted to see those pictures."

"And I thought you were looking forward to seeing me. I can give them to you on Tuesday, if I don't see you before then."

"Can't you just email them to me?" I asked.

"Sasha, think about it. I broke a lot of rules getting these for you. The last thing I want to do is leave a paper trail.'

"Right, sorry."

"So, are we still on for the Leafs and Habs game?" The *Habs* is a nickname for the *Canadiens*, Montreal's hockey team.

"Sure thing. If I can push my luck—"

"Sasha, you're going to push it no matter what I say."

"I'm sorry. But I really think I'm on to something here."

"Why don't you fill me in?"

"That's why I wanted to do lunch," I said.

"Well, my day is quickly doing a downward spiral. Tell me what you want. Keep in mind though, if I think this is getting too heavy, I'm going to have to tell the brass. I can't help you hide evidence."

"I don't have any evidence. Just a very strong feeling."

"Fire away," Mark said.

"Did any of the cops check with stores near Mimi-Minerva's condo to see if they have security cameras?"

"I'm not sure if they did. Probably. Why?"

"Maybe someone's camera has footage of the other cars parked nearby? I'd love to get some of the licence plate numbers of cars that were in the area when Ian left Mimi's place."

"I'll try to find out, but give me some time. I'm working on something else right now that's either going to nail a bunch of drug dealing scumbags or will fizzle into nothing."

"Okay."

After my call with Mark, I tried the Wendi number yet again, but I clicked off when the computer voicemail came on. I'd left several messages for her already.

Then I called Alessandro, an old high school classmate. While others in my graduating year had gone on to college and university and had generally done more or less interesting things with their lives and careers, Alessandro had taken the lazy way out. He had started scalping tickets years ago, long before the Internet became mainstream and people could get tickets off Stub Hub and Craigslist. Alessandro had kept up with technology over the years, and had a created a dotcom business as a ticket reseller. For all intents and purposes, he was still just a scalper. The sad thing is, I think he earns more per annum than anyone else from our class.

"Tell me you can get me tickets for the Leafs versus the Montreal Canadiens game Tuesday night without my paying and arm and a leg."

"I can get you nosebleeds pretty cheap, or primo seats for a few dollars more."

"How many dollars more?"

"I've got a pair in the second row just off centre ice. Five hundred bucks."

"Tell me that's not each?"

"For you, a fin for the pair."

I wondered if I'd be able to bury such an exorbitant expense into my fee for Hugh? The cost was a direct result of investigating this case. Hmmm. "I'll take them."

Mark had better deliver the goods if I was going to have to spend this much money to attend a sporting event that, for me, promised to be less exciting than cutting my toenails.

Hugh joined me just after I finished my patty melt. "So, any news?" He asked.

I self-consciously wiped crumbs from my mouth before answering. "I can't exactly tell you about the latest
development. However, I can tell you that what I've
stumbled upon makes me more than certain his murder
had nothing to do with this place."

"Have you got any ideas yet who did it?'

"Nothing definite, but I have some very strong
hunches. Gimme a day or two, and I have a feeling it
will all be wrapped up."

"I'll be glad to put this to rest. A liquor inspector
came by yesterday." I wondered if it was Eleanor. "And
an insurance representative wants to see me next week
to review my coverage."

"If things unfold as I expect they will, you'll be in
the clear and the bar won't be mentioned in any more
news reports."

"I can't wait for this to die down. Your lunch is on
me."

"You might regret that once you see my bill."

Friday,
3:10 pm

It was raining lightly. I bought an umbrella at a dollar store on Yonge Street. Given the sogginess of the
day, I didn't hold out great hopes of seeing teenaged
punks hanging out and about. Nonetheless, when I left

The Pilot, I took a detour to have another quick look for Macy. I walked through the parkettes near Yonge and Wellesley, then walked east a few blocks, and then traipsed around the side streets near Cawthra Square. Macy was around somewhere, and I was certain that sooner or later I'd stumble upon her. In my bag, I still had the photos the Edquists had given me, even though technically this case was closed.

Some street kids had appropriated an old abandoned house on Mutual Street. The windows on the upper level were all boarded over, as was the front door. Someone had knocked out the boards from the windows on the main floor. A pair of squatters was sitting on the wide, brick window frame, smoking a joint. The roof overhang kept them and their joint dry.

"Does she look familiar?" I asked, handing them the photo. A guy with a frizzy mane of ginger hair exhaled a hefty toke, shrugged, and passed the pic and the joint to his companion.

"Yeah, that's Macy, ain't it?" said a tie-dyed butterball. The girl who passed the picture back to me was fat, there was no nice way to put it. Her several chins merged into a flabby neck that stretched the collar of her psychedelic shirt. "Why ya asking about her?" Her upper arms had a lot of jiggle to them and I couldn't help but think of Wavy Gravy.

"I'm worried about her. No trouble, but I've got to find her," I said.

"I saw her day before yesterday on Sherbourne. She was with Shank."

"Right, yes, with Shank."

"They were going to squeegee somewheres."

Of course, squeegeeing, the career choice of street kids all over Toronto. Rough-looking teens armed with a squeegee, a bucket, some Windex, and a few dirty rags are the bane of Toronto motorists, or at least they were until the City passed a bylaw banning the activity. The bylaw is mostly effective. Nonetheless, at some intersections resilient kids still approach cars stopped at red lights and aggressively offer to clean their windshields for a buck or two.

"Too wet to wash windows today. If either of you see Macy, please give me a call." I gave them my card. I had no doubt they'd lose it in less than a day.

As I walked away, I started humming "Truckin'."

Friday,
6:40 pm

According to the news clippings I had seen at Ian's place, Tim Nealson was due to speak this evening at the library at Runnymede and Bloor, about a twenty-minute walk from Ian's apartment. I was slightly annoyed about making another trip to the west end, but chasing my tail and backtracking are inherent in my job.

Rather impulsively, I decided to visit Tricia Lado on the way.

"Sorry to drop by unannounced. Can I come in?"

"Sure, but only if you promise to ignore the mess. We just finished dinner."

In terms of the layout, Tricia's apartment was very much like Ian's, but hers was considerably larger. She had also clearly put some effort into making the place feel like home. The kitchen was a bright sunny yellow. There was a row of potted plants along the window-sill. I pretended not to see the dishes piled up on the counter next to the sink, nor the dirty pot on the back burner of the stove.

The living room was rather cluttered, but in a homey way. There were several framed family photos on one wall. The sofa and matching loveseat each had a crocheted blanket thrown across them. The television was on, but the sound was muted. There were toys and teddy bears strewn around the floor in front of it. Kayla was ignoring the toys and was intently filling in pictures in a colouring book. A glass-topped coffee table had lots of little finger prints all over it, plus several gossip magazines. One tabloid had a newsflash about Britney's lack of parenting skills. Another rag implied that Miley Cyrus has a fondness for drugs not available at her local apothecary. A third had stories on Snooki and Kim Kardashian, plus all the latest about Blake Lively and some photos of her *au naturel*. Racy pics seem to be a theme these days.

"Do you want a coffee or anything?" Tricia offered.

"A glass of water would be great." I had been thirsty as hell all day, no doubt a physiological reminder of my stubborn hangover.

"So, how's the investigation going?"

"I have a ton of theories, but nothing concrete. Was Ian into politics?"

"Not as far as I know. Why?"

"By all appearances, he was a big fan of Tim Neal-son's."

"What makes you say that?"

I told her about the clippings in Ian's bedroom. "You can go on over yourself and check them out. In some cases he circled the details, like where and when Neal-son will be putting in an appearance."

"Hmmm. That's really strange. If you had asked me back when he and I were a couple, I'd have bet that Ian couldn't have named our Prime Minister, much less Toronto's mayor. He didn't give a shi…" She remembered Kayla was within earshot. "I mean, Ian didn't pay attention to politics."

"Well since we're talking about strange, how's this for a strange question: aside from his, uh, hobby, was Ian ever v–i–o–l–e–n–t?"

Kayla was still colouring, but kept looking up at us now and then. It seemed like she was afraid she'd miss something fun that the adults had excluded her from. Maybe shifting from words to the alphabet is an orange alert to a child.

"Not that I know of, outside of his group of, uh, special friends. And he was a receiver, if you know what I mean. He didn't, um, get up to bat."

"What about if he had been drinking? Any rowdy nights out with the boys or anything?"

"Not really. He could be a real a–s–s–h–o–l–e when he'd knocked back a few, mouthy and obnoxious. But harmless. He'd usually pass out after awhile. But imbibing wasn't really his thing. There was a lot of alcoholism and alcohol abuse in Cape Breton. He made a point of only partaking once in a while. So, no. No bar brawls, or alcoholic rages, or anything like that."

"What about Ian's finances? Did he pay child support?"

"Kind of. We had an arrangement, but we never had lawyers write up an agreement or anything."

"It's usually a good idea to get things in writing," I said.

"Yeah, well. Ian paid for her clothes and bought her toys and stuff. Usually with clothing, I'd actually buy it and I'd give him the receipts."

"Sounds to me like he was kind of getting off easy."

"Yes and no. Remember, my family is pretty comfortable. Kayla is my parents' only grandchild so far. They spoil her, and they would do anything necessary to make sure she's well cared for, even if they couldn't afford it."

"Did Ian do okay financially?"

"I guess. His paycheques weren't exactly whopping big, as far as I know, but I don't think he was maxing out his credit card either. Why?"

"No reason, really. It's just that money often comes into play in a murder case. Did Ian have any other sources of income besides his job?"

"I don't think so."

I nodded towards Kayla before asking my next question. "Is it okay if I ask about plans for the f-u-n-e-r-a-l?"

Tricia lowered her voice when she answered. "She doesn't really understand it yet. I've tried to explain it, but I know she still thinks she'll be spending the weekend with Daddy."

"Poor kid."

"I know. She hasn't really cried or anything. She has no idea what dead means. Anyhow, I got a call today from the coroner. They're ready to release the body. I spent the afternoon trying to make arrangements to ship it down East. Do you have any idea how much it costs to fly a corpse down to Nova Scotia?"

"Not really. Wouldn't they just charge regular baggage rates? Cargo or whatever?" I asked.

"You'd think so, wouldn't you, but the price is almost as much as a roundtrip ticket in business class."

"Maybe you should check with UPS?"

Friday, 7:50 pm

Runnymede is one of the nicer branches of the Toronto Public Library. Since 1975, the building has been listed as one of Toronto's heritage properties. The old stone library, with its steeply pitched roof and totem pole entryway, is indeed beautiful. The original building had even been featured on a Canadian postage stamp a few years ago, as part of a series showcasing Canadian architecture. A few years ago, the library had extensive work done to preserve the original edifice while adding an extension to the back. It felt like simply crossing its threshold would be an edifying experience.

Not surprisingly, Tim Nealson's audience tonight were members of the Toronto Heritage Society. Nealson was talking about what he would do to preserve Toronto's architectural history. Judging from a quick glance at the crowd, it wouldn't be long until someone needed to marinate this group of silver-haired septuagenarians in formaldehyde to preserve them. Some of these seniors looked several years older than the buildings they championed.

"He never gets off the campaign merry-go-round," I whispered to Gwendolyn.

She was standing near the entrance to the meeting room, greeting late arrivals. She was as well put together today as she'd been last night. Obviously she wasn't hungover, unlike *mucho stupido moi*. Even though it was early evening, I still felt kind of rough, although by now it was more because of fatigue than because of a nasty hangover. Tonight, Gwendolyn was in a smart black pantsuit and a silvery blouse with a French collar. She had traded yesterday's teal sling for a black one.

Tim, standing at a dais at the other end of the room, had already delivered his canned political speech, and was now taking questions from the crowd. Members of the audience, seated on rows of neatly arranged folding chairs facing the podium, kept asking Nealson to speak up. The dais didn't have a microphone, and people in the rows furthest away continually asked him to repeat himself. If I were Nealson, I'd have offered a tax break to seniors who maintained the batteries in their hearing aids.

"It's just over two weeks until the election. We can't afford to slow down now," Gwendolyn said to me. "I'm surprised to see you here tonight. Didn't you say last night that you live in the east end?"

"Indeed I do. In Riverdale. But you live not too far from here, don't you?"

"Yes. Tim and I recently bought a house on Clendenan, just north of Bloor."

"Good for you. Anyhow, I just happened to be in the neighbourhood tonight, so I thought I'd drop by." Gwendolyn gave me a quizzical look. "I lost my campaign button somewhere in my travels last night. Do you have any extras?"

"Sure." She passed me an orange and blue button with Tim's picture on it. "Tim appreciates your support. The dinner last night at your brother's place was wonderful. We raised a lot of money for the campaign."

"Glad to hear it." There was an awkward pause as I'd run out of bullshit. Gwendolyn just kept smiling at me. "Your feet must be getting sore, standing around like this," I said finally.

"Thank God for insoles," she said. "I'll sit down for a while when Tim's winding up."

"What other events have you got on the agenda this weekend? I might try to round up a group of friends to check him out."

"That would be wonderful. Tomorrow we'll be campaigning out by the airport, so that probably wouldn't work. Sunday morning, Tim's meeting with people at a homeless shelter near Moss Park, then in the afternoon he's going to be talking with the Kensington Market Business Association."

"Maybe I'll try to attend that."

"If you come, you should take the streetcar instead of driving. The traffic there is chaotic, and it's impossible to find parking." There was no point in mentioning that I don't even have a licence.

The political glad-handing didn't look like it was about to wrap up for a good while yet, so I told Gwendolyn I'd be on my way.

"I hope you and your friends can come on Sunday," she said as I was leaving.

"I'm sure I'll be able to get a few people to come down. See you then."

I left the building, and did an about-face to go to the parking lot behind the library. I had no idea which car I was looking for, but it's a safe bet the Nealsons don't drive a rusty old beater.

I peeked into the front of a few minivans, but didn't see anything that would make me think the vehicle belonged to the Nealsons. I ignored small compact cars, sports cars, and trucks, certain they wouldn't be driving one of these. A black Lexus looked promising, but yielded naught, ditto a Benz and a BMW. As I peeked through the windows of one sedan after another, I was struck by what kinds of things people leave out in the open to tempt car burglars. One car had four or five shopping bags from designer stores sitting on the passenger seat. Another had a case of wine resting on the backseat. I saw iPods on dashboards, leather jackets, and more than a few briefcases. If this had been a dodgier neighbourhood, it's a safe bet that more than a few car windows would have been smashed and the contents spirited away.

I found what I was looking for when I got to a metallic grey Audi parked near the end of the lot.

This car had to be the Nealsons'. There was a slight dent in the front bumper, plus a few scratches, no doubt souvenirs from Gwendolyn's recent fender-bender. There were "Nealson for Mayor" lawn signs stacked on the back seat, as well as a box of pamphlets, and another box of campaign buttons. I snapped a few photos of the car, the damage, and the licence plates, and then headed back downtown.

When I got off the subway at Yonge and College, I discovered I had missed three calls. The first message was from Macy. She spoke haltingly, in that raspy, gasping voice of someone trying to choke back a flood of tears. She didn't say why she was calling, but said she'd try again later. Of course, she hadn't left a number where I could reach her.

The second call was from Justin–King Arthur, asking if I had reconsidered going to the fetish party with him this weekend.

The third was from Dawn Valentini, wondering if I had any news for her.

I deleted all three messages.

Friday,
11:58 pm

The first thing I did when I got to Monsoon was make myself a pot of coffee. For about the seventeenth time today, I regretted going out on the town with Lindsey last night. The hangover I'd had for most of the day was one thing, but the lack of sleep was another. I'd known yesterday that today promised to be a long day, but did that stop me from being an idiot?

After two coffees guzzled in quick succession, I sat down to do the most painfully boring, but necessary part of this job: reading through the day's sales receipts and journal tapes. I didn't see anything suspicious in the paperwork, so I took out a scale and started measuring the contents of each and every liquor bottle. Scamming on the liquor inventory is irresistible to more than a few restaurant employees. Time and time again, theft – especially theft involving alcohol – is the reason for restaurant bankruptcies. Everything here seemed on the level, though. The number of wine bottles on hand matched with what the inventory and purchase orders indicated. The array of Scotches and vodkas and rums behind the bar matched the expected tally on paper. So either there was no funny business with the liquor, or I just hadn't yet figured out the funny business. My gut told me to keep checking. Sooner or later, I'd find something.

Next, I went into the walk-in freezer and counted all the slabs of meat and all the packages of frozen fish. Nothing seemed amiss here either. Invoices from various suppliers told me there should be so many pounds of this or that, and indeed that's what I found. Hmmm. If everything behind the scenes was as it ought to be, then where were Percy's profits disappearing to? Even in a walk-in freezer, something still smelled pretty fishy.

I made some notes that would eventually form part of a case report for Percy, and then I turned off the lights and called it a night. I'd come back tomorrow night to dig a little deeper.

Saturday, October 6, 2:26 a.m.

I should have walked the couple of blocks to College Street and taken a streetcar home, but I felt like shit. It had been a long day, and I'd spent most of it enveloped in the hostility of a nasty hangover. I had only walked about half a block before an empty cab rolled by. I flagged him down and hopped in.

"We're ultimately going to Riverdale, on Carlaw, just north of Gerrard, but we need to make a detour along the way."

"Sure lady. Where first?"

"Just boot down around Bathurst and Queen. I'll let you know if we need to stop." I was concerned by Macy's voicemail tonight. She hadn't sounded stoned, she had sounded scared. It wasn't too much out of my way to swing by and see if I could spot her.

This cab driver would never be able to do covert surveillance should he one day wish to try. I dug around behind me, trying to find the seatbelt strap. The irregular rhythm of the driver's halts and lunges made me feel like a bean inside the maraca of an overly enthusiastic mambo dancer. The cabbie honked and swerved as he spun through back roads and side streets. Once we got to Queen, where traffic was much heavier, he alternately floored it and braked so quickly that my head jerked back. My brain felt like a soft-boiled egg rattling around the inside of an empty oil drum.

"This is fine, I'll get out here." We were about a block from Bathurst. I passed a ten-dollar bill to him.

"Thought you were going to Riverdale?" he said accusingly.

"Change in plans." Cabbies around the world have rather negative reputations as drivers. With this guy, the reputation was well deserved.

I did a quick tour of Queen and Bathurst, but it was all for naught. There were a couple of winos passed out on the steps in front of the drop-in centre, but I didn't see any young folks.

Strangely, I kind of had a feeling someone was following me. I tried to remember if I'd felt like that when I left Percy's restaurant, but I couldn't be sure. I walked into Tim Hortons and grabbed a coffee. I sat at one of their window seats for a while, scanning the life on the streets before me.

I saw lots of twentysomethings dressed in urban chic. No doubt most of them were suburbanites who had come downtown to blow off steam in a hip and happening 'hood. There were groups of college and university kids who had spent the evening trying to get as drunk as they possibly could so they could brag about it to their friends the next day. A few couples walked by, holding hands. Date night. A vagrant wearing three dirty raincoats and a pair of flip-flops pushed a shopping cart full of empty bottles and cans as he made his way across the street. The usual Friday night at Queen and Bathurst. I didn't see anyone suspicious. I didn't see Macy either.

I finished my coffee and stepped outside. Right in front of Tim Hortons, I saw an empty cab stopped at a red light. I hopped right in.

"Kensington Market first, please, and then River-dale." I said. I wanted to end up back at my house, and sleep in my own bed tonight.

"'Kay." He flipped around on the radio dial, and tuned into a station playing classical music. He turned the volume up a notch. Ahh, Glenn Gould doing Bach. Gould's artistic genius on *The Goldberg Variations* floors me every time I hear it. This driver was clearly not into chatting, which was just as well, because I was deep in thought. I had a very strong feeling about the Ian Dooley case. As I listened to Gould's fingers fly across the ivories, I still had a rather vague feeling that I was being followed.

And although I was still feeling concerned enough about Macy to do a half-hearted search via the taxi, my gut told me I wasn't going to see her tonight. I sensed that if Macy didn't want to be found, then she most certainly wouldn't be.

"Turn right onto Dundas, please."

"'Kay." This driver was much less aggressive than the earlier one. He was so mellow in fact that it might have been quicker to walk. I eyeballed the park and schoolyard as we drove past them. I scanned people waiting at the streetcar stops. I saw lots of punks and street kids, but no Macy and no Shank.

We then turned north on Augusta. The street was kind of quiet. All the stores were closed and none of the buskers were out. I didn't see anything or anyone that made me want to take a second look. In fact, Kensington Market was unusually quiet tonight. There was hardly any traffic.

And then it hit me. Not once, but twice.

Gwendolyn said she had been shopping in Kensington Market last Sunday. Last Sunday was September 30, and it was the last Sunday of the month. Pedestrian Sunday in Kensington Market. She wouldn't have driven here to shop; it was the monthly car-free day in Kensington. Secondly, even if she had driven here and parked a few blocks from the market, she probably wouldn't have taken Lake Shore to get home. Lake Shore Boulevard was too far south, too much out of her way, if her house is on Clendenan Avenue, which runs north from Bloor Street. But someone coming from Leslieville would most definitely drive along Lake Shore.

"Change of plans," I said to the driver. "We need to go to the west end." This was going to end up being one damned expensive taxi ride, but I was sure it would pay off. "Can you turn around and go to Lake Shore?"

"'Kay."

The meter was climbing, but I didn't care. I had the driver take me from Kensington Market to Clendenan Avenue via Lake Shore. There wasn't much traffic on Lake Shore, but even so, I knew for certain this route took longer than as the crow flies through city streets. We exited at Parkside drive, and headed north. Then we rode the length of Clendenan until I saw a house with the Nealsons' grey Audi parked in the driveway. The house was dark, even the porch light was off. I squinted to check the digits on the licence plate. They matched.

"Okay," I said when we got to the end of the street. "Let's go back to Kensington Market, this time via city streets."

The driver zigzagged along Dupont to Dovercourt, then cut across Bloor Street, and headed south to Harbord. Then he took a series of side streets until we were back on Augusta.

"Mission accomplished," I said, cringing as I looked at the meter. I also looked at my watch. The timing just didn't make sense. Gwendolyn wouldn't have been on the Lake Shore if she had in fact been in Kensington Market.

"Can you drop me at 29 Wood Street instead of going to Riverdale?" I impulsively decided to stay at Jessica's after all. I just wanted to get to sleep, and was too wiped out to spend the extra few minutes to get to my house. Besides, cutting the trip short at her place would save me an additional twenty dollars in cab fare. This ride had been very expensive, but it was worth every cent. Anyway, maybe this cab fare could slip into my final invoice for Hugh.

"You know there's construction on Yonge near Wood Street, right?" I asked the cabbie as we neared Jessica's building.

"Yeah. I was gonna go around the block so we could enter from Church Street."

"Don't bother. The building is at the end closest to Yonge. You can just let me off at the corner. I think I can safely walk the ten yards to the entrance."

"Suit yourself."

Saturday, 3:55 am

"Hey, wake up. Are you okay?"

A trendy looking gay couple were leaning over me. My head was pounding. Was my hangover back? As far as I could tell, I was in the bushes in front of Jessica's apartment building.

"What happened to you? Want us to call the cops?" The guy doing the talking was bald and spoke with a clichéd gay lisp.

"I'm...I think...somebody hit me. My head is pounding. Fucking hell..."

"Did someone try to mug you?"

"Is this your purse?" The strap of my shoulder bag was twisted around my left ankle.

"Yes." I tried to sit up, but felt a bit dizzy. "Can you tell me if my phone and my wallet are in it?"

His partner poked his head in my bag, nodded, and handed it to me.

The Bald Lisper was running his fingers through my hair. "No blood, thank God. Head wounds get really messy when they bleed. There's a bit of a bump now and it will probably be a lot bigger in the morning."

"My head fucking hurts like hell."

"You might even have a mild concussion. I know

about this stuff, darling. I'm a nurse at Scarborough General Hospital."

"Then I'd damn glad you're the guys who found me."

"What city is this?" Baldy Lispy asked.

"The centre of the universe. T-dot, Hogtown, YYZ, or Canada's version of the Big Apple."

"How many fingers am I holding up?"

"Two fingers with badly chewed nails and one thumb with a hangnail."

"Were you cheeky before you got clobbered, or is this just a side effect?"

I tried to smile in reply, but my head hurt too damn much to move any of the muscles in my face.

I had next to no idea what had happened. All I could remember was getting out of the taxi and heading to Jessica's building, literally only a twenty-second walk from where I had hopped out. I vaguely remember someone grabbing me from behind, but that's all. I had no recollection if the person had been male or female, tall or short. I don't think they spoke to me, but maybe they did. I couldn't even remember being conked on my head.

There was no way in hell that this had been random. If my purse had been taken, I may have chalked it up to a bad-luck mugging. But someone had wanted to scare me. Someone had definitely been following me tonight and they wanted to make sure I knew that they were onto me.

Fuckers. Now it's personal.

It turned out the gay guys live in the penthouse level of Jessica's building. They escorted me to my door.

"There's really no point in going to a hospital. They'll just tell you to put ice on it to keep the swelling down, and to get lots of rest. I can come down and see you if anything changes."

I thanked the guys and unlocked the door.

Damn, what a night.

Saturday, 12:06 pm

I couldn't shake the feeling that I had missed something at Ian's apartment, something besides the paint can of cash. So, once again, I found myself in the west end. I had to walk around the block a few times before it was safe for me to repeat my bedroom window routine. Even though it was lightly raining, there were people out and about, walking the dog, coming home from grocery shopping, taking little Suzy to ballet class and little Jimmy to his swimming lessons.

Once inside, I didn't poke. I just sat on the living room sofa and looked and thought, and clutched my head. I had a rather large bump at the back of my skull, and even though I'd taken some Advil, I felt a persistent dull throbbing.

I considered motives. Generally they relate to one of the seven deadly sins. I thought about how each of them could relate to this case. Pride? Maybe. Wrath? Probably. Envy? Possibly. Lust? Most likely. Gluttony? Nope. Avarice? Pretty much a given. Sloth? Nope.

I looked around the room, from left to right. I turned off all the lights because the artificial brightness seemed to make the headache worse. It was daytime, but the sky was grey and not much light entered the living room. I glanced at the plain old furniture, at the toys on the shelf. I noticed a beer bottle cap in the corner of the living room floor.

Then something clicked and the missing piece hit me right between the eyes. The Disney videos. What first struck me was that they should have been on Kayla's side of the shelves, but they weren't. The second thing that hit me was that they should have been DVDs not VHS video cassettes. For the last couple of years, movie companies were shifting to DVD and even Blu-ray. These movies were too old to jibe with a four-year-old daughter. If Ian had bought these videos for Kayla, they wouldn't have been VHS tapes.

I slid the first Disney tape into the VCR.

Porno.

Juicy, hot, steamy, super XXX-rated porno.

It was an old video, probably at least fifteen years old or so, judging by the setting and the picture quality. For the opening scene, the camera zoomed in on a couple fornicating on a waterbed. I don't think I've ever used the word "fornicating" before, but that's just what they were doing. Raw, pared down, atavistic caveman copulation. They were humping and grunting like two mammals at African Lion Safari. The video quality was rather poor, but then pornos aren't known for their fierce dedication to high art. Or for their music. The cheesy thumping soundtrack was just like the background music of any other porno flick. Not that I've ever watched a dirty movie.

The title rolled across the screen. This flick was called *Wild and Wendi*. The Wendi from Ian's caller list, no doubt.

The moustachioed man in the video was nothing special. He had a bit of a pot-belly and wasn't particularly well hung. I wouldn't have taken him home, not even at last call after a night of tequila poppers. The woman, however, had a great body, and she was certainly agile. With her teased and layered brunette hair and tons of blue eyeshadow, plus a pair of dangly earrings that looked like fishing lures, I was fairly certain the movie had been shot in the eighties.

"*I want to hear you moan, I want to hear you scream,*" the man breathed heavily as he spoke.

The broad obliged with some fake sounding screams of pleasure and some heavy panting. No Academy Awards on the horizon for this performance.

"*Oh yes, take me, take me…ohhhhhh yessssss, make me cum…!*" said a breathy but familiar female voice.

The naughty stuff on screen was timeless and amateurish, and if I may say so, it wasn't particularly imaginative either. But this wasn't just any old dirty movie. The brunette on whom the man was now enthusiastically performing oral sex was Gwendolyn. I fast-forwarded to the credits at the end. The female lead role was credited to Wendi Allcock. What a lame-assed porn star name, I thought, although it was easy enough to see the metamorphosis of "Gwendolyn" into "Wendi."

Everything was crystal clear now. Ian was black-mailing the Nealsons. That had to be it. Blackmail explained the money and was as solid a motive for murder as anything could be.

I ejected the movie and inserted *Weekend with Wendi*. The screen showed the same young brunette version of Gwendolyn. In this movie, Wendi and a pair of young studs were romping around on a living room sofa. I thought the scene in this movie looked like one of the pictures on Ian's Blackberry. A photograph of a video image from a TV screen would be grainy. Dooley must have played the tape until he got to a scene he wanted a still shot of, then hit *Pause* and snapped a pic. Poof. From that, it would be easy enough to send the picture to Wendi/Gwendolyn via his cell phone, along with a message saying "Pay up or these become public knowledge." And then it would be bye-bye mayoral race.

Whatever Wendi Wants was up next. Apparently Wendi wanted another threesome, but this time in a hot tub. She was locked in pretzel embrace with the guy from the first movie and a very chesty blond woman. Another scene from this movie looked like one of the photos I'd seen on Ian's cell phone, at least going by memory. I really wished I'd copied the pictures from Ian's phone. Or that Houghton would get copies to me. It was highly unlikely that I was mistaken, but anything's possible. Though not necessarily probable.

There was no point in looking at *Wet Wendi* or *Wicked Wendi*. It was now just a matter of deciding what to do next, and how to do it. Knowing *whodunit* and catching *whodunit* aren't necessarily the same things.

Now that I was fairly certain that the cash in the

paint can was evidence, I decided not to leave it here. I had to turn it over to the cops. The money was clearly the proceeds from what had to be Ian's blackmailing venture. And there it was: the missing motive.

I had a feeling of dread as I opened the closet door in Kayla's bedroom. Nothing looked out of place, but a little voice inside my throbbing head told me to expect to be disappointed. And I was. Someone had beaten me to the money. The empty can of green paint was on the shelf where I'd seen it yesterday, but there was no cash inside it.

Oh shit.

Who's been tailing me? Whoever took the cash had to be the same person who knocked me out last night. How much more of what I was doing did they know?

Saturday, 1:45 pm

I kept looking over my shoulder as I walked up to Howard Park to catch the 506 streetcar. I didn't think anyone was following me at this minute. But somebody clearly knew what I was up to.

I was the only person at the streetcar stop. It had stopped drizzling. I checked out everyone walking up and down the street. Dog walkers, families, joggers. No one was walking along in dark glasses, with a hat brim pulled low, wearing a trench coat and carrying a sawed off shotgun in a violin case. But still, to me everyone looked suspicious.

"Please tell me you can squeeze in time for a coffee or a drink or something this afternoon," I said when Lindsey picked up her cell. "I really need to talk to you."

"Why? Did you say 'I love you' to Derek again?"

"Go to hell. Seriously, can we grab lunch? I need to pick your brain."

"I'll be wrapped up for the afternoon by around three o'clock. I'm on my way to the last showing for today. Where are you?"

"I'm waiting for the College streetcar. I just left Ian's apartment."

"Perfect. The house I'm going to is in the Annex. Why don't you meet me at Café Diplomatico any time after three?"

Fortunately, I didn't have to wait long for the Red Rocket. I threw a token in the fare box and took a seat up front behind the driver so I could keep an eye on whoever else was getting on.

Besides my irrational case of claustrophobia, one of the reasons I take the streetcar whenever I can, instead of the subway, is that I can still get cell reception if I use surface travel. Derek picked up on the second ring.

"Sounds like things are really moving," Derek said after I'd given him a heavily edited version of this morning's developments.

No one on the streetcar looked like they were paying any attention to me, but I kept details to a minimum anyway. I told Derek about the porno flicks, but neglected to mention the missing money or the conk on my head last night. "Are you sure you're safe? I don't like thinking someone might be following you."

"I'll be okay." I hoped that sounded sincere. Maybe I was trying to convince myself. I was actually pretty scared, but there was no way I'd let that on to Derek. It would be pointless having him worry from hundreds of miles away. "I won't really be doing anything more about the murder case until I hear back from Mark, which should be tomorrow, I hope. Or maybe Monday."

"And in the meantime?"

"I have to work on the restaurant case. I'll be at Monsoon again tonight, and then I'll stay at Jessica's again. I'll take a taxi there and back. Nothing's going to happen."

"So you say, but I don't like it. I don't feel right about it," he said. I didn't bother to tell him that I was filled with misgivings myself.

"Sorry. I shouldn't have told you all of this. I don't want to worry you."

"Well, I am worried, but there's not a damn thing I can do from here. Be careful."

"I will." A pause. "It's too bad you're stuck up north for Thanksgiving weekend."

"I'm less than happy about it. Everyone involved in this trial was hoping to have it wrapped up by yesterday. But the jury didn't even start deliberations until two o'clock yesterday afternoon."

"I really wish you were here," I said.

"Trust me, I do too. This isn't going to be the holiday weekend I'd hoped for."

"But you won't stay put all weekend, will you? You're going to visit your parents anyway?"

"Yes. I'll be getting in the car as soon as I get off the phone. My mother said she has a big pot roast planned for tonight. Then they'll do the turkey dinner tomorrow when my brother and his family arrive."

"Save the wishbone for me, okay?"

Saturday, 3:22 pm

"This probably wasn't a good choice. I'm afraid to eat anything with tomato sauce on it in case I spill it on my clothes," Lindsey said. She was dressed in business casual, with an ivory blouse under a tan pantsuit.

"How about sharing a Caprese salad and the Firenze pizza? That has pesto instead of tomato sauce."

"Great, so I'll have a green blob on my clothes instead of a red one."

"Would you like anything from the wine list?" asked the waiter.

"No vino for me. I have to get back to the office to do some paperwork. Besides, I'm driving."

"Can you bring us a couple of cans of Brio, please?" I asked.

The waiter nodded and shuffled off.

"I'm in over my head with this case," I said once we'd settled in.

"How so?"

"I know who did it, and I know why, but I'm still not sure how," I said. I filled Lindsey in on Gwendolyn's starring roles in X-rated movies.

"You have to go to the cops," Lindsey said. "Why don't you call Mark?"

"I already have. He's got some info for me and we were supposed to get together yesterday, but he had to cancel. We have plans for Tuesday night, but I hope to get together with him before then. I just left him another message."

"If things are rolling along so quickly, maybe you shouldn't wait for him. You can talk to another cop, you know?"

"If I have to do that, then I will, but I don't want Mark to get in shit for any of the help he's given me. Also, I want to know how the murder happened, how the Nealsons pulled it off, before I say anything. They're very well known. Tim's got a very good shot at being Toronto's next mayor. If I'm wrong about this, I could ruin his chances. Hell, it could ruin his career in politics. And Shane would kill me."

"Is there any chance the woman in the porno isn't her?"

"Possibly, but it's also possible that the next lottery ticket you buy will win the jackpot. The close-ups when she's giving the guy a blow job are pretty unmistakable, even though she's now a blond."

"I still think you should call the cops," she said.

"Well, it's not like the Nealsons are about to flee the country. I would really like to figure out if they're both involved, or if it's just him—"

"Or just her."

"Right. Anyhow, it's all in limbo for the moment. Believe it or not, I have two other cases on the go right now too. I have to go back to Monsoon tonight. You know, that restaurant friend of Shane's."

"The guy who thinks he's being ripped off by his staff."

"Bingo. And then I have to get started on a new file for Mr. Belham early this week."

Saturday, 5:15 pm

After my late lunch with Lindsey, I'd decided to stay downtown, since I was heading to Monsoon later anyway. There was no point in going to the east end.

As soon as I'd gotten to Jessica's, I placed a call to Dawn Valentini.

"I'm ready to talk, and I need you as insurance," I said when she picked up.

"So, what's Mr. Nealson trying to hide?" she asked.

"Promise me you'll wait a couple of days before you take it to the press? The case is almost wrapped up, and I've written out the whole story – hunches and theories and everything – for you. I stuck it in an envelope and I'll drop it in the mailbox when I go out again. If anything happens to me, spill the beans."

"Are you worried? Have you been threatened?" Dawn asked.

"No comment. I just need the last piece of the puzzle. I've figured out 'means and 'motive,' but I'm still working on 'opportunity.' Once I fill in that blank, you can go to town. But please keep you lips sealed for another day or so."

"You have my word. So, what's going on?" Dawn hacked a bit, and then I heard her light another cigarette.

"The *Reader's Digest* version involves hot and heavy sex, and blackmail."

Dawn drew in a drag of her cigarette and slowly exhaled before answering. "Nealson has sex? Isn't he worried that he'll mess his hair?"

"Not mister. Missus. And not just sex, but sex tapes. A younger, dark-haired Gwendolyn seems to have had a budding career as a porn star. She's in at least five dirty movies."

"Holy shit."

"It appears the victim in my case was blackmailing the Nealsons."

"Hot damn! The story'll make the front page!"

"Hopefully it won't include my obituary."

I popped a couple more Advils and stretched out on the couch with an ice pack on my noggin. Bella curled up next to me, and we spent the rest of the afternoon watching old movies on the Classics channel. I caught the tail end of *The Maltese Falcon*, and then watched *Double Indemnity*, one of my all-time faves. Next up was *Twelve Angry Men*. Shortly after that, I'd be off to work.

The bleep of my cell phone cut in just as Fred

MacMurray arrived at the offices of Pacific All Risk. I looked at the call display and saw "unknown number."

"I need some help," Macy said. Her voice was a bit shaky and there was a lot of background noise.

"Name it. Where are you?"

"I'm at a payphone on Yonge Street. Near Dundas." That wasn't too far from Jessica's place.

"There's a McDonald's on Yonge, just a bit up from Dundas."

"Yeah, I can see it from here," she said.

"Go inside and wait for me. I'll be there in five minutes."

I grabbed my purse and threw on a jacket. Macy was literally just down the road from Jessica's apartment. I tossed the letter to Dawn in the mailbox on the way.

"What the hell happened to you?" Macy had a black eye and a number of bruises. They weren't fresh, maybe a day or two old. The scabs and scars of her self inflicted cuts showed through the purple and yellow hematomas. She was also missing two of her bottom front teeth. Her eyes were clear, but I could tell she had been crying. I was pretty sure, though, that she wasn't high, at least for now.

"Nothing."

"Don't tell me 'nothing.' Someone did a number on you. Who?" Whatever had happened to me last night was nowhere near as bad as what had recently been done to Macy.

"I don't want to talk about it."

"Okay. Tell me when you're ready. Have you had anything to eat today?" It's unlikely that food would do much to improve Macy's situation, but I had no clue what to say or do. I've never really been in touch with my Florence Nightingale side, and I felt totally out of my element.

"Not really."

"Let's grab a couple of burgers and you can tell me what's be going on."

"I don't think I can chew."

"Oh yeah. Well, you need to eat. Let's order something and we can talk."

I could hardly be described as maternal, and few would ever confuse me with a health nut, but the order of fries and Oreo Blizzard didn't strike me as sound nutritional choices. But on the plus side, each could be ingested without relying on a full set of teeth.

"I got rolled," she said after swallowing a handful of French fries. "A group of scary assed dudes near Moss Park rolled me for my stash and cash on Thursday night." The missing teeth affected her pronunciation. It sounded like she was whistling, not speaking.

"Did they mug Shank too?" I asked.

"Nope. The fucker didn't stick around for it to happen to him. He saw the three guys coming at us and took off like a candy-assed pussy. I only had a couple of hits on me and five bucks. They'd seen me with Shank and figured I had more cash or dope, so they beat the crap out of me to tell me where he was or where to get a few more hits. I can't believe Shank bailed on me. What a fucking asshole."

It would have been too easy to say, "I told you so." It was too late to tell her she'd been hanging out with bad influences. It would have been counterproductive to tell her to "Just say no." But I thought all these things.

"What do you want to do?" I asked.

"I dunno."

"Are you ready to go back to your parents?"

"I don't know yet. They suck. But this sucks too. Why can't there be something in between?"

"You don't have to make any decisions right now. Your health should be your priority. Do you want me to take you to the hospital?" Perhaps I should have suggested that before suggesting french fries.

"Nah. I'll be okay. I looked a lot worse yesterday."

"You're going to have to see a dentist."

"My parents will flip at that. I just got my braces off last year."

"Where have you been staying?"

"I rode up and down Yonge Street all night last night."

"Look, I think for now, you need to have a good sleep somewhere safe and warm. I know a place."

Stashing Macy at Jessica's may not have been a wise idea, but I was stuck. I didn't think she'd be willing to stay at my house in Riverdale if she knew there was a parental presence in the house. Besides, I really had to get back to Monsoon tonight. Unlike Shane's restaurant, which is open seven days a week, Percy's restaurant is closed on Sundays. And he was going to be closed this coming Monday for Thanksgiving as well. If I didn't try to wrap things up with him tonight, that case would be hanging over my head into next week. I wanted to get rid of it so I could finish the Dooley murder case for Hugh and then get started on the work for Belham early next week. I was certain that when I saw Mark at the hockey game Tuesday night, he'd give me the final piece in the Ian Dooley puzzle, if not before.

"Look, I'm minding a friend's apartment a few blocks from here. I can take you back there. I have a job to do tonight, but I should only be gone a couple of hours. You can hang out at her place, have a bath, watch TV, whatever. Then we'll figure out what to do with you in the morning."

"I dunno…"

She was a bit reluctant. Come to think of it, so was I. Leaving a teenaged runaway with a fondness for drugs and a penchant for slicing her arms alone in the apartment I was minding for my friend wouldn't have had the blessing of Solomon, unless it was Solomon Grundy.

"Come on. It's not too far from here."

Saturday,
9:40 pm

Now that I had invited Macy to stay with me for the night, I was stuck playing social worker, or at least entertainer. I had no idea what to do with her. She wasn't exactly hostile, but hers wasn't the most charming company I've ever shared.

"Have a seat. I'll get a cold compress for that eye. Looks like it still hurts a lot."

"Yeah." Macy took the armchair next to the sliding glass balcony doors. She sat cross-legged on the chair, and Bella climbed up onto her lap.

"Here," I said handing her a bunch of ice cubes wrapped in a dishcloth. "Do you want a Tylenol or a painkiller? Those bruises look like they hurt something fierce."

"I wish I had a joint right now. A good buzz would feel all right."

"Sorry, there's no dope on the menu here. And if you have any drugs on you, I better not see them. Remember, this isn't my home, it's my friend's apartment, and I don't want you doing anything that would cause problems for her."

"All right, all right, I get it."

"I'm not going to make you do anything you don't want to do, but I really think you should call your parents."

"I don't want to talk to them yet."

"Is there anything you want to talk about with me? I'm a good listener." Usually that's true, but tonight she'd only get one ear. Ian's murder, the Gwendolyn movies, the missing money, and Monsoon were weighing heavily on my mind.

"I don't know what I want to do."

"You need to get your shit together. You have to stop cutting yourself."

"I know."

Sunday, October 7, 12:22 am

It started raining again while I was on my way to Monsoon for my second night of snooping. After last night's taxi tour of Toronto, I couldn't afford another cab. I ducked out of the rain and stood in the entryway of a store while I waited for the streetcar. I looked nervously around me, wondering if anyone around me had played a part in last night's knockout.

A glance through Monsoon's reservation book showed they had been booked solid from five o'clock onwards. Several parties of two, plus a number of larger groups, from ten to fifteen people. The restaurant had emptied out around eleven o'clock, and it had been locked up and the alarm was set at 11:50.

The sales receipts showed a gross total of $7,802.38 for the night.

"Mama mia," I mumbled, "that's a lot of mahi mahi," I said to the empty room. A lot of people had ordered Firecracker Tiger Prawns tonight, but that was no surprise as it's the restaurant's signature dish. The Coriander Crusted Orange Roughy had also sold well. But they had sold only six orders of Beef Tournedos in Hoisin sauce, and three of them had been sent back.

Hello! Red flag.

The three beef dishes had been voided from the bill, and the customers had declined to order something else from the menu. The notes on the computer claimed the beef had been sent back because it was tough, and had therefore been deducted from the bill. Apparently, none of the customers had ordered a replacement dish. Another red flag.

Three wasted meals, each priced at $44, ouch. I noted that the remainder of this bill – an order of Coconut Lime Chilean Sea Bass, two bottles of wine and four decaf coffees – had been paid for by cash, something less and less common in the worlds of fine dining and expense accounts.

Voided items on bills that were paid by cash is one of the oldest scams in the restaurant biz. What happens is that the customer eats the meal or meals and pays the bill in full, using good old greenbacks. Then, if a slippery server or dishonest manager wants to scoop up a bit of extra money, they make it appear that the items were rejected by the customer and not paid for. The scamming staff members do this after the fact, once the customers have paid the total and have left the establishment. The cash goes into the waiter's pocket instead of the till.

You can't pull this scam with credit cards because the charge goes through for whatever the customer signs for, and the client has a copy of the receipt anyway. But when people pay cash, once they walk out the door, no one can prove how much they actually left on the table or in the little billfold. The customer leaves enough for the whole bill, but the server or someone on staff adjusts the amount of the bill once the patrons exit the restaurant, and the difference is pocketed.

Of course, sometimes the food really is unsatisfactory and it ends up in the garbage.

I knew what I had to do next, and I was overwhelmingly under-enthused. I turned on all the lights by the back door of the restaurant. The rain hadn't let up at all, but that made no difference to me. Even a crisp autumn night would not make the task at hand any more pleasant.

I beamed a flashlight in an arc around the back doors. In the middle of the night, in downtown Toronto, most women would probably have been afraid of being accosted by a creepy guy in a trench coat. Me? I was terrified of racoons. I had seen plenty of the little black-eyed buggers during my late night meanderings over the years, and I was terrified of their pointy little teeth and rabid bite. Damn. There was no avoiding this. Good thing I had worn sneakers. Even better, I found a pair of rubber gloves in the kitchen.

I banged a couple of pot lids together, like a toddler who knows just how to irritate Mommy, probably like Kayla would, or one of Robin's three little devils. Two big fat racoons scuttled out from behind the garbage dumpster. I leaned into the dumpster, and hoisted out the first rain-slicked bag. At least it didn't smell too bad. Soggy bread crusts, used teabags, stinky shrimp shells, wine corks, and coffee grinds. I dug a little deeper. Plastic wrappers. Paper towels. A wad of gum. Gross. Perhaps it was just as well that Derek was out of town. Looking the way I did right now, even I would have dumped me.

The rain kept trickling down.

Garbage bags two and three held more of the same.

Bones from the baby back ribs, cleanly licked of their tangy red pepper and chive sauce. Blech. Lots of fish scales and fish carcasses. Dirty Kleenexes. Potato peels. Used hairnets from the kitchen staff. Yuck. It was after one in the morning, and I was really riled about rummaging through restaurant rubbish in the rain. My alliteration was good, but I was starting to think yet again that my career sucked. Maybe I'd become a radiologist, a romance writer, or a race car driver. Or even a bartender at fetish parties.

Garbage bag number four yielded nothing except further resolve to consider changing careers. The bag reeked to high heaven and I gagged a few times.

I slipped when I reached for bag number five, and my ass landed in what I think had been the soup du jour. It had the colour and consistency of baby shit, but smelled like a puree of carrot and ginger. Ugh. I cursed some more, and ripped the bag open to find out what treasures it contained. Nothing but the usual miscellany one encounters when sifting through garbage.

Bag six was the last bag, and when I finished with it, I still hadn't found what I was looking for, and yes, by this time the U2 song was scrolling through my head. This meant, of course, that I had learned exactly what I needed to know.

If three $44 plates of beef tournedos had been sent back because they were "too tough," shouldn't I have found them – or remnants of them – in one of the trash bags? I went back inside and cleaned myself up a bit before locking up. I shouldn't have bothered trying to freshen myself up. By now, it was pouring rain and it had gotten pretty cold.

Sunday,
2:43 am

When I got back to Jessica's apartment, there were only two things on my mind: Macy, and a hot shower. I had caught a bit of a chill in my soaking wet clothes, and I looked and smelled awful. A soon as I opened the front door, I got a feeling Macy wasn't there. All the lights were on, and the apartment was silent, no TV sound or music playing.

"Macy? Hello."

No answer.

I could see pretty much the whole apartment from the front foyer. The door to Jessica's bedroom was ajar, and the bed was empty and still made. No one was sitting on the sofa or the armchair in the living room.

I wasn't altogether surprised that Macy had taken off. The entire context in which I knew her was based on the fact she was on the run. Still, I was a little bit mad that she was gone. And a little bit worried. But on a very selfish level, I was almost relieved that Macy had split. I'm not cut out to play nursemaid-cum-therapist. I was worried about her, but she wasn't going to listen to anybody, not her mother, not her father, and certainly not me. I mentally debated whether I should call her parents tomorrow and give them an update or not.

I kicked my wet shoes off in the front hallway. I was too soggy and garbagy and gross to traipse any further into the apartment. I immediately steered myself straight into the bathroom and peeled off my soggy jeans and sweater right away. My wet clothes became a squelchy pile on the bathroom floor, and I jumped into the shower.

The water was turned to as hot as I could stand, and I instantly felt the tension in my neck melt away. The bathroom was all hot and steamy in no time. Mango shower gel washed away my scent of eau du garbage, and I scrubbed away the layers of grime under my nails. I lathered my hair with herbal-scented shampoo and lemon-mint conditioner, massaging my scalp very gently around the bump. I was too tired to think about Macy or Gwendolyn or Dooley or anyone else. The last few days had exhausted me so much that I wanted nothing more than to finish my shower, then curl up in Jessica's bed and sleep for twenty-four hours.

The bathroom was all warm and steamy when I finally shut off the water. It was then that I noticed the stink. The litter box, tucked into a corner on the bathroom floor, was rank. I hadn't changed the litter in a few days, in fact I had hardly even scooped out the clumps. The steam from the shower made the stench of Bella's litter box that much more noticeable and I just about gagged from the odour of stewed cat pee and feces, especially after an already gross night burrowing into bags of garbage. I was too tired to change the litter box right now, but the smell was enough to make me vomit. I wrapped a thick, fuzzy towel around myself, and brought the litter box out to the balcony where I could safely ignore it until tomorrow morning when I'd feel like changing it.

"Don't make a sound," said the voice at the other end of the gun that was pointing at me.

I was so stunned that I dropped the box, and clumps of kitty litter and little lumps of feline poop scattered and rolled all over the balcony.

Gwendolyn Nealson was at the other end of the gun.

"What are you doing here?" I asked.

"You couldn't leave well enough alone," Gwendolyn said.

You've got to be kidding me. It's two-thirty in the morning, and a crazy woman is pointing a gun at me? This isn't really happening. It can't be happening.

"I don't know what you're talking about." My voice was shaky. I was chattering, and it wasn't from the cold.

"Bullshit you don't. It was the perfect crime. There was absolutely nothing to connect us to Ian Dooley. The guy was a fucking dirtbag. The world hasn't suffered a loss at his death," she said. Her eyes narrowed and she took a short step closer to me. "He was going to bleed us dry, or create a scandal that would blow Tim's chances for election. He was easy enough to stop. He was so fucking stupid. But then you came along, you nosy fucking bitch."

"I have nothing on you. Take off. Please. Let's just forget this all happened. I'll vote for Tim." I backed away a small step as I spoke, but that just made Gwendolyn move a step closer to me.

I'm not really standing in cat shit on a balcony, wearing nothing but a towel, with a gun pointing at me, am I? Please, tell me I'm not. Pinch me and tell me this is just a bad dream. How the hell could I possibly get myself out of this? I clutched the towel a bit tighter around me. Keeping my privates covered up made me feel less vulnerable, but only marginally so. I'd have gladly traded my soft, fuzzy cotton covering for a Kevlar vest.

"You've poked around too much. You could fuck up everything Tim and I have worked for."

"No, I haven't. Really, I haven't. He can still win the election, and you can be Mrs. Mayor. Everything's just fine. I won't say a word about anything. Really." Gwendolyn just slowly shook her head a wee bit from side to side.

I could scream. I could holler my lungs out and wake the whole building. A neighbour would hear me and call the cops. But if I screamed, Gwendolyn would pull the trigger. She could kill me before anyone got around to calling 9-1-1.

"Tim is going to be Toronto's next mayor. We've worked so hard, and everything is within reach. You're the only loose end now. And you're about to have an unfortunate accident."

No, no thanks, I don't want an accident. "Please. Think this through. I don't have any proof."

I could hear Bella purring in the living room. Damn it, you fat, lazy Himalayan, why can't you be one of those heroic super pets like you see on YouTube? Use your paw to dial 9-1-1.

It couldn't be that I was pinning all my hopes on a cat. Please don't let this be how I meet my maker, in a towel, on a cat-shit-covered balcony, hoping against hope that a cat would call the police for me. "Walk away now, Gwendolyn, and everything will go back to normal. The election is only a couple of weeks away."

"Fuck you. It's over, bitch. You wouldn't leave us alone. All those calls to my cell phone. Snooping through Ian's apartment. You asked for this."

Time to take a different tack. "I'm not the only one who knows what happened," I said. "I've told your whole story to a reporter I know. If anything happens to me, all your secrets will end up on the front page."

"Bullshit. We've covered all our tracks." I swear her trigger finger was twitching. I tried to ease back another step.

Bella pawed her way out to the balcony to see what was going on. She let out a raspy purr and tried to wrap herself around Gwendolyn's ankle. I made my move. As soon as Bella tried to curl up around Gwendolyn's feet, I lunged for the gun. There was a struggle and I dug my fingernails into her wrist. The gun handle was still in her hand, but I twisted the barrel around so it was pointing away from me. She kicked at me and I kneed her in the crotch. I shoved at her, and twisted at her arm, and then suddenly, the gun went off.

Bang. A single shot. The force of the firing loosened her grip and she dropped the gun.

I kicked it away from her, and she lunged at me, snarling, her eyes filled with a level of hatred unknown to mankind.

It would be corny to say that what happened next was a catfight, but it was. Gwendolyn kicked at me, and I punched her. She reached out to scratch at my face and neck, and as I twisted away, my towel fell off. I was doing my damndest to get away, but she cornered

me into the railing of the balcony and attacked. Her
fingernails dragged their way across my boobs and I
let out a screech in an octave I didn't know I could
reach. I hauled off and gave her a right hook in the
jaw. I heard something crack, and she spat blood right
on me. Then Gwendolyn kicked me in the shin and
leaned into me to grab my hair. She pulled at a clump
from the back, twisting my head around so that I was
now bent over.

Someone from the apartment above us told us to
keep the noise down. I just screamed louder, yelling for
help and asking someone – anyone – to call 9-1-1. Bella
let out some sort of feline growl and ripped her claws
across Gwendolyn's shins. I gave Gwendolyn another
good right-hook in the side of the face and she spat out
more blood, and then tried to bite my hand. I punched
her again and she dug the heel of her shoe into my bare
foot. Lights went on in the apartment next door.

The pain in my foot distracted me enough to give her
an edge. Gwendolyn's hands reached around my neck
and she started to squeeze. I started to gasp and then I
totally snapped. I don't know if it was fear or adrenaline
or desperation or what, but I pried her hands from my
neck. She stomped down on my foot once more, and
reached again for my neck, one hand grabbing a hunk
of wet hair and yanking mightily. I was pummelling at
her shoulders while trying to twist away from the edge
of the balcony. Her heel dug into my foot again, and
I screamed louder. The guy upstairs yelled down at us
again to keep the noise down. Gwendolyn pushed her
heel down harder and scratched at my face. I kneed her
in the crotch and she wrapped her hands around my

throat again, harder this time. All I wanted to do was get her hands off my neck.

I pulled at her hands and struggled as much as I could. I was starting choke and cough, trying to get some air. I just had to get her off me, away from me. I twisted and used my elbow to thwack her in the chest, then kneed her in the crotch again. She stumbled a bit from the blow and I seized the opportunity to get her off me. I drew upon every ounce of adrenaline I had and shoved her away from me. The push was so hard that the next thing I knew, she was doing a swan dive over the balcony.

She screamed as she went down then landed with a cracking thud. I started crying. More lights were flicked on in neighbouring apartments. I looked over the balcony rail and saw Gwendolyn lying facedown on the pavement below. I puked right over the edge.

"Oh my God!" said a male voice I recognized.

"What the fuck?" said another male voice.

Derek and the building superintendant had let themselves into Jessica's apartment. The superintendant took one look over the balcony rails and picked up the phone. I puked over the balcony again, and then fell sobbing right into Derek's arms. I was naked as a jaybird.

"What are you doing here? Where did you come from?" I was stunned by everything about this moment.

"I wanted to surprise you. I planned all along to drive down tonight after dinner with my folks. I would have gotten here hours ago, but there was an overturned tractor trailer on the highway. Anyhow, that's not important. What the hell is going on?" Derek asked.

"I don't know what happened. I came out of the shower... The litter box. I just wanted to get her off me. I didn't mean for her to go over the edge. I wasn't trying to kill her. She was choking me..."

"Shhh. You'll be okay. You're in shock." Derek put his jacket over me and looked down to the ground, twelve stories below. I could already hear sirens approaching. "Come on, let's sit inside. He steered me to the couch and I flopped down into it. The superintendant looked down at the floor. Bella curled up on my lap, and as big and fat and fluffy as she is, she didn't cover up all my privates.

"She's dead, isn't she? I can't believe what just happened. She had a gun..." I was simultaneously bawling and shivering.

"Here," the superintendant said, passing me a Kleenex, while politely trying to look in the other direction. "You're bleeding."

"You need to put something on," Derek said. "The cops will be here in a minute. It would be best if you weren't in your birthday suit when you give them your statement."

"My clothes are all wet. Get me something of Jessica's. Anything, I don't care. Grab whatever's in the closet that looks warm." My heart was racing, and I was choking back a flood of tears.

When Derek opened the door to the walk-in closet, he found Macy, bound and gagged. Gwendolyn had used pantyhose, a tensor bandage, scarves and belts to tie Macy to one of the chairs from Jessica's little dinette set. She had taped Macy's hands together behind the chair. A sock had been stuffed into Macy's mouth, and then layers and layers masking tape had been wrapped around her head, covering her mouth.

"That fucking woman was a psycho!" Macy screamed as soon as Derek had removed the coverings from her mouth. "I want to go home!"

And then the police arrived. Thank God.

(Thanksgiving) Monday, October 8, 6:30 pm

"Here you go," Shane said as he passed the gravy boat to me. I drowned my turkey and potatoes in the sauce.

"So then what happened?" asked Lindsey as she helped herself to a drumstick.

The dining room table was laden with platters and five of us were seated around the table. Shane, Dad and me, plus Lindsey and Derek. This was Derek's first time meeting my dad and my brother and I was nervous.

Shane had teased me, and I had fussed all afternoon. Derek was the first guy I'd brought home to the family since Mick. No one could ever accuse me of being Little Miss Domesticity, but after lunch I had raced through the house, fluffing cushions and straightening pictures. In truth, I just didn't want to be corralled into helping prepare dinner. My cooking skills are sub-par at best. I really wanted this evening to go well, and helping to cook dinner would be an act of self-sabotage.

"That was when all hell broke loose," I said. "When a person dials 9-1-1, the call goes out to pretty much all the emergency services: cops, firefighters, and ambulances. The fire guys didn't stick around. Neither did the ambulance guys once they determined that Gwendolyn was dead and that Macy was ostensibly okay."

"But they all showed up."

"Oh yeah. The cops were there for a while. They took our statements at the apartment instead of bringing us down to the station."

"Macy's parents showed up just as the cops were finishing and the crime tech boys were securing the scene."

"It was you who called them, wasn't it?" Dad asked Derek.

"Yes. I guess, understandably, Macy wanted to take off as soon as she was unbound. She was less than keen on talking to men in uniform."

"Poor kid. She's so messed up."

"What do you think happened to the money?" Shane asked. "You said you found some money at Dooley's place, but then it was suddenly gone."

"That one's easy. The cops found over $50,000 in cash at the Nealson residence," I said.

"But which Nealson took it and how?" Lindsey asked.

"One or the other of them was following me. Maybe both. I'm sure I tipped my hand on the library night. That was the night I got knocked out in front of Jessica's apartment. The cash was gone the next day."

"I can't believe you didn't go to the police at that point. You could have been killed," Dad said.

"After what happened on the balcony, I'm well aware of that. Anyway, the Nealsons knew Ian had a lot of cash, since they're the ones who paid him."

"So they broke into Ian's place to take back what they thought was theirs," said Shane.

"Yup."

"Why didn't they take the pornos?"

"I'm not sure. They weren't easy to find, for one thing, since they were hiding in plain sight. They were labelled as Disney videos, sitting right there on the shelf. Also, they probably went in and out of his apartment as quickly as they could," I said.

"But still, to break in and not take the movies?"

"I don't know. You'd have to ask the Nealsons that one."

"What about Saturday night? How did Gwendolyn get into Jessica's apartment?" Lindsey asked.

"She banged on the door. Macy thought it was me and just let her in. Didn't even look through the peephole or anything."

"Did Gwendolyn know Macy was there? Or did she think you were there?"

"I'm not sure. And with Gwendolyn dead, we'll never know," I said.

"I bet the guy from The Pilot is relieved," Dad said.

"Most definitely. I spoke to Hugh last night, and he said he'll drop off a cheque for me tomorrow. He also mentioned something about letting me drink at The Pilot for free from now on."

"Can I come?" Lindsey and Derek said at once.

Monday,
11:05 pm

After dinner with my family, Derek and I went back to his place for some alone time. We had done everything I'd suggested in my naughty drunken call, plus more. He had attacked me like a Viking finding a lonely damsel shackled in the tower of a medieval castle. We'd acrobatically fucked our brains out the first time around. Then we'd made love, slowly, tenderly, taking our time, enjoying every inch of each other's body. Derek's touch sent shivers down my spine, and his lips on mine – after being apart for so many days – felt hungry and inviting.

I reflected on my hungover "I love you" comment from when we were on the phone the other day. Derek hadn't mentioned it, so I was feeling a bit relieved that he apparently hadn't heard it. But as I looked deep into his hazel eyes and gazed at his perfect face, I thought to myself that I had indeed meant what I had said. I just didn't want to be the one who said it first. I was terrified he might not say it back. But lying here with him right now, I felt love more surely and more completely than I ever thought I could.

"So, how did you figure it out, anyway?" Derek asked, snapping me out of my reflection. He passed a lit Cuban Maduro to me.

"It was easy. All the proof just sort of fell into my lap," I said, sitting up and taking a puff of his cigar. That could be a euphemism for what I'd been doing for the last half hour.

"Tell me again about the car part of it. I think I missed something." Derek passed a crystal ashtray to me.

"Well, first I caught the lie about the fender-bender Gwendolyn Nealson was in." I tapped off some of the cigar ash and then took another puff. "She said it happened after shopping in Kensington Market. First of all, that day was pedestrian Sunday, so anybody with a brain wouldn't have driven there."

"They could park a few blocks away and walk there."

"True, but why bother doing that? She and Tim live in the west end. There are about a hundred other places between her house and Kensington where she could have bought salad fixings. It just didn't make sense. That, plus, even if she had shopped there, she wouldn't have driven home along Lake Shore."

"And that's where the accident happened."

"Right. The timing fits with Ian Dooley's death. And the accident report puts her near the scene of the crime."

"So how did she pull it off?" Derek asked.

"Tim was her accomplice. Ian was blackmailing her, well, actually he was blackmailing Tim, but it's essentially the same thing. Mark Houghton and the boys in blue checked security videos from some of the businesses at Yonge and St. Clair, where Mimi-Minerva lives. One of the security cameras, ironically from a camera store, had some footage of the street. The camera didn't capture the whole car, but it showed the front of Neal-sons' Audi, and the first three digits of the licence plate."

"Wow."

"Another camera shows Gwendolyn in profile. Basically, Mister and Missus Nealson ambushed Ian when he left Minerva's place. According to what Tim told the cops when he was arrested, Gwendolyn held Ian at gunpoint, and rode with Ian in his truck. Tim followed behind them in his own car. Gwendolyn forced Ian to drive to the Port Lands, where she killed him. She then drove his truck to Leslieville, with Tim following in their Audi."

"Unbelievable."

"Her mistake was in parking the truck illegally. And in not moving the seat and mirrors back to their original positions. Anyhow, according to Tim, she dropped him off the Mayfair Racquet Club, this was supposed to be his alibi. He was supposed to have a game of squash, but his partner never showed up, or so he says. This part is a little fuzzy."

"All the cops would have to do is find out who he was supposed to play with. Nobody would lie for him now."

"No one will vote for him now either. All I know is what Tim said to the cops, and he contradicted himself a few times. I think maybe he showered there and changed his clothes and went home. Basically, he showed up there long enough to establish an alibi."

"Wow. And how did Gwendolyn know you were onto her?" Derek asked.

"She must have known almost from the start. Remember her number was on Ian's BlackBerry caller list. I had no idea who she was. I called her a few times and told her who I was, and left messages. She must have shit herself when she met me at Pastiche for that fundraiser."

"How come you didn't recognize her voice?"

"I never actually spoke to her. That cell number for Wendi didn't have a personalized outgoing message, just the computer voice asking me to leave a voicemail. Gwendolyn heard my voice, but I never heard hers. And I gave her enough info to find me and follow me. Especially after I saw them at Runnymede library. She knew the heat was on, then."

"So what about the gun she pulled on you?"

"It was the same one as she used on Ian Dooley." I took a sip of my wine. Derek had opened a delicious Malbec, and we were making short work of the bottle. "She was an idiot for not getting rid of it. It would have been better if she had done like Mark said, and tossed it into Lake Ontario."

"How do you think Ian Dooley knew about her and the dirty movies?" Derek asked.

"My guess is that they knew each other from down east. I twigged onto that when Tricia Lado told me about flying his body to Nova Scotia for burial. At that fundraising dinner at Shane's, Gwendolyn said something about being from Nova Scotia too. I'm not sure, but when the cops investigate, I have a feeling they'll find out that the movies were made in Nova Scotia, before Ian or Gwendolyn moved away. They might have known each other there, or maybe he just came upon her films there." I took another haul on the cigar and passed it back to Derek.

"So how did he connect that with Gwendolyn here and now?"

"My guess is that he saw her picture in the news when Tim decided to run for mayor."

"And what about Tim? What's he saying about what happened at the apartment?" Derek was gently rubbing my shoulders as we talked. After the craziness of the weekend, I couldn't have felt happier or more relaxed than I was right now.

"That's an interesting question. He admits to being involved in the Dooley situation, but he's downplaying his role in everything else, pointing the finger squarely at Gwendolyn. She can't really deny anything now that she's dead."

"Of course."

"I kind of have the feeling that what happened at the apartment was her own doing. I don't know if Tim knew about it or not. And I'll never know," I said.

"How did the Nealsons know when and where to find Ian that night? After the fetish party?"

"My guess is that they had been following him. They may have tried to set up a meet with him to pay some more blackmail or something. Tim has contradicted himself on this a few times too."

"I see."

"The cops will be able to piece it all together from phone records," I said.

"That's true. Anyhow, enough about this. How about some more wine?"

"Fill me up." I passed Derek my glass.

"By the way, Sasha?"

"Yeah?"

"I love you too."

Excerpt from

Frisky Business

Sasha Jackson's next adventure.

Coming in 2012.

Friday, June 29, 5:22 pm

"That was blowjoberrific! Love the final shot." The hairy-necked, T-shirt-clad butterball nudged the cameraman standing next to him. "Heh heh, 'shot,' get it? *Shot*." He snorted as he laughed, then the laugh turned into a rusty hacking fit.

Antonionio Agostino Antonelli made the same joke every time. Fortunately, his partner wrote most of the scripts; Antonionio's sense of humour and wordsmithery were pathetic even by porno standards. Had he not carved out a career as the slimy but successful executive producer at AAA-XXX Films, it's quite possible Antonionio would never have gotten laid.

"Okay, guys, that's a wrap," said Frankie Jones, the director, and Antonionio's partner. He turned to the two cameramen. "You guys can start packing up."

A gorgeous blond woman lying naked and spread-eagle on a picnic table tossed her head to the side to move the sticky wet hair out of her face. She was handcuffed to the table.

The forty-five-by-twenty-five "studio" had been covered with Astroturf and a few unadorned artificial Christmas trees in order to create a backyard barbecue setting. A wooden deck chair near the picnic table was covered in discarded clothing and a still dripping garden hose. The melted strawberry ice cream on the floor would probably attract ants or cockroaches. AAA-XXX didn't bother with a regular cleaning crew.

Frankie and Antonionio high-fived the male actors as they exited the low-budget set.

"Good job, Brad."

"Way to go, Stone. Ya gave it to her real good."

"You got the stuff, Lance. Keep it up. Get it? Heh heh. Keep it up." Antonionio launched into another plump and juicy coughing fit as each of the eight well-hung naked guys grabbed a clean towel from the director's assistant and headed off to the showers.

"Can someone uncuff me, please?" Nicki Spumoni asked. Nicki was the twenty-two-year-old star of twenty-four adult movies produced by AAA-XXX.

"Yeah, one sec," said Danny, the guy in charge of lighting and props.

"This table's really uncomfortable, and my back is itchy."

"I already told ya, just a sec."

AAA-XXX was one of the leading porno production companies in the world, and certainly the most successful smut business in Canada. It was founded in the mid-1990s by Antonionio and Frankie, two unemployed truck drivers who had somehow landed a government grant for young entrepreneurs to develop small businesses. They had convinced the grant-awards committee that they planned to produce sensitive artistic films that celebrated the physical union between lovers, or something like that. They'd both been more than a little bit stoned when they filled out the application.

However, in the bourgeoning days of the Internet, with is anonymity and immediacy, high-end, stylish nudie films were no longer on anyone's radar. Frankie and Antonionio made a few movies with titles like *Shakespearean Seduction* and *Twilight Tryst*, and only a handful of people ever saw them. But for Frankie and Antonionio – guys who were both quite accustomed to receiving fake phone numbers from the girls they met – the adult film industry opened up a whole new world.

"I'll get the video files to you later tonight," Frankie told Antonionio.

"I won't gotta do much editing with this one. It's pretty awesome as it is. I'll have it available for downloading by tomorrow afternoon."

"You've decided on the title?"

"Yeah, we gotta go with *Cumsicles* instead of *Yogen Splooge*. Our lawyer said the frozen yoghurt chain people might try to sue us if we use that one.

"*Cumsicles.* Cool. I like one-word titles."

"I'm getting really sore. Can you take these damn things off, please?" implored Nicki.

"I don't got the key. You got it?" Frankie asked the others standing nearby.

"I thought you had it. It should be right around here somewheres..."

Friday,
11:03 pm

"They're all such assholes," Nicki slurred. She kicked off her four-inch heels and put her feet up on the coffee table. There were already two empty twenty-sixers of Stoly on the scratched surface. "Fucking assholes. I'm a human being for Chrissake, not some damn rag-fucking-doll!" She tilted the current vodka bottle up to her lips and took a big swig.

"I know. They treat me the same way, the scumbags," said Kitty Vixen, Nicki's roommate and occasional co-star. Kitty had almond-shaped green eyes, long black hair, and she wore custom-made 38DDD bras. Everything about her was store-bought, from her coloured contact lenses and her silicone breasts, to her acrylic fingernails and collagen-plumped lips. She kept the receipts for all of her maintenance work and tried to deduct whatever she could as business expenses at tax time. "Lemme have some more," she said, reaching for the bottle.

The vodka bottles were part of a nightly routine. Occasionally, so were hash, cocaine, and ecstasy. On filming days they usually knocked back three bottles and several lines, but on days off they limited their in-take to just the bottled stuff, and never more than one or two.

The two porn stars shared a funky loft-style apartment above a clothing store in Little Italy. Despite being in-demand adult entertainment actresses, the girls were perpetually broke, and usually had to scrounge just before the first of the month to come up with rent money, after having blown their earnings on clothes, personal grooming, and miscellaneous intoxicants. The guys running AAA-XXX knew of Nicki and Kitty's fiscal fluctuations, and saved their raunchiest films for the end of the month, when the girls were in no financial position to refuse the work, no matter how vile or degrading.

"Think about it. I did the whole bloody *Fun in the Sun* series with them," Nicki said as she hoovered another white line.

Fun in the Sun was targeted at horny viewers with food fetishes. The movies featured edibles associated with summer, and were filmed against a number of low-budget picnic and beach volleyball backdrops. The extremely thin storylines found imaginative uses for hot dogs, banana splits, lemonade, and raspberry sno-cones.

"That series has some of the worst titles," Kitty said after snorting her third rail.

"I know. I mean, *Cumsicles?*"

"Not as bad as *Rub-A-Dub-Tug.*"

"Oh yeah, the hot tub one. That was bad. But whatever. They've been downloaded more than a hundred thousand times," Nicki said. "They make a fucking fortune off us and don't even treat us like we're human. I had to ask that asshole four times – four fucking times! – to uncuff me. I thought for sure they were going to forget about me and leave me locked to the fucking picnic table all night." She gulped another mouthful of vodka. The girls had long ago lost interest in adding any mix to their booze – too many calories anyway.

"I remember after shooting a flick once I was so wet and gross and covered in you-know-what. And I asked them for a towel, and the son of a bitch said *get it yourself.*"

"Asshole."

"We gotta do something about it. Those bastards wouldn't make a fucking penny if it wasn't for us."

"I know. Today I had to fuck eight guys for this shitty picture. And I know two of them deliberately ate garlic before the shoot."

"More assholes."

"I know. But the point is I had to have sex with eight scummy guys who didn't even have enough manners to wipe their cum off me after the shoot. Eight! And I get paid the exact same for this flick as when Chrissi Frost and I did that girl-on-girl flick with the red velvet sofa. There wasn't hardly any penetration in that one. Was mostly just tongues."

"That's why I like doing girl-on-girl videos. I'm usually never sore afterwards. Easier work."

"Exactly. We should get a raise for each guy that bangs us."

"Can you imagine? My record's from when they did those "history" movies. Twenty-five guys in one day. *Napoleon Bonerparte. Attila the Hung.* Can't remember which one had the twenty-five. It's all a blur."

"I made one of those stupid historical pornos too. *The Munchurian Candy Date*? I did guys and girls in that one."

"You're right, though. We should get paid more if we have to fuck more people. It's only fair."

Monday, November 12, 5:35 pm

"Sorry I look like shit. I just got off work." The chesty, raven-haired girl didn't exactly look like shit, but she did look like freshly scrubbed garbage. Her hair was damp, she wore no makeup, and her extravagant boobs strained the fabric of a very tiny pink and black striped T-shirt. The stripes were horizontal. She certainly didn't need any optical illusions to emphasize her physical endowments. "Candace Curtis gave me your number. She said you could help me."

Candace Curtis is a former madame I met during the Hispanic Hooker in Hiding case this past summer. She had suffered some collateral damage as the case morphed from missing person to murder.

I initially had mixed feelings about the sex industry when I met her, but Candace and I had developed something of a friendship in the few months since then, and she had opened my eyes to the realities of the sex trade. As well, I helped Candace reconnect with the son she had abandoned years before. She felt indebted to me for that, but in my opinion she shouldn't have. At the risk of sounding trite, the smile on her face when she and the boy were reunited was reward enough.

Nonetheless, I had happily cashed her irresponsibly generous cheque when it came in the mail.

"Grab a seat," I said indicating the empty chair opposite my desk. I glanced around my rather plain but functional office and wondered what impression it gave to the occasional clients who came in. It occurred to me that perhaps it wasn't very confidence-inspiring. Maybe I should set up a mini-bar with a crystal decanter, and get a leather couch.

"My name is Kitty Vixen. Nice to meet you."

"Want to tell me your real name?" I said.

"Oh yeah. Michelle Berger." She extended her hand, and I shook it.

"What's the issue?" I asked.

"My best friend was murdered a couple months ago."

"Tell me more." As soon as she started talking, it occurred to me that I should have spouted some sort of sympathetic platitude about her loss. Occasionally I am an insensitive twit.

"Nicki Spumoni. Her real name was Julie Allison McPhee. She was beaten to death and found in an alley. The police say she died two days earlier, on September 10. No one's been charged, but I know who killed her."

"And that was…?"

"Either Antonionio Antonelli or Frankie Jones."

"Then you don't know who did it if it's an either/or."

"They're one and the same. They own AAA-XXX Adult Films. Everyone calls it Triple-A Triple-X. Antonionio is the president. Frankie is his partner and Chief Executive Asshole."

"I see. Keep going."

"Nicki was causing too much trouble. Neither of us liked Triple-A Triple-X, but the money's good, it's just not good enough. Nicki was trying to get the guys to pay us more."

"And I assume they didn't want to?"

"Hell no."

"What's the going pay rate for a porn star these days?"

"A thousand bucks a day."

"That's kind of a lot of money in one way, but then again, not really." Through my work for Candace, I had learned a lot about money and sex. I also know how much I've earned in private investigation fees over the last while.

The high-ranking escorts who had plied their trade at Candace's bordello could earn a thousand dollars or more for a night's work. So could a few of the strippers I've met. In either case, it was significantly more than my fees. But in those scenarios, unlike in the dirty picture biz, there is nothing, um, residual in their workday. When the guy leaves, or the lap dance ends, the event more or less ceases to exist. I couldn't imagine thousands of people – strangers – watching me have sex. Or people watching it over and over again. I shuddered at the thought. "Do you get any royalties from the movies or anything?"

"Nope."

"So, a grand for a day's work. How many days a week do you work?"

"Depends. Most flicks are shot in about two or three days. I usually do two or three films a month. Nicki did about the same."

"So you make between six and nine thousand dollars

a month? Not bad. I know a lot of people – families even – who make much less than that. I'm not saying it's good..." I wonder how much I'd have to be offered to make a porno flick?

"The pay is standard for the industry. And the guys pay us in cash – no deductions – when the filming's done. Plus we can pick up a few extra bucks for doing podcasts and webcam stuff."

"So how much more did Nicki want to be paid?"

"She never really said. Well, not like she wanted a fixed amount. We get paid a daily rate, no matter how many guys we fuck. If you think about it compared to the way a hooker does things, it's not fair. Prostitutes get paid for each guy they have sex with. We get the same pay whether it's one guy or lots."

"Okay, I can see the logic in that," I said.

"Keep in mind, we don't use condoms. No one will download a flick with rubber in it."

"You've got to be kidding."

"We get tested for STDs every week, but that doesn't mean anything. I know lots of girls who've caught stuff, and I have, too. Luckily it's all been curable."

"You girls are taking your lives in your hands. No amount of money could make me take a risk like that."

"Well, you don't know what it's like. But that's kind of what Nicki's point was, is that the risk factor increases when there are multiple partners, and it really wears you out, being rammed so much. Everywhere. So, Nicki thought the pay should increase, since the risk and wear and tear go up with more guys."

"I see. So you think one of these guys, Frankie or Antonio –"

"Antononio."

"Are you serious? Who in their right mind calls their kid Antononio?"

"His mom had a stutter, or at least that's what he says," Kitty said.

"I see. So you think one of these guys killed her because she wanted a raise?"

"Yup."

"What about the police?" I asked.

"They've gotten nowhere, and I don't even think they're trying anyways. To them she's basically just a dead whore. But she's not. She was the best friend I ever had."

"Okay. I'll give this a try." I told Kitty my rates.

"I've got a thousand bucks on me now. Can you start with that, and I'll give you more after I do the next flick?" She handed me ten hundred-dollar bills.

"Deal." I tucked the money into the front pocket of my jeans.

"The money isn't just from me. Some of the other actresses kicked in. Nicki was one of us."

"I won't be able to get started on this until Wednesday or Thursday. I have a couple of things I need to wrap up."

"No worries. Nicki's been dead two months already. She's not going to get any deader."

Wednesday, November 14, 8:45 am

I was in slow motion this morning. Derek and I were sitting in his kitchen, flipping through the newspaper and half-listening to the morning radio show. I was too tired to pay attention to anything, and my thoughts kept drifting back to the way I'd been woken up. Derek brings new meaning to the expression "rise and shine." Sleeping over at Derek's place generally means that neither of us gets much sleep. It also means that we'd both be walking around with goofy grins for the rest of the day.

"Ready for a refill?" Derek asked.

"Yes, please. More caffeine." He filled my coffee mug for the third time this morning. I added real cream and far too much sugar, and almost immediately choked on it.

"Aw, come on, my coffee's not that bad."

"It's not the coffee, gorgeous. Look at this. My latest client has been murdered." I handed Derek the newspaper.

The article at the bottom of page eight was short on details. Twenty-one-year-old Michelle Berger had been strangled to death. Police currently had no suspects but were "pursuing several leads." There was a small headshot of the girl, under the tawdry heading "Sex Star Strangled While Sleeping." Apparently she had been killed sometime late Monday night or early Tuesday morning. Her body had been discovered around lunchtime on Tuesday when her new roommate, a porn actress whose screen name was Athena Starr, showed up to move in her few suitcases.

"Jesus."

"Wow. That's now two dead triple-X actresses in as many months."

"That's not good. You'd better call Houghton."

Derek was referring to Mark Houghton, a cop on the Toronto Police force and an old friend of sorts. We'd actually had a brief fling when I was in my late teens and I swore I'd never speak to him again after he dumped me. I ate my words years later when I reconnected with him in my professional life, and he's proven more than once to be a valuable ally.

"I will. This is awful. I met her only once but she seemed like a nice kid. Her life was totally screwed up, but she was nice enough."

Wednesday,
12:00 noon

"Hiya, handsome," I said as I joined Mark at a quiet table at a pub in the Beaches, although Mark and several of his neighbours call this area around Queen Street East *The Beach*. I find it pretentious to use the singular, as if it's the only bloody beach in the world.

We had picked this spot because it was close to Mark's house and Mark had the day off work. He was spending it painting his kitchen, but he welcomed the interruption. There were little globs of sage green paint in his hair, and on his hands and forearms. His arms were thick and strong and I tried to remember what his touch had felt like. I came up blank. It was too long ago, and I'll admit there had been a fair bit of alcohol involved.

"The murdered porno star Kitty Vixen was my client."

"Oh really," Mark said. "That's very interesting." He took a sip of his draught beer, and I waited him out. I could usually get more out of him if he volunteered things than if I prodded. "We haven't got anything solid, but my gut tells me the perp was one of the hotshot movie guys she was working for."

"That would be my first guess." I took a long swig of my Guinness and waited for him to continue.

"The two guys who run the film company, Triple-A Triple-X, look good for it, but both have concrete alibis."

"For both murders?" I asked.

"We looked at them both pretty closely when the other girl was killed in September."

"Julie McPhee."

"Yeah. Julie, a.k.a. Nicki Spumoni. Different manners of death. One beaten, one strangled."

"That doesn't necessarily mean different killers. Do your instincts tell you it's the same guy?" I asked.

"Most definitely."

"So if the producers, Antonionio and...who's the other guy?"

"The money guy behind the scenes is Antonionio Agostino Antonelli. He calls himself the company president and executive producer. His partner, Frankie Jones, is the director and vice-president. Jones also gets credit for all the scripts. Calls himself the head screen-writer."

"Highly doubt they have a stable of guys sitting in a conference room pitching storylines and consulting thesauruses. "

"Wouldn't the plural be *thesauri*?" Mark asked.

"You can use either, but the plural of Beach is *Beaches*."

"You've made your point. Anyhow, we couldn't find a way to pin Nicki Spumoni's death on either Antonionio or Frankie. We'll have to see about Kitty Vixen. I'm not involved. The brass has got me doing stolen property these days. Next up for the homicide guys, though, would be to look into Kitty's private life and see what comes up. We know from the first murder that drugs come into the picture from time to time."

"This doesn't sound like a drug deal gone wrong."

"No, but it's a place to start."

"How did the killer get into the apartment? There wouldn't be a superintendent or anything if it was just a single apartment above a store."

"Actually, there are two units. The other one's been vacant since August. The girls apparently never locked the door to the street, just the door for their apartment. We tracked down the former neighbours and they said the lack of security, plus the noise from a lot of late-night partying next door, was the reason they moved out. The guy who owns the building and rents the apartments and the store downstairs lives in Richmond Hill and doesn't really need the money and doesn't seem interested in the property. He inherited it. Says he wants to fix it up and then get rid of it."

"Be harder to sell now that it's been the scene of a crime."

"Yup."

"So how did the killer get in?" I asked.

"That's a good question. It appears the perp was let in, or had a key. The door was unlocked when the new roomie showed up to move in."

"So Kitty probably knew her killer."

"Yes, and that's why we've ruled out a random or unknown."

"Kitty gave me a retainer to look into the death of Nicki Spumoni. I have no way to give the money back, so I'm going to be poking into this."

"As soon as I saw your number on call display, I knew you'd be involved. Just try not to do anything that leads to disciplinary action for me. I caught a lot of heat last time."

Mark had indeed broken a lot of rules for me when I had worked the Spank Me, Shank Me murder case a few weeks ago. I had literally and figuratively bared all when I caught the killer and gave the cops my statement. Houghton should probably have been suspended for the ways he had helped me. Luckily, the ends justified the means, so the brass had chosen to ignore his police procedural peccadilloes.

"We never had this conversation and I didn't meet you for lunch today. My treat, by the way," I said.

"If that's a bribe, it's a little on the small side," he said with a wink.